About the Author

Mynah Gadu has a degree in creative writing, but her fascination with the creative concept has been a long-lingering obsession. The art of shaping a world and characters that interweave within the boundaries of reality creates a sense of magic, something that is mostly undermined, yet in its infancy it holds the potential to create an object of inherent beauty.

The Next Mynah

Mynah Gadu

The Next Mynah

Olympia Publishers
London

www.olympiapublishers.com
OLYMPIA PAPERBACK EDITION

Copyright © Mynah Gadu 2024

The right of Mynah Gadu to be identified as author of
this work has been asserted in accordance with sections 77 and 78 of
the Copyright, Designs and Patents Act 1988.

All Rights Reserved

No reproduction, copy or transmission of this publication
may be made without written permission.
No paragraph of this publication may be reproduced,
copied or transmitted save with the written permission of the publisher,
or in accordance with the provisions
of the Copyright Act 1956 (as amended).

Any person who commits any unauthorised act in relation to
this publication may be liable to criminal
prosecution and civil claims for damage.

A CIP catalogue record for this title is
available from the British Library.

ISBN: 978-1-80439-763-3

This is a work of fiction.
Names, characters, places and incidents originate from the writer's
imagination. Any resemblance to actual persons, living or dead, is
purely coincidental.

First Published in 2024

**Olympia Publishers
Tallis House
2 Tallis Street
London
EC4Y 0AB**

Printed in Great Britain

Dedication

I dedicate this book to my husband, Paul.

Acknowledgements

Thank you to my husband, Paul, for being the inspiration in my life and for encouraging me to dream.

CHAPTER ONE

The rumours were flying. Gossip so ripe the wind tore into the choicest chunks and brought them to her. Her nose lifted, as the happy titbits sailed by like paper boats. She did not mind. Let them gossip until they passed out under the hot sun, dressed in their Sunday best, with their poisoned words poking the air, their eyes glazed with envy, put there by a future that would be hers. Oh, she did not mind being the victim of their gossip this time. Yet, as she walked down the blazing tarred road, she knew it was too good to be true.

It all started exactly a week ago. At home, at supper, seated around a table for four that had to take five. Hers was the high wooden stool with the polished circular seat, raising her up and above the rest, so that she felt like a lighthouse, a badly built one, about to slip into the sea. It was the way she was sitting, crouching over her plate, afraid to fall off.

'How many times,' Nancy scolded her youngest, 'must I tell you to sit up straight? Who would say you are twenty-two? You behave like a ten-year-old.'

She straightened up at her mother's words, staring down at her plate. The rice grains seemed far away now, scattered, like white islands, with the small pieces of meat pushed to the side of the plate.

'I didn't make gravy for supper.' Nancy poked a finger at the plate. 'I cooked a chicken curry. In this house we eat what I cook. You think I enjoy spending hours in the kitchen? Yes, you think that. No thanks for what I do. Imagine seeing my own child behave so selfishly.'

It was a path they went down often. Coral would be the first to admit that her head was full of thoughts without roots, that her idea of becoming vegetarian was more like kicking the apple cart and watching the bright red heads roll, as if they were the fractured heads of a lineage, cursed and flawed. For in Nancy's house, the only thoughts that survived were the ones that came from her. She took over now, her voice sounding like the wail of something choking, under a full moon, her face puffed into an orange shade, ready for combat. Shaking her head, she rocked herself into a small state of composure, told everyone that she had never hoped to live to see the day when a child of hers would be so disrespectful. That she, as the mother, knew what was best for them, after all, where did they come from, but from herself. That no matter how old they got, she was never to be questioned.

'Tell them, Ed,' she said at last, jerking her chin towards her husband, 'instead of sitting there with your mouth full of food, tell them I am right.'

Her husband, an obedient figure occupying the chair by her side, kept his dark head over his plate, his small shoulders hardly moving as he ate. He seldom said much, usually leaving the household matters to his wife. And if he said anything at all, it was after he had exchanged notes with her.

'Ed, don't act like you deaf. Sitting there, as if you pay rent to live here? Don't say anything now,' Nancy put up a hand, even though Ed gave no indication of speaking, 'just think about how you should be teaching these girls some manners.' Nancy was getting worked up. Especially this one,' she nodded towards Coral. 'As it is, you chose the name for her, without telling me about it. You think I don't know how they all laughed behind my back. That day in church, when you made the grand announcement, and suddenly everybody had the itch down their throats. You think I didn't hear them. I should have put you right that day, but it doesn't matter. Better late than never, I will sort things out myself, make sure you pay for that mistake, every single day, every single hour, for the rest of your life.'

A frown drew itself upon Nancy's features as memory took her back, her face suffering deeply from the seriousness of the situation. 'I want to know, after all these years, where you got *Coral* from? You never said anything. The last time I checked, I never see any Indian girl in our family with that name. As it is, your daughter doesn't know who she is, and with no proper Indian name, what hope does she have, tell me? I told you to think before you talk, but when the spirits jumped out of that bottle and into your brain, something turned, and you went and opened your mouth.' She paused, catching her breath. 'Opened it wider than any river mouth. Who can forget that performance, tell me? I know I can't, and now, we're stuck, with a child and a name, and the two don't match. I am fed up with it, I tell you, *but*, there is hope.' She turned her head back towards her girls. 'I won't listen to any stories from the three of you. Not when it comes to your weddings. Nobody tells me what is right or wrong. I know all of that for myself,' she nodded her head. 'If your father won't give the news, then I got no time to waste.'

Into the stunned silence, she made the announcement that nobody except Ed was expecting, and it had nothing to do with Coral's unfinished dinner, 'Sunday is around the corner, already sitting on the other side of tomorrow. *They* are coming for you,' she pointed a finger at Coral, 'bringing a nice enough boy, from what I heard. Don't know what they will say if they come and see how useless *my* daughter is?'

Coral's head was up. Her words when they came out, were soft, hardly audible.

'Ma, I don't want to get married now.'

The Kwa-Zulu Natal air, cool and shaken, sauntered into the room, carried along by a pocket of grace, and they were able to draw new breath. The break from the heat put some common sense into the matriarch, faster than an alcoholic shot had the power to. In a rare moment of compassion, she tried to explain herself.

'I know it's very quick,' Nancy admitted, 'but think about your father's, father's father. How that man left India to come find work in a new country. Three generations gone if you count. Every time the car goes past the sugar cane plantations, I think of my father and what he said. Listen to the sound of the leaves, he told us. It tells the story of a heart broken in two, one half here and the other half in India.'

'Ma,' the second daughter interrupted Nancy's walk down memory lane, 'what does that have to do with Coral and her getting married?'

Arya's voice snatched Nancy back, and it was not something the older woman was used to.

'I mean they had guts,' Nancy snapped, 'and that is something lacking here tonight. We are not the only ones to have one foot stuck in the mud. Look at *them* next door. Three times they went through this.' She stopped and let it sink in. 'Three times the same aunty found three nice boys for those girls. Look at them now, all married, who knows how many grandchildren are running around everywhere. Nobody counted. But Maya and Dick got no complaints, everything is perfect for them. So perfect they can't keep their mouths shut. Always bragging about their luck. Always standing and waiting by the gate, whole day, every hour, so they don't miss anybody, so happy to catch the next innocent person walking on the street. Looks like nobody can hold their hands, not any more, they gone to the top, they can afford to shout and tell everyone about their good luck,' Nancy dropped her voice to a whisper, as if she were letting out a secret, 'the daughter who married last, her husband landed a big job, very rich,' she snapped her fingers, 'money is nothing to him. he can buy anything he wants. Why, the way things are going, looks like Maya and Dick, one of these days, will have their own wishing well, set up right next to the new house they're moving into, straight to the other side of town. Not like us. We're stuck here.'

She stopped to wring her hands in desperation. 'And my girls, nothing yet. I don't know which evil eye stopped outside our gate.'

'*Ma,*' It was Arya persisting again, the only one of the three sisters who, at twenty-four, had full rights to speak without the potential of being struck down, '*please* tell us who is coming to see Cori?'

Nancy rolled her eyes to the ceiling, quietly suffering under the agony of the words that stuck in her ears like hardened wax. She did not have the willpower to chastise her favourite, not her angelic girl upon whom her dreams were built. It would be better to lie in wait for someone else to make a move. She did not have long to wait.

'Yes,' Veru, the eldest at twenty-six, opened her mouth and enquired lazily, as was her habit, 'exactly *who* is coming to see Cori?'

Nancy swallowed her relief, covered it up with spite and

launched herself into a new space, her voice raising itself. She secretly savoured the thrill of a retaliation that only she could give, enjoyed basking in the glory of her dominance, 'Where you got Cori from? Tell me? Last time I checked, I heard the name Coral.'

'But, Mum,' Veru insisted, 'exactly what is in a name?'

Nancy scrunched up her eyes, and turning to Ed, her voice laced with distaste, she barked, 'You see, already thinking she is too big for her shoes, questioning her own mother? In this world, I'd rather be six feet under than have such insolence.'

'Please, Mum,' Veru said carefully, 'I don't mean to be rude.'

Nancy ignored her, keeping her face turned towards Eddie, she launched a fresh attack, 'Look at your children now. Hear how they are asking questions. In our day, no such thing. A tight slap and everything got sorted out same time, no fuss, no worry. Nowadays, we give our children too much rope, so much rope they end up getting knotted in it, can't move, too stupid to do anything, all they know is to hop everywhere, like rabbits. Making too many mistakes because they can't think for themselves. That's the way we are bringing up our children in this modern world, and let me tell you, everything is your fault. Watch when I say, everyone else's girls are getting married and keeping the family name. And here? I must bend over backwards to find a starting point, and they got the nerve to *ask* us why.'

Another shot of cold air drifted into the small room. Attached to this new arrival came the promise of a night storm. Eddie put down his spoon at last, finished his mouthful and looked up. He turned towards Nancy, cleared his throat, the scraggly white beard that had formed only recently, begging for a shave, and was about to say something when Arya intervened, still focused on Nancy, deliberately dismissing her father, she insisted, 'Ma, you are getting too angry for nothing. Forget about the name issue, tell us, *what* is happening on Sunday?'

Arya was the family mascot in a way, they all knew that. She was Nancy's golden goose, the one who would marry a handsome, rich man and live in a castle by the sea. Nancy held no secrets in that aspect, being very public about these ideas. Every morning she unpacked them, shaking them out and fastening the pegs, stringing them under the growing sun for everyone to gawk at. Those ideas came in her dreams too, arriving in a show and tell parade of pictures, going by in full colour. They told a story of the future, where she saw half the town, dressed in servant uniforms, scurrying around a castle, watched over by a very disciplined mother queen. It brought a blush to her cheeks, the picture of her entitled self. And then, to account fully for the missing lot, the other half of the town she saw as peeping Toms, those others staring from their windows, waiting to catch a glimpse of herself and her girls, whenever they chose to give off their time, striding up and down the streets, decked out in heels and big hats, just like in the movies, looking flashier than peacocks. She kept her dreams close, but always in the centre of those dreams, a bottomless hate brewed, like a pot of stew seasoned with bad magic, it simmered over the years, bubbling and spitting, the thick glug turned into poison. And that was not her fault. She knew about the gossip that travelled between her neighbours, false faces with strong teeth, chomping on her fate, as if the words were chewy meat, but in those mouths, it melted like salt. Oh yes, she knew they gossiped about her and Ed, but mostly about her.

Those women talked, and they said poor Ed was worked

harder than an old donkey, starting from the time he married her. They said Ed came home so late, that by then, their suppers were already gone to their toes, fully digested, and their men fast asleep, tucked inside their blankets like happy roti rolls. That they as women, with their strong senses, could tell that if Eddie had picked any of them, he would have been better off, and from that first day, his palms would have started itching, and nobody cared if it was the right or left, but that the itch would have stayed with him his whole life. She never did believe in that superstition, and if money was going to come Ed's way, it would not be an itchy palm that brought it, but a beautiful daughter blessed with the charm of a snake. That was her Arya, taking up after her mother.

    She was getting distracted from her story. But the tattlers hold on her was firm. She had been given news of her own this morning, from the most spiteful of haters, a woman so threatening that not even lightning could put a bolt into her. Yet even that creature had come to her door, telling Nancy what they were all saying – Ed, being a jack of all trades, and she a housewife with very bad luck, the pair of them had their path set out, and it went straight, just like the salary Ed brought home.

    That was the last straw. The walk down memory lane had brought back the poison, woken up her mind, sending it back to the way it functioned when she was a teenager. She had hopes then, looking for the best picks life would give her. She would be the first to say she had not picked well, or she could have been looking out from a window on the other side of town. But, bringing her mind back into order, she patted herself on the back for progress made. It gave her joy to think that she had stuck to her mission, letting her daughters know that if she was miserable, there was no chance of escape for them. From Monday until Friday, Nancy complained that Ed lived in clothes soaked in cement and dust, and that although they all took turns at scrubbing, it was still her hands that took the greatest bit of suffering, and it made no difference to how those clothes looked the next morning, That Ed's undersized boots were a sign that the man's time was almost up, considering he had outgrown his shoe size and his lifespan, with the number of hours he spent under the hot sun. It was their duty to release their parents from such a worrying fate. She told them that the man himself never complained, but one look at his face and the story was written there. She could tell. Nancy made it clear too, that of the three potentials she was looking at, her hopes were pinned on Arya. The chances of the other two, she prophesied blankly, of landing a rich husband, were non-existent.

Now the slim, bright-eyed girl with the light complexion and long dark hair said blankly, 'Ma?'

Nancy softened up, turning to her favourite, 'Oh, you know auntie Shammy from next door? She knows a family. They not that bad off. Got two shops, not bad at all. They're not looking for too much, only a girl for their eldest son. Twenty-one, same age as Coral, so Shammy, very decent thing she did, she told them about us. On Sunday they will be here, for tea.'

As her fork hit the plate, all eyes moved to Coral. She was sitting up straight, her voice so small, 'Mum, I really don't want to get married.'

'Well,' Nancy shrugged, 'who asked you? As it is, it's a disgrace having the youngest marry before the eldest. But in this case, luck has landed on our doorstep. It is far more than I hoped for you. You should be grateful.'

CHAPTER TWO

Coral came back to the morning heat and the buzz of voices. *Sunday* had arrived, bringing with it the life- altering tea and the meeting of her prospective other half. She was too nervous to give him a profile in her mind, dared not picture what his face might look like, or how kind his eyes might be. She had not slept much during the past night. Instead, her mind kept digging deep, unpacking the many changes that were coming. She was getting used to the idea of having someone all to herself. She liked the feeling of belonging, and her hope for a good match grew. That morning she had insisted on going to church. The others stayed behind to get the small green house with its two bedrooms and tiny kitchen ready for the visit. She could see the roof ahead, red tiles like old fish scales, calling for a scraping. Each step took her closer, the windows came into view, small squares punched into the brick walls, shiny glass windows covered with iron straps. She was already at the gate, and without turning to the others, she swung it open and closed the voices off behind her.

She went down the small, dirt driveway and disappeared into the cool dark interior of the house.

Nancy came hurrying towards her. 'How long does it take a person to get here?' she yelled. 'I can tell you church finished a long time ago. You supposed to come straight home.' Nancy gathered herself together. 'Get into the bath, now, and try to look decent. I don't know what I did to deserve this, when my own daughter won't listen to me.'

She found out later about the last-minute change, the fact that her prospective family had called and decided to make an early appearance, but she did not mind. In a village such as hers, Karumpu, where so many girls her age were blessed with good looks, why would anybody go out of their way to see her? The more she looked at it from that angle, the more attractive the proposition seemed to grow. Yet, marriage would take her away from the village. She had mixed feelings about this. Karumpu was a small village, tucked inside the greater town of Tongaat, lying not more than a twenty-minute drive to the coastline. There were days when, during late summer afternoons, the ocean kicked the wind into their neighbourhood, and it came calling, riding on the promise of a thunderstorm, rich with the scent of salt on the rocks, spiked high by a day's worth of heat. She thought about her mother's words then, often wondering about the faceless ancestors of her past, their voices combined, a ghostly plea, to be heard and remembered, their voyage across the sea from their homeland, had brought them to a new land, to descendants, such as herself, many who would never know more. Sometimes, when she had walked to school, she thought she heard that same ocean wind thrashing about in the fields, mimicking the waves so closely, and in that chorus, she latched on to feelings that were new to her, felt the courage of an unknown past nibble into her veins. It still came in rare moments, this notion, that she had more going on in her mind, and heart, than what she realized, and it was then that her head went up high, and she felt the strength warm her bones. She knew she was made differently, that a sleeping force had been deposited into her being. She had no idea what this force was capable of, just that she knew it lay there, curled up inside her, contently napping like an overfed cat. . And it scared her.

Her thoughts shifted back to the village. It was a strange place to live in. The people were sorted differently, with a single main road dividing the small suburbs. If one did the trip on foot, as most of them did, the suburbs changed quickly once the two rows of shops were left behind. Single storey houses came into view, placed on either side of the main road that sloped and dipped, with smaller roads branching off, uniform houses crawling up and down the banks. She lived in one of those, at the end of a long street, where they were fortunate enough to have a narrow stretch of road that minded its own business on the one side. For the community suffered from an infestation of gossip, and for those houses wedged in with others, there was no treatment for the problem. Things changed if one kept to the main road, following it as it ran through a small intersection, where suddenly blocks of flats sprang up, about ten in all, filling the landscape on either side. The road started to gain height from this point on, stretching forward into an overhead bridge, so that the railway tracks that ran beneath stayed in the dark. Once past the overhead bridge, the road straightened itself out, the landscape hosting a church and school on the one side. Bigger houses, double storeyed, sprang up on the other, where the land sat higher, the hill dipping out of sight into a valley. A new suburb thrived there. These houses were different, with long driveways, lined by tall palm trees from which thick curtained windows looked out onto manicured gardens. Shrubs trimmed like lollipop heads competed with blooming roses and marigolds, bright yellow and orange dots in their flower beds.

She had walked through this part of the neighbourhood many times. It was like something out of a movie, a part of a world she would never belong to. She often wondered what the people were like. With that much money, she had to assume they would be different, otherworldly, separated from people like herself. It fascinated her. And as children, when she was still at primary school, her friends would pretend the houses were spooked, taking turns to run up and down the roads, keeping their eyes on the sleeping forms of the dogs. They never trusted those. Once the sleeping dragons woke, their eyes rolled up in their heads, going faster than a hunting tiger shark, their primeval instincts activated, they dashed for the gates, their tails cutting through the air, their legs speeding faster than they intended, so that to keep their pride, they snapped like flytraps, sprinted like cheetah, let their tongues hang out as if each needed a scrub in the bathtub, before seeking refuge in big stainless steel water bowls. She was never one of the provokers, never thought much about working up those grand performers, but her friends, they were of another breed, never bothered to tame their ambition. She was the one who lagged, carrying a stinking pile of shoes, watching as her friends moved, like rodents, from one house to the other, jumping better than grasshoppers, on the sun-baked tarmac, raising an uproar of barking and yelping.

Her thoughts returned to her. She knew things were starting to change in her own neighbourhood, and if she put the stamp of honesty on the face of things, the scale of change shaped itself after the suburb with the long driveways and giant houses. She watched as single storey houses began to hide behind high fences, the barricades going up faster than the house extensions. The change brought dogs groomed for the theatre, their barking and biting talents were put on exhibit behind high steel gates, where everyone could see the rampage safely from the other side. The days were fast receding, of a time when there was a field of mushroom houses, with fences so low it could have been put there for rabbits. And the people, they were starting to hide behind burglar- guarded doors, peeping out like moles, wincing in the daylight, no longer knocking on doors for conversation, under the pretence of borrowing half a potato and getting six instead.

One thing got a boost though, and that was the channel of communication. They had telephones now, new lines of interference that created more havoc than blocked gutters after a storm. News spread faster, and the hearing, connected as it was to the memory, took longer to unblock. Everybody lived in fright, that the gossip, flying from house to house, might brand family honour. This made the fear palpable, and those who had been branded, moved like mosquitoes, waiting to bite the goodness from the next victim. She could never miss this part of the village life, and if she was being truthful, was grateful to be leaving it behind.

She came out of the bathroom and stood in front of the full-length oval mirror. The water had been freezing, the geyser was having an off day. The dress she saw, was comforting, made of a thick material that cloaked her body like sheep wool. Slowly, she felt herself heating up, as if the gap between her clothes and her skin had stoked a fire, one that quickly caught, the tip of the flame poking into her brain. She leaned forward, going closer to the mirror, the jabbing in her head getting stronger, spreading into her eyes, the sockets became hot springs, the pupils rebelled, became itchy with grains of salt in them, and she put the palms of both hands to her eyes. When she dropped her hands back to her sides, the face staring back showed a pair of offended red eyes, blinking away perspiration, fat drops that dripped off her forehead, a few soaked her sight, others crawled down the bridge of her nose, plunging off her chin, and sailing like drunken sailors into her dress, leaving happy dark splotches everywhere. Her reflection made her feel sick. Sicker than before.

The thought brought something rolling into the base of her throat, where it lodged, like a fat candy apple, stuck in place, creating a tension that filled up her insides, the vibrations travelling to her head. She had a fully bloomed headache now, complete with the feeling of a cockroach scratching around somewhere inside, extra-long feelers moving like cotton threads in the wind. The idea puffed up in her head, worsening the headache. This feeling, when it happened, was a signal that she had to get under the covers, and stay there, just until the scratching and the thumping subsided.

But she could not do that now. Her face stared back at her, and the question raised itself again. How could she find love, when she appeared so plain. The feeling of anxiety dug deep, raising observations with legitimate grounds. Her sisters, twin beams of light, glowed like fireflies catching attention with their light complexions and happy faces wherever they went. They ruled the hours. It did not matter what they wore. They looked good in anything, and in their Indian community, it seemed as if everyone cherished them, the lighter, brighter duo. At least, that is what her experiences had shown her. Her sisters were icons in their field. She glowed too, just in a different shade that nobody cared about. It hurt.

It was not for the lack of trying though. She had tried everything, the last idea left her with a yellow stained face, a temporary problem, but she had to stop with the turmeric powder, the moment the school called her parents in, to find out if she was jaundiced. But there was that other time, when she found out about the wishing well, a small, stagnant pool of water on the edge of the village, over which, in another time, a small bridge had been built. Her friends at school had called it the wishing well, telling stories of wailing ghosts that had been stitched into the missing bricks. Nobody went there anymore, but everybody spoke of a young girl, who lived a hundred years ago. She wanted a handsome and noble husband for herself. She got him, after dipping her feet into the magical water. Coral had gone there, desperate to try for herself. She went armed with the bravery of youth, determined to strike a bargain with the walled spirits if she had to. She was not afraid of them. The reality of her world, on the other hand, now that caused her anxiety and fear. Like one in a daze, she slipped both her feet into the murky water, a sickening pool of litter and abandonment, probably scared off any watching ghosts when she did, and been sick herself for a week after. If she thought about it now, it was worth it. Her dream was about to come true.

The present dragged her back, and she saw a green dress. Nothing more. Just a woolly green dress from which a head peeped out. She felt like an insect. The door opened, and Nancy walked in.

'What is that?' her mother looked alarmed. 'You look as if you stole that dress. It does not suit you. I told Kesh that colour is not right for you. Put on the Punjabi. And wear some makeup.' She shook her head in disapproval, shoving Arya's red lipstick at her. 'I don't know why you are so lazy. Just try and look decent for once.'

Nancy looked at her sharply, remembered something, and rushed out. Into that short silence, Veru and Arya, came into the room.

'Oh, that won't do.' Arya shook her head. 'The red Punjabi will look better.'

Veru nodded. 'Yes, this time I think I agree.' She sat down on the twin beds that they all shared, 'Yes, it looks to me like the red will be better for your complexion.'

Coral left the room to change, and when she got back, the sisters were deep in conversation.

'You know, I always found it so confusing.' Veru was saying, 'Being Christian, *and* Indian.'

Arya giggled, 'No silly. Look at it the way Mum does. She got herself rolled up in the best of two worlds.'

'Oh, look.' Arya became distracted, as she pointed at Coral, who had just come back into the room, 'look at all that sequin. It even makes Cori look good.'

'But something's missing,' Veru observed, eyeing Coral intently, 'I wonder what it is?'

'The shoes?' Arya pointed at the spot where Coral's shoes should be.

Both girls giggled, as Coral hitched up her loose pants, a few notches to reveal her feet, 'It's here, see.'

It was a rare moment when she joined in the fun, and the smile that spread across her face was begging for a few more rounds, but her timing was off, and both sisters missed the joke, pouncing on her instead.

'You don't look like a bride to be,' Arya frowned, grabbing the lipstick out of Coral's hand, then taking a firm hold of her chin, Arya snapped Coral's head towards her, keeping it steady so that she could paint her lips.

'She needs more than that,' Veru laughed, diving under the bed to produce a pair of pointed, sequenced heels.

'Wear these.'

'No!' Coral turned her head, the look of alarm spreading over her face. 'Those are yours. It's too big. I'll fall. I can't walk in them.'

'Don't look away when I am busy,' Arya moaned, forcing her head back. 'Now look what you did. The lipstick is all over your face.'

Whilst Arya started rubbing her cheeks as if her hands were erasers, Veru got her feet into the shoes, so that she wobbled with the change.

At last, both girls stood back and surveyed their handiwork.

'I don't know,' Veru said slowly, 'the lipstick – that colour is not right.'

'Too bright?' Arya chirped.

'Yes,' Veru nodded, 'it's perfect for us. But on her, it just looks...'

'Too much?'

Veru nodded.

'Well then,' Arya said brightly, 'we do this.'

She rubbed more lipstick into Coral's cheeks, and then dappled some onto her eyelids.

Veru giggled, 'Mum is going to kill you. She looks like a painted vase now.'

Nancy's hysteric voice travelled through the half open door, as if she were on an egg timer, 'They here! Coral, stay in your room. You two, get to the kitchen now.'

The girls raced out of the room, leaving Coral to take a final look in the mirror. The face in the mirror peeped out of the loose, sequined top, whilst the long red sleeves covered her hands, and the wide pants hung loosely above her pointed heels, drowning them. If the shoes failed to finish the job, the length of her pants would. She sighed, hearing her mother call, and left the room behind on wobbly steps.

They were all there, arranged in a circle in the family lounge. The visitors were given VIP seating, having the soft cushioned seats for themselves. The rest put up with the circular topped stools.

Coral saw her mother's gaze settle on her. Nancy's expression gave nothing away. Coral knew what she must be thinking, and when the nod was given so that she might move to the centre of the room, she watched her mother's features harden, and it grew more entrenched, the more she wobbled towards the centre stage. At last, her feet took her there, and she faced the new trio, the visitors all plump and arranged in a row like chickens for the feeding. It was easy to see they came from the same genetic pattern, shaped with round cheeks and large, expressive eyes. But now, they were undergoing some kind of shock, their eyes frozen, their mouths numb as if ice had been shoved in to keep them shut. Her heart dropped into the foundation of the house and stayed there.

After a while, the matriarch spoke, her head bobbing, as it moved in short spurts from Coral to her son, 'I see,' Maya was saying, in a thin, stretched voice, 'but you see my son is my only child. The bride, we choose for him must be perfect.'

Nancy laughed, a nervous alien sound that fetched three pairs of eyes onto her, 'I mean, you are a mother too. What child is perfect?'

Maya stood up, in genuine anguish, 'Mine is,' she returned, her chubby face breaking out into a sweat, her eyes narrowed, 'I don't think this will work.'

She ought to have said something charming, to change the mood, but her lips were sealed shut. She watched the scene play out as if in a theatre. By now the son and Father were on their feet too, both of heavy built, both of same height as if levelled out by a ruler. The son leaned across and whispered something into the father's ear, who then transferred the sounds into the mother's ear.

A lightbulb switched on somewhere inside Maya. Her face grew a smile, and it spread across her cheeks like melted margarine. Excited, she announced, 'Can the two mothers have a chat in the kitchen, huh? Girl talk, huh?'

The Father and son sat down again, as the two ladies rushed into the kitchen, which was still in plain earshot of the lounge.

'Dinesh says Arya is the one. She is tall and fair, just like him.'

Dinesh had some sense to look away from Coral, as his mother's words filled the air.

'No, no' Nancy could be heard saying, 'she is spoken for.'

'What a shame,' Maya returned, 'but then your other daughter…?'

'Veru?' But she is older than your son. More than three years, the age gap?'

'What is age, huh?' Maya returned wisely, 'she is also very beautiful, fair too like my son.'

The ladies came back, glowing like schoolgirls, not caring if they had been overheard. They were behaving like new best friends.

'Oh, it's settled Dino baby,' Maya gushed, 'Veru is yours.'

But she needn't have bothered. The two had already found each other, locked in a dreamy gaze from across the room, whilst everyone else tuned in, forgetting about the figure still holding centre place in the room. Nancy finally remembered, and keeping her voice in a whisper, so as not to break the mood of the new lovers, she hissed behind an upturned palm, 'Coral, why are you standing there like a tree? Get to the kitchen and help Arya make tea.'

Before Coral could make a move, Veru jumped up from her place, almost knocking Arya over in her haste, she reached her future mother-in-law in one massive stride. The gracious lady placed a kiss on Veru's forehead, announcing proudly, 'The Almighty has given us a perfect daughter-in-law. Perfection, I tell you. I will name our next shop for you.'

It defied logic how Veru managed to speak and breathe in the next minute. She was ecstatic, her common sense pressed flat on the floor like shoe tramped gum. She laughed and talked with gathering speed, the words falling out in phrases of nonsense – dry pieces of wood that were torched into a blaze by the firelighters in Maya's eyes. Maya's head pushed up higher with pride, her fat cheeks glowed with the heat of the afternoon, and from the triumph that was hers. She had secured a future daughter--in-law whose performance was a miracle. How Veru kept her breath and her voice in that commotion was a mystery.

Back in the tiny kitchen Arya was in a good mood, 'Who cares which one of us it is, right sister? All that matters is that Veru is going into a rich family and will have a shop named after her. Mother must be in Venus right now, singing and dancing like a Christmas elf.'

Despite herself, Coral smiled. Of all the choices she had, Arya had chosen the one planet where anybody would be most likely to fry. It seemed a good precept, for herself, for nothing in her life would ever change now, but somehow, she was okay with that. Her thoughts turned to Arya, how she had wanted to be an astronaut. Her final school report, though, was worth practically nothing, covered as it was in figures, that if you counted, came to a total far less than the cost of a pair of second-hand shoes. Still, everyone said she was made for the stage or the big screen, and that the proof did not have to show in a report. The piece of paper was quickly stashed away, somewhere secret, and Arya was instantly elevated to a pristine status of devotion. Her looks gave her that boon, being so finely crafted that many people said she was destined for the extraordinary, something better than a mundane school report could ever provide.

But Arya had ended up as a receptionist, for a Mr Devan, last name unknown, a struggling estate agent, with his own office. Nancy proudly announced to everyone that since he was already married three times over, such a busy man would have no time left to go after a fourth. Therefore, he was safe enough to have Arya work for him.

'Cut those scones and butter them,' Arya was saying, 'and make it quick.'

She didn't know why her head was swimming. It was odd, and so she picked up the knife and started to split the scone sideways. The knife slipped. She watched transfixed as the bright red liquid oozed down the side of her palm, falling in drops on the kitchen counter.

At that precise moment Nancy sailed into the kitchen.

'What's this?' Nancy shrieked in a whisper, 'you stupid child. You don't know how to even butter a scone? What I did wrong, I don't know, to suffer like this,' she complained to the ceiling, and then grabbed the knife out of Coral's hand, giving it to Arya, 'You take this, at least you know how to do things. And now, Maya wants to go, and what will they think of us, tell me, letting them leave like dogs without food.'

Nancy disappeared, leaving Arya holding the butter knife,

and now her mood seemed to match her mother's, 'What are you staring at?' she hissed, pulling Coral's hand, and shoving it under the running tap, 'let the water take care of it. It's just a stupid cut, not the end of the world.'

As Coral took back her hand, she bit down on her lip, pulled off some kitchen paper, and wiped the oozing cut. It was not something to fuss about, she told herself, and her hand shook when she fixed a plaster roughly over the angry rip.

'Pull yourself together,' Arya snapped, 'I must do all the work because you are useless.' She washed the knife and started buttering the scones rapidly, 'anyways, I think you just pretend to be half here and half somewhere else all the time. You are just lazy and a horrid sister.'

Coral watched as Arya's face grew redder, there being no time to stop, since Nancy was back for the buttered scones and the rest of the platters. There was the gulab jamun that Coral had made herself. She learned the recipe from her grandmother, years back. She liked to make it whenever she could. It brought back the good memories when her grandmother was still around. The hand rolled pieces, fried, dunked in syrup and then rolled in coconut powder sat perfectly on the serving tray, filling the air with a nutmeg and syrup infused delicacy. She had gone too far with the nutmeg, and it brought a smile to her lips. She could hear her grandmother telling her that she had finally worked up the courage to put her own spin to her craft.

'Go, help Ma with these,' Arya ordered, handing her a tray of fried samosas, the triangular portions of mince and potato filled variations were piping hot, 'and come back for the rest.'

In the lounge the conversation was buzzing, the tea had been poured and the treats set the mood on a new level. Coral was holding the tray with the samoosas. It was a light silver tray, with a pretty paper serviette layering the bottom, on top of which sat the hot, fried snacks. Coral stepped towards Maya, forgot that her heeled shoes were in the way and tripped, sending a rush of fried pastries into Maya's lap. Maya gasped, dropping the cup and saucer she had been holding. Her gasps brought husband and son to her side, taking up their places, standing idly, they watched her, then turned horrible eyes towards Coral. She could not move, dared not speak. Instead, she let her mind wander. She thought about love and obedience. How it affected families and their relations with each other. She let herself meditate, realized she preferred a cross relation between the two ideals, and that, if she had to choose, she would choose obedience. Whilst her thoughts were piling up, events were escalating, very rapidly, around her.

Maya stood up, pushing the small serving table onto its side, everything that had been on top, now joined the brown carpet, covering the space like floating islands.

Gasps and screams filled the air, then silence. Maya smoothed down her clothes, raised up her shoulders, puffed out her sweating chin, and began marching to the door. She stood still at the doorway, turned around, speared Coral with her large eyes, gone rounder now from the drama, so that Coral stared into them, fixated. Maya's body expanded, drawing breath, she spat words into the air in her needle voice, 'You are too much. I pity your mother.'

The words echoed like a wheezing wind. But higher than that, Veru's sobs cradled the air, reaching the frequency of something nearly unearthly. She begged and cried for Maya to reconsider leaving. Nobody wanted to see Veru upset, and all faces took on the agony of the venting girl. Maya was shaking her head, but she made her voice soft, 'Veru my pigeon, we cannot choose our family. This is not your fault. We will take you home soon.'

Veru smiled through her tears, looking like a pacified baby, whilst Maya turned her attention to Nancy. Her words were delivered swiftly, clipped by nasty edges, the verdict was pronounced, and it was deadly, 'We keep our word. Our family is a proud one. The engagement will go on.' She paused long enough so that Veru had time to put a hand to her chest, as if to stop her heart from displacing itself, and the earth released Dinesh, so that he took his place by Veru's side, from where they both stared at Maya like trapped animals, 'but, keep your daughter' Maya was nodding her head, 'and you know which one I am talking about. Keep her far away from everything and everyone. Please, I am telling you, from experience, our family is very big, and us being shop owners, people like to talk and drag our name through the mud, first chance they get. I don't want a bad name, and I don't like people talking about us. So, I am sure you understand.'

When they were gone, Veru fled to the room and locked the door. Arya complained of a chipped nail, said she got it from all the work she had to do on her own, then banged on the door until Veru let her in. The door slammed shut, the key could be heard turning with a deep finality. Her parents retired quietly to their quarters, leaving Coral to fend for herself. She stared at the evidence of a deconstructed tea party that lay on the carpet, and brought herself to quickly tidy up, before settling down on the couch. She would have to do without a blanket for the night, but it was warm, and as sleep knocked on the door, the tune of whistling snores that came from Arya and Veru chased it away. Nancy's voice carried across thickly through that racket, 'It's all your fault. She came out, just like your family. The other two, take up after mine.'

CHAPTER THREE

A month had gone by. Another Monday brought skies of pale cloud, dusting everything in shades of grey and black. Coral opened the door to the bookstore and went in. For two years, she had run the place, being offered the job by an employment agency. She had no idea who owned the store, and found she preferred it that way.

The bookstore was housed in a cottage, built at the end of a busy street. It had a thatched roof, creamy walls with old wooden floors that had seen the heads of too many mops. The walls were lined with bookshelves. Some books were so old, the history lay more in the fingerprints decorating the pages, rather than in the printed content, whilst others newly purchased and never read, kept their stories bound within the covers. Together, they wafted their slightly musty, bookish scent into the air. She loved that unnamed, unique scent, but it was the grove of mango trees, with their roots guarding the yard, surrounding the cottage, like ancient guardsmen, that really fed her spirit. With their dark, glossy leaves shimmering in the sun, or whispering together in the wind, the trees created a cove under which tables were set. It seemed only natural then for the bookstore to offer coffee and biscuits to raise the appeal.

She finished dusting and mopping, to the sound of the front gate clicking shut. She looked up to find her sisters entering the store, both flushed and excited, dressed in denim shorts and orange summer tops, with matching white jackets. Their feet were covered in white takkies, their voices bringing in the bustle of the outside world. They stopped talking as soon as they spotted her, and the double stare they fixed on her was intense. Before she could say anything, Veru made the announcement as if she were naming the seasons, 'I am getting engaged. It has been confirmed. In one week, I think?'

She looked towards Arya for confirmation.

'She's really pairing up, in one week,' Arya laughed, as Coral moved towards her sisters, a smile on her face too. 'That's the best news, sis,' Coral heard herself saying, 'I am happy for you.'

'You should be,' Veru shrugged, moving off, 'imagine if you weren't. And you are my sister, so you don't have a choice.' She stooped and picked up a book, 'how do you manage to work in this drab place, anyway?'

'Yeah,' Arya joined in, picking up another and leafing through it, 'What's the point of writing all these words, if you can just draw pictures and tell the same story?'

'Exactly,' very agreed, 'we think alike. Our travel brochures have the best pictures, and there's hardly any writing. They can make you happy just by looking at them.'

Coral opened her mouth to speak, but Veru was not done, 'Anyway, when I get married,' she paused, tasting the words, her red lipped mouth moving from one side to the other, 'I will join Dinesh's family business. In the future, I won't have to look at pictures of places. I can go there if I want to.'

'But you love what you do,' Coral put in, surprised, 'did you really leave work?'

Veru snorted, her voice rich with sarcasm, 'No girl, I didn't leave work, I went and told them I would rather work there forever, making them rich, rather than helping out my new family.' She shook her head in disbelief. 'Sometimes I wonder if everything works all right in there.'

Arya joined in as they enjoyed a good laugh, then Veru picked up from where she left off, 'Of course I left. I gave up my job as a travel agent to manage a shop that has been named for me. But if I think about it, it's too much to take in. I can't blame you for having a blank spot. Like, sometimes, I feel that I am walking in someone else's shoes.'

'But you are,' Arya chipped in, 'you took what was supposed to be hers, and she let you get away with it. I know I wouldn't have done that,' Arya finished off, thumbing over her shoulder at Coral.

Veru's face changed, 'Well, they didn't want her. They wanted me. She was aiming too high, I know for sure, cos I thought about it. It's not my fault, it's hers for being so naïve.'

'You could have said no,' Arya reminded her quietly, 'It might have been her only chance.'

Veru's sharp tongue could make life uncomfortable if the listener was not prepared for it. The words, like a sting delivered by the Gympie plant, might even make a person itch to death. Coral waited for Veru to deliver the final words. 'It's not like they would have changed their minds. Dinesh told me in private, that he was planning to run away, he didn't like her at all. But his mother got him what he wanted. So, now he is staying, and we have a wedding to plan.'

Coral knew she had to be strong, to not let the bitter words upset her, but even so, it left a dent somewhere.

'*Ohhhh*,' Arya cut in impatiently, 'enough! I am bored and starved. It's not every day that Devan lets me jump a day from work. Get the words out, Veru.'

Veru tucked a hand under her long hair, drawing her

fingers along the length of it, as if the words were bound up inside it. Finally, she said, 'Okay,' as she fixed a bull's eye on Coral, 'It's about the engagement. You need to make yourself scarce for that weekend.'

The silence lasted, with Coral trying to digest this latest piece of news. Meanwhile, Arya and Veru were growing irritated. It was Arya who finally broke the silence, 'Don't be melodramatic Coral. It's not a biggie. If I were you, I'd book a bus ticket and go anywhere I want. Mother can't say anything since she wants you gone for the weekend too. It'll just make things easier for everyone.'

'Okay.'

'*Ahhh*,' Veru looked pleased, 'thanks. Honestly, Ma didn't know how to tell you. My head is still sore from all that discussion we had about how to get you to understand. But you're a big girl, and besides, between Ma and her nagging, and your clumsiness, I'll tell you a secret, I'm actually better off without the two of you.'

Once again, Arya joined her voice to Veru's, and they giggled.

'You know what?' Arya put in lightly, speaking to Veru now, 'If I had to choose, I'd choose Ma...'

'Cos, she has more gumption,' Veru put in.

'And not as...'

'Boring as this sister of ours.'

'Geez, you would think we were sending a baby off for the weekend, not a fully grown adult,' Arya winced, 'It's quite regrettable, the situation.' They nodded like twins, knowing their work had been done. Throwing kisses into the air, they left as if they were attached at the hip. Coral remained still until she heard the gate click once more. The floating kisses they had thrown her popped like bubbles and were gone. Struggling to find something to hold on to, her mind ransacked the bookshop and brought up the face of her best friend. Relief washed through her, and like a flower that opens its face only to the morning sun, she allowed the comfort from the thought of that face to wrap her up in its warm glow.

Matti. The name took her back three years into the knitting of their lives. Back to that December of their matric year. With the last paper written, it felt as if they had been kicked out of school, straight onto the fenceless field of the real world. It was wide and endless, no uniforms, brick walls or plastic chairs to put up with. They were free at last to roam through life at their own leisure. That liberation only lasted until the dawn of the next morning, when Coral's mother hammered reality back into her head, issuing orders that she was not allowed to set one foot past the front or back door, not until her results arrived. The results came, and she had passed well. But she learned that Matti had not. She felt bad for her best friend. She knew about the house Matti had grown up in, the cold block of brick and cement Matti had told her, was more alive than her parents were. She referred to them as a pair of zombie moles with torches, a new breed. In Matti's stories, she turned herself into the earthworm. But because of that, she explained, the moles had lost their taste for their favourite snack. So, they did not want to eat her, just lived to torment the worm. Coral did not know what to make of these references, and sometimes, she wished, she had pressed Matti more on the matter. Coral never knew what to say, always feeling inadequate, never thinking that much of herself, to call for her best friend's confession, as if she were qualified to pass any comment on it. She told herself that Matti was just making stories up. Matti wanted to be a writer, so it made sense that she had already started making things up in her head to fit the profile. Matti never brought it up again, and so, she took her parents back into the abyss, they went somewhere, too far away, and in Coral's mind, that's where they stayed, neither real enough to cause harm to either of the girls.

But once, in the year that they both turned sixteen, she had gone to Matti's house unannounced. It was Matti's birthday. She had never done that before. Matti had told her to never come to her house. She had pushed caution up the chimney that morning and gone anyway. After knocking smartly on the door, she stood back in time to see it flying open, as if it had been kicked. Matti's mum stood there, her eyes bulging like the underbelly of a pregnant dog, her mouth pursed into a button. Her bleached hair stood rigid, and it showed off her madness like a crown. Coral stood in the shadow of this crazed woman, feeling the hate steaming off the doorway and seeping into her skin. 'What do you want?' Matti's mum barked into the afternoon air, 'and speak up. You are wasting my time standing there, opening, and closing your mouth like a fish.'

Coral swallowed, 'Hello, aunt. I am Matti's best friend. May I please see her?'

Matti's mum rolled her eyes from top to bottom, taking in Coral's dishevelled hair and dusty shoes, 'I am not your aunt,' she sneered, peering forward, 'and don't you have your own house, coming to other people's houses and disturbing them.'

'I'm s, s, sorry' Coral stammered, not remembering Matti's mom's name, 'I brought her a birthday present.'

'How nice,' Matti's mum said sarcastically, standing aside as if she had problems moving. 'You better go, give it yourself then.'

As Coral walked unsteadily past, her heart thumping in her chest, she heard Matti's mum muttering, 'Go see what happens when people your age don't listen, and think they are gone too big for their shoes. That girl, only a spring chicken and already she wants to walk in my shoes.' Matti's mum paused, calling out for Coral to stop. Her feet froze. The words came at her, directed to her back, 'Don't think you can use this as an excuse to sit in my house and dream. When I was in school, we never had the guts to walk into someone else's house and roam inside it. That's what happens when the world gets too modern. Now go, hurry up. I got nothing better to do than open doors for people. Next, I'll be expected to make tea and scones for them too. Waste of time.'

Coral's feet rattled into action. She saw Matti's dad sitting on the couch in front of her, a beer can in his hand, his nose inside the daily newspaper. She hurried past, not knowing which way to go to find Matti. But then she got her orders from the doorway, telling her to go straight to the first door on the right. That was Matti's room. She got there, and knocked, calling urgently, 'Hey, it's me.' The answering call came from the wrong direction. It was Matti's mum shouting from the doorway, 'Keep your voice down. This is my house and my roof. Nobody shouts under my roof.'

As Coral stood and stared at the unpainted door, it opened, and Matti stood there. She looked strange, like something that crawled out of a cave. She stood hunched, cowering, with her curly hair hanging over her face, the locks covering both cheeks, so that as she looked up at Coral, who was in truth shorter than her, it was as if she were melting into the ground.

'What do you want?' she hissed, 'what are you doing here?'

Coral held out the gift-wrapped book mechanically, forgetting why she was there. She watched as a hand shot out to grab it. She did not know what to say.

'Get out now,' Matti told her fiercely, 'and never come back.'

As Matti moved back, her hair moved with her, so that a cheek became visible. It had an angry red bruise on it.

'Your face!' Coral whispered, and almost without thinking, she blurted, 'Your mum, was it her?'

'Don't pick on my mum!' Matti shouted, loud enough to bring the said person running at full speed to the door. Coral felt her shirt being yanked at the collar and turned around to face the woman.

'What do you think you are doing, stirring trouble in my house,' Matti's mum yelled, 'you little eavesdropping goblin! You get out now and mind your own business.'

Before Coral knew anything, she was pulled out and thrown onto the porch, with the front door slamming shut in her face, the reverberations of which hooted inside her head. The door had not fallen off its hinges, and for this she was grateful, but she turned around, and ran back home, as if she had someone jabbing her from behind. That afternoon had displaced something inside her. It stayed with her, the rock that wedged itself where her heart should be, made breathing difficult. She had sensed something awful in that house, but worse, she could not put it into words. The episode haunted her. She should not have gone there. She hated herself for doing that. To make matters worse, Matti did not pitch up at school for three days after that, and if the weekend were counted, then five days later Matti emerged again, picking up their friendship as if nothing had ever happened. A month later, Matti vanished once more.

This time she returned after three weeks, and by then, she had moved in with her father's aunt who lived in another town, about half an hour's drive away. She travelled from her aunt's house to school, but that was all she said, and Coral did not ask more. They became sisters again, talking endlessly about their dreams under the evergreen leaves of the pine trees that shaded the school backyard.

After they wrote those final exams, Coral had not seen Matti again. They were out of school, the reports had come, and still nothing. But two years later, Matti arrived to pick her up, in a tiny car that was hers. They went to the mall, where they window shopped until their feet grew too heavy, and then, they went to the beach. As they lay on the sand, watching the waves, Coral turned to survey the girl she had known. Matti had outgrown her thinness, taken on a rounder profile. She wore clothes that reached her ankles, and material that covered her wrists. She had a big sunhat on, shaped like a flying saucer, so that she sometimes misjudged where she was going, and bumped into someone or something. But she removed her hat now, leaned back on her elbows, and put her face towards the sea.

'It's beautiful,' she murmured, 'the blue. But I don't trust it,' she said turning towards Coral, 'it's like the poison dart frog. Pretty and toxic.'

Coral sighed, 'What does that gorgeous sea have to do with the poison blue frog? There's no logical comparison. It reminds me of what you said years ago– that your parents were moles or what was it? Zombies with torches?'

But she shouldn't have brought that up. Something stiffened in Matti.

'I'm sorry. I shouldn't have said that. But you know me, I

always speak before sorting things out in my head. '

'Yes, every day is market day in there,' Matti suddenly laughed, prodding at Coral's temples lightly, 'and today it must be busier than usual.'

Coral laughed too, but she knew Matti had dismissed her already.

Matti got up and started running to the water. She waded in, her flowery clothes bubbling in the waves. She stayed there, bobbing in the waves, for a long time before calmly walking out, her clothes stuck to her body, her hair dripping, and her face sun burned. 'It's wonderful,' she remarked, 'the water is amazing.'

'We didn't bring a towel.'

Matti was not one to stick to rules. She simply did as she pleased. That had not changed. The one time, on a school excursion, the bus carrying a load of kids and teachers, came to a halt at a congested intersection where the robots had fizzled out. In the pouring rain, in the confusion, Matti went running out of the bus, bounding into the centre of the four- way intersection, to pick up a scraggly cat from the traffic island. The cat had been sitting there, looking peaceful, but now it went mad. The cat arched its back, and fought for its freedom, by shooting into the air and clawing Matti on the arm. Matti was not phased, but then the inevitable happened. The cat bounded across the road, with Matti chasing after it, disappearing into the adjacent sugar cane fields. It took a whole hour to find Matti again, as the string of reluctant teachers made their way into the fields, wandering through the waving grass, until they emerged with the girl, a group of soaking wet adults, their faces so stung with anger, it burned holes into the images of that day. From the school bus windows, the rest of them got a good view of Matti, looking merry, clutching a sugar cane stalk which she must have plucked from the field herself, taking giant bites, chewing with her mouth full, she kept spitting out the leftovers onto the road.

She came back from that reverie to find they had left the beach behind and were on the way back. They reached Coral's house and to her horror, Matti jumped out of the car, headed straight into the house, and leapt onto her mother's pride and joy – the couch.

Veru was the first one there.

'Do you want a change of clothes?' Veru asked cautiously, as one by one everyone emerged from the rooms, to stand and stare at the wet, bare footed girl lounging on the revered piece of furniture.

'No need,' Matti answered cheerfully.

'I'll get a towel,' Arya chipped in, quickly disappearing from the room as Nancy arrived.

'That couch cost a lot of money,' Nancy said through gritted teeth, her face like stone.

Matti jumped up, went running to Nancy, and put both wet arms around her neck, 'Aunty Nancy, you'll give yourself a heart attack behaving like this.'

Everybody stared, including Nancy, who besides standing stiffly, both hands at her sides, for the first time, found herself empty of words. Arya dropped the towel she had been carrying, as Ed started moving towards the gate, loudly rattling the lock as he prepped the gates for Matti's departure.

Matti waved cheerfully at the lot of them, the row of stone heads, before jumping into her car, backing out of the driveway as if the ground were made of soap, she pumped her hooter loud enough to start all the neighbourhood dogs, as the old car rolled slightly back on the inclined road, before rattling and skidding away, out of sight.

'The nerve of that girl,' Nancy puffed back into life, directing her words to Ed, 'Imagine having such bad manners. No respect for your elders. You can see why her mother kicked her out.'

'Ma!' Coral gasped, 'How can you say something so horrible?'

The fire coursed through Nancy as she put out a hand towards her daughter, finger pointing to the sky, her voice cracking from anger, she croaked, 'what did you say? Standing here in the sun and questioning me in broad daylight, with everyone listening and no shame to backtalk your own mother,' Nancy shouted, 'No better than the dogs roaming in the street. None of my other daughters behave like this.'

There was nobody else around, not even on the road, just the five of them. Coral lowered her head, swallowed the words that were rising like a summer tide.

Later that week, when they met up again, Matti announced she had written a book, 'complete from cover to cover,' she said quietly.

A book?' Coral asked with awe, 'That's amazing, 'when can I read it?'

'Yeah,' Matti said flatly, 'Like never. I showed it to a big brain and got turned down,'

'What do you mean?'

'Never mind. It doesn't matter anymore. There's red lines and marks all over my work. I lack structure, apparently. In any case, who cares? It's not maths, where one plus three equals four. It's not that straightforward.'

'But can't you make the changes, and then submit it for

rechecking?'

Matti looked hard at Coral, her eyes turning cold with hatred, 'You are just like them. Thinking in a straight line. That way you all feel safe,' she drew breath dramatically. 'You don't know what it's like, having this thing inside your head. And then when your fingers start to move, the thoughts, they just flow. And you want me to follow a pattern of thinking?'

'That's not what I was trying to say.'

'Really?' Matti rounded on her, 'In your perfect world, with your nice house and your family, stuck together like overcooked spaghetti, you want to take away the only thing I have? My work?'

'But, I...'

'Yes, I know. I never forgave you for what you did that day, coming to my house, even though I asked you not to. You wanted to see for yourself. So, you could pity me.'

'That's not it.'

Matti scrunched up her eyes, as if to shield them from the sun, her long face with the pointed chin creased, thin lips pursed, and the tip of her freckled nose seemed to be touching the top of Coral's head, as she stared down at her, new intimidation in her voice, 'You never bothered to ask.' Matti leaned away, shaking her head, 'not even when you saw that I was miserable at school, every day, I waited for you to ask, so that I could tell you. But you're selfish, only bothered about your world and yourself.'

Coral was stunned. As usual, the words that could have saved her never came. Instead, the vision of a bunch of chopped flowers stuffed into a vase, from someone else's kitchen, floated into her head. She saw their long stalks, climbing out, rotten at the bottom, limp, and rising, to show flower heads that betrayed the truth. Disgust built up in her brain, this weakness killed any hope, sending vibes like shock waves, where they stayed concentrated at the base of her throat, hardening there like the bile of a sick person.

She came out of her reverie, to find Matti collecting her breath, 'Anyway, as for my writing, it is mine, and it will stay that way. You can't follow instructions to produce a masterpiece. No, you live it. For starters, let's ask the biggest question – where do the words come from huh? Those words that jump into your brain. Where does it come from? Tell me.

Coral remained silent.

'It got put there. Like a seed goes into the ground, so that the words grow, bend and twist, to create something extraordinary. And then judgement day arrives, and *they* undo everything with a toothpick, when they can't even explain it themselves. What do they know of the suffering, words banging into your head, until your heart races and your fingers itch. I say it is supernatural, a power that comes from another world. As if a dead person with no body, wants to reach out, to tell a story, and the poor homeless spirit finds another one that matches it in misery,' she paused, smiling broadly, 'one that's alive of course, like me. I think it sort of rents space in the head of the living, comes and goes, whenever it pleases, takes possession until that story is told.'

'That is powerful, Matti.'

Matti sized her up with a long sideward stare, 'For once, you said the right thing. I am feeling better already. Not everybody is so lucky to write their story, you know.'

Matti was growing excited, 'A dead person's craft, that's what I have, and I will tell the story, in the way it's meant to, and I don't need permission to do that, not from anyone, dead or alive.'

'I agree with you, Matti.'

Matti looked at her with new scorn, 'There you go again. I knew it. You are the kind of person who will agree with everything. You have no mind of your own.'

Coral found the grace to look away.

'Yes,' Matti was saying, more to herself, nodding her head as if she were trying to convince them both, 'I'm tired of waiting for something good to happen. And I'm tired of all the bad that never goes away, and of all the boundaries. I have the power to set myself free. I'm going to do great things,' she dropped the words slowly, as if she were making the pact with herself, in that space of time, and Coral played witness. A dangerous smile played on her face, 'I'm going to take what was never mine in the first place.'

Coral did not want to spoil the moment. She waited.

'You know, my aunt gave me the starting point, only I didn't see it clearly until know. A place to reach out and grab something for myself,' Matti was starting to sound delirious with anticipation, 'She has connections to get me in. It's a couple of networked towns, small remote ones, sort of, somewhere between Port Elizabeth and Cape Town,' Matti paused, twirling her fingers in the air, giving Coral a brief background to her story. Just then, a roaming fly came out of nowhere. It started making circles around her head.

'Stupid fly.'

She deadlocked the buzzing insect with a tilt of her curly head, then brought her hands together without warning, squashing the fly in her palms, before wiping the remains off on her shorts. 'See,' she looked at Coral, enjoying the look of horror on the girl's face with growing satisfaction, 'that's what sets me apart from everyone else. I am not afraid.'

'Yes.'

Matti shrugged, 'So, coming back to what I was saying. The main town is huge, the beach, forest, and private waterfall, everything bought and paid for by some rich guy, so rich that he started the biggest of the towns, brought in the labour, laid the foundation for fruit farming, forestry, the works. The man was a genius, a dead one now. But his family,' Matti sighed deeply, 'they are still here, and they have everything, passed on to them. There's lots of them, running things – they made a place for us, young people, in a town where they still follow the old man's philosophy,' Matti held up her chin – Take nothing more seriously,' her voice had lifted, 'never more seriously than old socks. For those can be thrown away when you don't' need them, and nobody will mind,' Matti was so excited that she had to catch her breath, 'I want to follow his logic. I am ready to be free.'

'Is he still alive?'

'No, I just told you, not anymore, been gone a couple decades ago. I cherish his mindset. That is how I will live from now on.'

'Are you really going then?'

Matti ignored her, still wrapped in her ideas, 'Why should I settle for less, huh? What's the point of making do and being complacent, tell me. I don't like feeling stupid and naïve. You know,' she turned her face towards Coral, and the hatred that was written across it put fear into the other girl. 'I have two choices. One is to follow blindly, to swallow my pride and wake up every morning, telling myself that my breakfast eggs look brighter than the sun, and the other, is to lay down and die, like an abandoned street dog. I don't want either. I will break free, turn myself into something else. I will bend the rules to suit my purpose, and if that means I must turn my back on what's right, I don't care. And when I have everything,' Matti's eyes changed, grew shiny, 'I will see who has the guts to take me on. And that's what separates people like you and me. You will stay where you are, and me, I will escape.'

'You are saying too much. I can't follow you.'

Matti shook her head, 'Sometimes, I think everybody must be like you. That explains, why I am in my own league when it comes to looking at life. You are too simple to understand where I am coming from,' and here Matti narrowed her eyes, scrutinizing Coral's face as if she were searching for some physical sign, 'it's not your fault or theirs, I see that. It's just how you are made.'

There was a short silence.

Coral was used to this criticism from Matti and did not allow herself to fall into the trap. Instead, she brought the conversation around to something Matti had mentioned earlier.

'But do you really want to wipe away your history and tradition. You are lucky enough to have two cultures. Your mum is white, and your dad is Indian?' Coral's eyes were growing large, 'Why would you want to walk away from that?'

'And you are one hundred per cent Indian, who is going to snatch that from you. But if you had just one extra brain cell, you would see the artistry and challenge in this experiment. It is freedom, a chance to start something new. I will not be branded like a cow, forced to follow a destiny I did not choose.'

Coral stared at her best friend. She had always known that Matti would play truant, that she would never conform. Her ideas were too big to fit inside the tight scheme of things. School had been a nightmare for her, but she managed somehow to stay half inside the lines, and the first thing she did on the last day of school was to make a small fire a few feet away from the school gate, just behind the screen of small trees that gave them some privacy. As she fed her school shoes to the fire, a huge puff of smoke filled the air followed by a horrible smell. As the rebel stood over the struggling fire, others drifted into the scene, some to watch, others to follow. With the pile of shoes growing, and the voices of the chanting kids getting higher, the security guard came running. They scattered, fleeing like determined cockroaches. Thinking of that day still brought a smile to her face. Now that their school days were behind them, it made sense that Matti would live her life on her own terms.

'You see,' Matti was saying, 'Everyone suspects that we never see things for what they are. I suppose everyone does that to protect themselves against the truth,' she paused, 'frankly, I don't need protecting. I am after something else. I want to create my own version of what I see, not just in my writing, but also in my life. I refuse to look at it through someone else's logic. You get what I am trying to say?'

'But does that mean you want to change your culture?'

Matti shrugged, 'What is culture? A way of living? My aunt tells me there is no predefined concept of a culture at this new place. Everyone is free to choose."

'I don't know. I never thought about it so deeply before.'

'Well,' Matti said shrewdly, 'that is the problem with everyone these days. You never think enough. Everything is handed down because somebody else did it before, it must be done the same way, like ducks that live their lives, the same way ducks have always lived their lives. We are not ducks, at least, that's how I prefer to see it. Anyway, you are lost, still stuck in the first part of my conversation, so I'm wasting my time. All you need to know is that, as I was saying, my aunt knows a friend who works at this place. You see,' she explained quietly, 'it's a close bonded place. You can't get in unless you know somebody.'

Coral didn't know why but the words had affected her somehow. Before she knew it, she gushed, 'Please let me come with you.'

There was a pause, during which Coral wished she could take back what she had said. But the incredulous look that was reshaping Matti's face stopped her, 'You mean that? You will leave your family and come with me?'

'Yes.'

'Why?'

Coral swallowed, 'Because I want to. It's that simple, I promise.'

Matti looked away, 'We will have to work to earn our keep there. I'm probably going to be on kitchen duty, and I don't know what my aunt can organise for you.'

'I don't mind,' Coral replied too easily, because once she got started, it was getting very easy to go with the flow, 'I want to go with you.'

Matti shrugged, 'Okay. I'll see what I can do. But be warned, where people are involved, there's always a catch. The place is freedom, but the catch is – you won't get to have more than what you take with you. I am talking about your social rank. That cannot be changed, except by a miracle. And that's my challenge, for myself, not yours. You won't be able to pull that off in any case. For now, just know that there are those at the top, they are like royalty. The rest are bottom feeders. That's us.'

'Yes. I understand.'

Matti laughed, 'Okay then. I will make sure my aunt's friend gets us both in.'

The matter was settled. She had earned Matti's respect.

CHAPTER FOUR

Three months later, Matti arrived at the bookstore, flushed with excitement.

'We're in,' she smiled broadly, 'we go as kitchen help, but hey, who cares?'

After their last conversation, Coral had not seen or heard from her best friend. The weeks had piled up since then, , getting higher than the plate of pancakes she dreamt of most nights. Her dreams came and went, a slide show of pancakes, platefuls that almost reached the ceiling, drenched in a fountain of syrup. She was always seated at an enormous table, watching the swaying towers make their way to her, carried by half a dozen smiling faces per plate, faces that extended into bodies, dressed up with colours of the rainbow. She learned that this was her escape, a happy place, an unreachable destiny. She always woke up to the job at the bookshop, and in some odd way, she was content, living in a world caught between her books and dreams.

'So, we leave in two days,' Matti was saying, bringing her back to the moment, 'you better get home and pack.' She bit on a nail, throwing her glance about the room, 'at least you'll be out of this dump.'

Coral stared at Matti, feeling the dread creeping into her body. Their last conversation meant nothing to her, neither did the plans made. She did not want to leave her family. She should not have taken her promises so lightly, for looking at

Matti now, she knew that on Matti's part, every word said was a word Matti had built into a wall.

The silence fetched Matti's eyes onto hers, as she turned her head away like a guilty cat, 'You haven't changed your mind, right?'

Coral wanted to run.

'Are you being serious?' Matti sounded like she was going to choke, 'This whole thing has been a big fat joke to you?'

'I'm sorry, Matti,' Coral tried to plead her case, 'but I never heard from you since then. I honestly thought you had forgotten about it.'

'Don't use that word,' Matti glared at her, '*Honestly* is a word you don't have the privilege of using. You think you can make promises and then just change your mind, huh? But I knew it. You are nothing, you hear me? Just a small nothing who will get what's coming to her. You carry on thinking that you are better than everyone else.'

Matti's voice had changed, and her features had hardened. Her light brown eyes grew dark, her small mouth pursed in hatred, and the cheeks in her long face glowed red, as if they were lanterns hanging from a porch, 'You're nothing.'

'Please understand. I like being here, in my bookshop.'

'No,' Matti shook her head, 'you wanted me to feel like this, even more alone than I already am. You made a promise, remember? And forgot it just like that. It takes skill, I must say. You are bad, the type they make movies about. I never want to see you again.'

She knew Matti was right. She should not have promised that she would go with her. She wished for the tears to come, if only to remind her that besides the thumping in her chest, she was hurting. But the tears would not come. Instead, she stood still, looking as if she did not care. She watched as Matti dug into her knapsack and brought out a parcel, wrapped in brown paper.

'Here,' Matti said, as she threw the parcel onto the counter, then as if the thought had just occurred to her, began tearing at the paper herself. The wrapping paper was light, and it gave way easily, to reveal a wooden frame decorated at the edges with seashells. The beautiful trimmings were meant to detract from the centre piece, from where an iridescent blue-spotted, black-winged butterfly was pasted.

'It's a forest queen,' Matti said quietly, 'I couldn't believe it when I picked this up at a flea market last month. I didn't know why I thought of you. But now I do.'

She fixed Matti with her brown eyes. 'I wanted you to have it, and it makes sense. It's nothing more than a dead butterfly. You should keep it.'

She came out of her reverie to hear the front gate swinging madly. When she got there, it was to discover the wind had made a racket, sending leaves everywhere, a thick carpet lay on the footpath. She would have to sweep that. She closed the small gate and went to fetch the broom.

CHAPTER FIVE

Friday swung around bringing a fine stream of raindrops. The house, on the other hand, was anything but calm. The engagement was set for Sunday, and Nancy was beside herself, a nervous pocket of energy into which everyone put their wary smiles, and best manners. They kept away from her, as much as they could, but the house being so tiny, they were always in her path. She went everywhere in a mood that would have made any thunderstorm proud. She was at her peak now, pushing open the door to the girls' room, standing there, hands planted on her hips, looking like a teapot with a chipped lid.

'Coral,' she yelled, the words coming from deep inside her, 'what are you doing, dressed up so early? And you only leaving at eleven. Who's going to polish the brassware? You think it'll clean itself. Go, find the rags on the kitchen table – useless lot of children I made. Not one of them can do anything right.'

So much had happened since she last saw Matti. The changes that came into her life after that meeting in the bookshop had everything to do with Veru's engagement. The matter was no joke, her family wanted her gone for the weekend. Left with no place to go, she was desperate and on the doorstep of madness when Matti called her, straight out of nowhere. The call saved her. She made her plea and got her wish. Matti assured her that she was not angry any more, and that thinking on the past was a big nuisance, that she had moved on, going forward, rather than backwards. She was sending for the driver to pick Coral up and take her to the Mansion, as they called it, to start a new life. She had not told her family the truth. They knew that she was going to visit Matti for a week, after which she would be back. They did not know that she was going to join Matti on the other side. She had told another lie. But for her part, this time it was a lie she intended to keep, being all wrapped up like a gift at Christmas. There was no turning back now.

'Why are you standing there and daydreaming?' Nancy shrieked, bringing her back again, 'Wake up, and start your work.'

Her voice brought Veru and Arya running.

'What's she done now?' Veru asked, grinning.

'Waiting for you two,' Nancy replied, knowing fully well that she had just kindled a fire.

'No ways, I can't help,' Arya said flatly, 'My nails won't survive it.'

'Really?' Veru joined in, 'You expect me, the bride to be, to polish brassware?'

'Looks like it,' Arya drawled, 'since everyone knows I'm allergic to that stuff.'

'You're allergic to what suits you,' Veru snapped.

Nancy picked up her voice once more, raising it to the ceiling as she normally did to gather the reins, and reinstate herself as the single voice of reason. 'Arya and Veru, go iron the clothes for Sunday. And stop talking so much, focus on your work. That fancy outfits should come with a lifetime guarantee, the way they make them, so easy to burn. And the engagement is almost here, and nothing is done, not yet. As for you Coral, 'if I don't see my face reflected in that brassware, I'll make you wash the floors too.'

She shooed them off, and for the next two hours a certain calm reigned over the house, that is, until a fierce loud hooting penetrated the still morning air, bringing Nancy rushing out of the kitchen, yelling, 'Kesh is at the gate. Nobody else tramps the hooter as if they having a heart attack.'

'Ma,' Arya floated her eyes to the ceiling and back, 'let's keep quiet and she'll think no one's at home.'

Nancy controlled her smile, and there was approval in her voice, 'Your father's sister will definitely get that treatment somewhere, someday,' she told them sagely, before quickly pulling herself together, 'But it won't be at this house.'

With that she turned her attention to the older girls, who were still dressed in their night clothes, 'Go change quickly. Nobody visits my house to find everyone still in their pyjamas. That Kesh thinks she will catch me off my feet, make me look bad when she comes to visit so early. She thinks the house will be upside down, so she can go tell everybody her stories, but she doesn't know who she is dealing with.'

When Nancy emerged from the house, it was to find Eddie already at the gate, closing it, as the door of the car in her driveway opened, and slammed shut. Kesh stood in the morning light, dressed as if she were going to a wedding.

'Oh, my darling,' Kesh came gushing at Nancy, planting a kiss on her cheek, before moving into the house, as if she were on tippy toe, her stalk like figure draped in an orange and silver sari. She wore a sleeveless silver blouse that was cut low at the back. From both wrists, at least two dozen silver bangles dusted in fairy dust shimmered and dangled.

'*Yooo hooo* girls, where are you all? It's too late to be in bed. Oh, Coral, you appeared like a ghost, out of nowhere. You not sleepwalking, are you, girl?'

The other girls came running out of the room. After she had kissed each one on both cheeks and hugged each one as if the last day on earth had come, she handed over the gold dusted paper box in her hands to Ed, who remained in her shadow, 'Happy Diwali to my brother's family!'

'To you and the family too,' Nancy returned, taking the box from Ed, and setting it neatly on the centre table in the lounge, 'You went all out this year.'

'Every year, darling,' Kesh sang happily, 'Once a year, when the date comes out, I start early, and I bake and bake and bake. If I don't, who will?

She cast a long look at Nancy, who fought hard to stuff the words that filled the back of throat, rising so fast that she had to gulp them down and find new one.

'Thank you for the treats.'

'As always,' Kesh nodded, 'Not like you don't know about Diwali, but I must say, the lights and fireworks and baking and nice clothes,' her hands pumped the air, as if she were at a rock concert, bangles jingling as they went, 'I don't know how you can be so still in this house. Oh, where is Kino? Kiiiiiinnnnoooooo!'

Kino materialised, quickly flowing through the doorway, a tall thin teenager of sixteen who by some miracle was able to stand up straight under the weight of gold piled on him. He was the only grandson for both sets of grandparents. The twin set of gold chains at his neck symbolised family pride in this feat. The coin earrings and heavy wrist bracelet were gifts from his parents, and now firmly part of the public domain since everyone knew about them.

'*Ah*, Kino my boy,' Kesh said proudly, 'give your cousins a hug.'

Kino obliged, giving each of his relatives a very fleeting hug. He returned to his mother's side, and dutifully waited for her to sit first.

'Imagine that,' Kesh cooed, as she sank into the couch, 'if Kino hadn't been born, there would only be girls in the family, as far as the young generation goes,' she nodded towards Nancy, 'right?'

'Yes,' Nancy said through pressed lips, 'but our girls brought us luck too.'

'Yes, I have two and you have three. Everyone knows that, but honestly,' Kesh leaned forward, batting her orange tinted lids furiously, her red lips in a very light face quivering with emotion, her blushed cheekbones looking like two red dots in the dim lounge light. 'There's something about a boy. I was lucky, and I hear you were secretly hoping for a boy during all three trials, yes?'

For once Nancy found nothing to say, and it was Arya who came to the rescue, her voice, buttery and smooth, it tipped the air, 'Aunt Kesh, are boys better than girls?'

It came and went but at times, Kesh's instincts could be as sharp as a Gaboon adder and she picked up on the undercurrent, 'Why no silly! Girls, boys,' she flapped her hands, 'they're all the same. But mind you,' she wagged a finger at the three girls, 'There is no excuse for a badly behaved girl. I heard just now, there's a house down this street. They got three girls too,' and here she paused and made eye contact with Nancy as a premonition warning of sorts, 'the one girl wakes up in the middle of the night with a packed suitcase and runs away. *Boof!*' Kesh waved her hands dramatically, the red pointed tips of her fingernails making patterns in the air. 'The next day everyone sees the neighbour's son is missing too. Poor boy, must have been forced into leaving with that horrible girl.'

'Really?' Nancy sounded intrigued, 'what's the people's names, the ones in the house down this street? I might know them.'

'Oh,' Kesh shook her head, 'I forgot the name. In any case, I never met them myself, so it doesn't matter, but words don't lie. My brother here understands,' and Kesh tilted her chin towards Ed, 'family reputation is very important. Girls must behave like girls and keep the family name. When my Kino is ready to marry, I shall make sure the girl is of the highest breeding, the most exquisite with excellent manners. She will be marrying into our family after all,' Kesh gestured around her, 'and we are one of the last ones left with old school values and beliefs.'

'Very true,' Nancy rose to the challenge, 'but my girls won't be marrying any thief either. It will be a very nice family. Look at our Veru's engagement this Sunday, who could have known such a nice match will come for her.'

Born to push the knife deeper when she got the chance, Kesh leaned forward, eyes scrunched for better sight, 'I hear the match was for Coral?'

Her eyes found Coral's and locked in, 'How do you feel, my darling? What a shame, I think if it happened to my Kiara, she would be crying her eyes out.'

'I don't mind,' Coral said softly.

'Oh, you are a sweetie,' Kesh said sympathetically, her voice suddenly weighed down with gravity, 'you are so good, life is going to leave you with breadcrumbs,' and here she turned to Nancy, 'you should teach her to toughen up. My Kiara would have gone down fighting like a Komodo.'

'My girls don't fight like Komodos,' Nancy bit back, 'they

don't need to. Coral's time will come. But her fate won't be as good as the ones picked for her sisters. But what can we do?'

'And what is wrong with Coral for her to have a poor fate?'

Now that Kesh's teeth were sunk into the matter, she would not pull them out of it. Having picked a side, and seeing more joy in it, she was determined for war, especially since Nancy had brought it upon herself, by implying Kesh's daughters, being of the fighting spirit, were weak and ill brought up. When it came to anybody picking on her children, Kesh became a wasp. She leaned forward, her elbow resting on the knee, her fist supporting her chin, and waited.

'Nothing is wrong with her,' Nancy said loudly, 'but it is not her time.'

'*Ah*, not her time? How easy to say,' Kesh clapped her hands so that the bangled wrists jingled and jangled, 'What you telling me, is that if someone comes home for my Desh, and thinks that I will give them my Kiara, you think I will not send that good for nothing goat running into the street? Just think how I would feel, as if my one eye was not the same as the other.'

Nobody was brave enough to ask what would happen if the sainted Kino had a change of heart at any time, would she still see things from the other perspective. It looked as if Nancy just might when a single loud hoot that came from the roadside rescued them all. This was followed by someone lighting up firecrackers from somewhere which exploded like a misfiring engine. The early Diwali celebrations had started.

Whether it was the hoot or the firecrackers that prompted Coral into action, nobody could have guessed, but she darted into the bedroom and came out holding a suitcase. The sight of it sent Kesh shooting up from the couch. 'What's happening?'

she gasped. 'Where are you going?'

The alarm in her voice, brought Nancy around quickly, 'Work called her. Only for one week. Nothing to worry about.'

Kesh looked madly towards Eddie, 'But it's a family engagement. How can you let her leave like this? And a young girl, all alone?'

'She must go to work,' her brother lied, looking uneasy and turning to Nancy for reassurance. 'Coral forgot to put in her leave. She is going for a conference.'

'What? Since when bookshop caretakers go for conferences,' Kesh muttered, 'even if this is true, how can she forget?'

Coral did not wait for the tirade to finish. She did not want to keep the driver waiting. She went forward, and kissed each family member on the cheek, but when she got around to her aunt Kesh, the family dramatist stood her ground, and with lifted chin, she snake eyed Coral, then said sharply, 'Listen, you young nipper, if Kiara was here standing in front of me, with this attitude, by now I would have given her a nice kick in the backside, and sent her to bed. Look at that big suitcase you got, looking like a big shot, holding it so tightly like it is filled with gold. You go back inside the house now, and make time for your sister and your family, or you can kiss my shoe goodbye.'

There was silence. Coral was not sure what she was expected to do. She could not walk away from Kesh, for that would be rude and unthinkable. She could not tell the truth that her family wanted her gone, for it would set Kesh up against her mother. The dread crept inside her veins, panic installing itself in her head. But, on the outside, nothing showed on her face.

'It's just for this week, and I'll be back,' she heard herself tell the lie. 'I'll call when I reach.'

'Girl, listen to your mother,' Kesh was saying harshly, and it sounded as if her voice was coming from somewhere far. 'Young girls don't carry suitcases and walk around as if they were young boys, you hear? Think about your family and what everyone will say.'

Coral looked at Nancy for help, saw the almost imperceptible nod telling her to go, and she forced herself to walk away, straight towards the black shiny car that waited for her. She had never seen anything like it before. It sat on the road, glittering like a bug from out of space. She walked out of the driveway, sensing all eyes boring into her back, hoping that someone would stop her, but nobody did. She opened the gate and got into the car, and it moved off, leaving everyone behind.

CHAPTER SIX

They had been driving for hours. Coral sat quietly, staring out the window, watching the landscape change with each hour. It was all new to her. The sights that flew past flashed like a slide show of rolling green pastures, patchworked with watering holes and roaming cows. The mountains sat like squat monsters, some covered in trees and shrubs, huddling so close that it looked as if the mountains had been sick and thrown up a jungle. Other monsters showed their hard edges too, sleeping giants of rock, showing rugged backs, bare and stony, with boulders sticking out like pimples.

They came to a bridge, where a narrow pathway had been built on either side of the bridge. A fencing of net climbed up from the railings, and the sight of it shook the nameless driver into life. He made no mention of his name, only that he had worked for the Mansion for more than half his lifespan and counting. He spoke as if words had been extracted from his mouth under extreme torture, and she realised, he was one of her own. The driver crossed himself, saying a prayer in Latin, for which he extracted the fullest of her admiration, and then he told her his story. The footpaths running down the length of the bridge that had been given a netting, those barriers were there to prevent jumping feet into the deep gorge below. There was a winding stream at the bottom of that gorge, he said, and if anyone stood at the railings and peered through the net, they would catch a glimpse of a frozen piece of the sky, for the water even from that height, took on the image of shattered glass. He was sure nothing survived in that water and crossed himself again to make sure. He told her the only thing that looked right, when somebody looked down, was the pieces of jagged rock that piled up there. He could see plenty of that around him without having to get out of his car and take the cursed look. But here, too, he paused, adding that people spoke amongst themselves, and somewhere in between what was said, a new belief got stitched into the tale. People's imaginations stretched, he knew that, but this one was too good not to be told. His voice grew serious, as he said some believed that the rock that broke through the ground, next to that stream might have a direct connection to the stalactites, coming from deep inside dark caves. 'It gets better,' he pointed out, 'those rocks down below, with their jagged tips, with their history of cave origins, they wait there, to spear the next victim, turn them into bats,' he nodded, 'since most of the victims, it was rumoured, were never found anyway.'

She said a prayer too, in her head, and was glad when they left the bridge behind to emerge on the other side, with mountains bordering the road, their surfaces crawling with aloe, an adult population, with some already two metres above ground. But she found the aloe to be a strange-looking plant, as if the dead leaves were arranged around a waist, tailor- made. New fat arms of green flourished above the dead, poking the air with narrowed tips. Growing straight through the lot, like the stalk of a sugar cane plant, summer had fashioned a candlestick holder, with orangish- red tubular flowers at the end. She gazed at the arrangement in awe, felt compelled to ask the driver to slow down so that she might get a better view of her rocky bedded friends. She did not have the courage to do that, so they sped on, past bustling townships and rolling hills.

When the ocean came into view, the sight used up her breath. Her eyes locked into the bed of unnatural blue, sending her mind into the childhood image of wizards, their long gowns dazzling, as if made up of all the sapphires in the world. She saw those wizards, so many the number ran into thousands, jumping into the ocean, like colour fizz balls, bewitching the waters with a magical tint, but she knew, not even such wizardry held the power to conjure the kind of beauty she was looking at. Gradually, she lost sight of the ocean as the weather changed, the beautiful sky went into a sulk, and when the ocean came up again, the allure was lost, the water took on a blandness, threatening in its ordinariness as the wind gathered speed, whipping the water into a frenzy. The waves grew higher, the car reached a stretch of road outside the town of Port Elizabeth, where a concrete barrier of pillars remained the only buffer between the raging madness and the road. She knew fear then, wondering if the car would be smashed against the barriers, taken by the waves, like a toy in a bathtub. She saw the water split itself on the concrete, sending a shower into the air, and a deluge onto the windscreen. The car sped away, leaving behind the showers as they headed off into dusk.

In that narrowed light, she had her last sighting of a rocky shoreline, where the dark formations made patterns in the sea. The tide had drawn back, revealing phantom shapes, mimicking underwater shipwrecks, their nakedness exposed to the mist, the drizzled fog settled over the exposed bones, gently healing, touching the rawness, a game not to be seen with day eyes. She turned her head away, not wanting to be the cursed on-looker. Soon, her eyes grew heavy as she fell into a deep sleep. When she woke up, her head was resting against the window, collecting the morning sun's rays. so that as she lifted it up, her hair felt like it had been set on fire. Her lips were dry, her neck felt stiff, and she quickly rolled down the window. The morning air drifted in, and she took a deep sniff. The air smelled different, cool, curious. It made her think of lemon peel, more pungent, crossed with a kind of mild bug spray. It was not unpleasant, just different. She yawned, forgetting her place and it brought the driver's attention to her.

'You're awake,' he called from the wheel, 'That's good cos we almost there.'

She quickly put a hand over her mouth, gathering herself. She had no idea where they were, but the car wound its way along a dirt road, broad enough for two, the road cutting through a dense forest. The road was pebbly, and the tyres wobbled, as the car swerved, avoiding the exposed large rock heads that peeped out from the ground. Creeping vines twisted up the trees, crawling along branches, and when those branches reached across to touch tips with their cousins across the road, the overhanging arches shaded the road, like snakes forming a tunnel, they were distracting, making the driver more anxious, causing him to lean so far forward he might as well have had his head out the windscreen. She remembered Matti saying something about the drive to the Mansion being an otherworldly experience. Matti had certainly not clipped her words on that one. She wondered if they might be somewhere between Port Elizabeth and the Cape.

'You know,' the driver complained, as if he had read her mind, 'when they say we are somewhere between the two provinces, they should have added that we are smack in the middle of nowhere.'

Coral nodded, not wanting to add to the tension.

'And the best part is,' he continued, 'a world swallowed into a world. You will see what I mean.'

The car climbed uphill, went around a few bends, each worse than the previous, found straight gravel road, went downhill, dipping and rotating around the bends that folded and straightened with alarmingly short notice, until the driver said with great relief, 'We are here,' as a set of large gates loomed ahead, their heads sparkling in the midday sun.

He took out his cell phone, punched a few digits in, then put the phone back into his pocket. 'In this place, reception is rare,' he grumbled but then added with pride as the gate swung open, 'Good thing is, if you know where to look, you can find it.'

He withdrew into himself after this, and peering ahead, shoulders hunched as if he were going into the wild again, the new course began as the road twisted and curved like a wobbly piece of dough. She held on to her seat, under the illusion that they were travelling at great speeds. There were more bumps, more time passed, until eventually the road levelled out, and they were heading towards an imposing structure that dominated the skyline. A monstrous rectangular building came into view, the roof ought to have given the house dimension, but instead, it turned the architecture into a forbidding omen, as if the massive iron grey sculpture housed something haunting, with rows of windows blinking like dozens of cats out of every level, and it was not until they got closer to the building that she saw the face of the building was greyish blue, with every giant window set in a painted trimming, looking out across the driveway. At the end of this driveway sat two massive, hand-built stone towers. The pair of watchdog towers, with cone shaped roofs, had a long window set into each body, and a grey door with a brass knob punched into each. The towers were linked by a curved arch, the word *Eleutheria* looked down from here. When the visitor's eyes had calmed down enough, and blinked itself back into focus, it was only then that the tall stemmed, skirted aloes came into view, with the teething greyish-green leaves and the rounded, hollow flowers that poked the air like a pipe, their orangish-yellowish hues reminiscent of a coastal sunset.

'Aloe Africana, I think,' the driver pointed at the tall aloes, 'Can never remember exact names,' he stopped to dip his chin towards the ground, and her head followed his, to see the large fields covered in yellow and white flowerheads. 'Now those, with their faces to the sky, that's Gazanias.'

She could not understand how she had missed that. The ground was covered in those faces, their petals arched and ready for flight like the wings of a butterfly. It looked as if Heaven had done a day's work of spring-cleaning, tossed them out in a mad moment of charity.

'This is as far as I go,' the driver said, jumping out and heading towards the boot for her suitcase. 'Will you be all right on your own?'

Coral looked at the kind face – the eyes almost blank from the need for sleep.

'I will be fine,' she assured him, feeling nothing of the sort for herself. Her voice surprised her, for in it there was strength.

After having waved him off, she passed between the watch towers, up the path of flowers and aloes, arriving at last in front of the massive front door. She stood like a zombie, staring at the white door, the impressive purity of that colour stunned her eyes, made them search for defects, for any run of paint or a cat's scratch that would show the true colour of the wood beneath. The satin smoothness stared back until the door was suddenly wrenched open, and a woman stood in the threshold, tall and straight. She wore a long grey dress that started beneath her chin and ended at the tips of her shoes. She had short hair that framed a thin face with a pointed chin, from which a prominent nose poked out. A dainty mouth finished the portrait, but her talent lay in her voice; a strange rattling sound that came when she opened her mouth, as if her breath had collected into the space of her narrow waist and was now threatening to send her shooting to the stars.

'Coral?'

The prominent nose sifted the air for a better quality, as round eyes fixed themselves on her victim.

'Yes, maam.'

The plucked eyebrows puckered slightly, 'There is only one madam here, and that is not the one standing before you.'

'I am sorry…'

'You will address me as Miss Nan, as everyone else does.'

'Thank you, Miss Nan.'

'And what are you thanking me for?' she enquired, leaning forward and frowning, so that her eyes became coin slots. 'You seem very young. Matti attached an age of twenty two years to your name?'

'I am, Miss Nan.'

Miss Nan straightened up, looked very unimpressed and turned about, beckoning her to follow. 'Well, if you are going to survive here, you should work on that child's voice. I have no tolerance for whispers, you understand. Time is everything, and I cannot and will not have my hearing challenged, you hear me?''

Coral said nothing, stepping over the threshold, unaware at

the time that she had changed the course of her life forever. Following the lady with the determination of a puppy, she went gladly, complacently, until they reached a massive hall, where her feet and her heart both froze. In that second, her mind breached the gap between horror and reality, and she reached a new breed of recognition, for the pair of massive lions holding her sight were grey stone creations. They were standing side by side, on a bed of tumbled rock, their heads turned up, their eyes of reddish orange fixed on her with cunning intent as if they might pounce in the split of a second and settle on her throat. It was as if she could hear the roar in her head, feel the power of those paws, flying nails swiping and tearing. Her feet remained still, silkworms in their cocoons, gone to sleep. Her heart told her it was fine, but it beat like the drums of jungle thunder.

'What is it now?' Miss Nan was asking, shaking her head, eyebrows almost reaching into her hairline, her sharp, thin face showing impatience. 'I tell you, you are too timid to be here if you do not understand that Zircons and stone do not make a living beast, so pull yourself together and follow me.

Coral pulled herself together, her feet now in action as she hastened forward, 'Don't think I will play fetch for you,' Miss Nan's voice reached her, forced her to rush ahead, as if she had been kicked from behind, and in that haste, she knew she had forgotten something. The lady spoke again, this time she added a pointing finger, and it was directed towards the suitcase Coral had left behind, 'The suggestion is incredibly presumptuous of you, as if I were a porter?' Miss Nan sounded annoyed, 'Get your own luggage, we don't run a business of offering porters here to the house help. And hurry up if you intend on staying here.'

Coral retraced her steps, picked up the suitcase and

dutifully followed the leading lady as they passed the entrance hall of stone, to enter a calming zone where an impressive staircase in dark wood, like a magic tree of a hundred years, split at the base, both halves climbing towards the sky, gave the traveller two options. Miss Nan took the left path, and they were soon marching through a long corridor.

'The kitchens are along here,' Miss Nan told her as her long legs picked up pace, 'Come now, you must put some life into you, or it will never do. I cannot have my staff display such sluggishness.'

The words were no sooner spoken than, from around the next corner a young girl appeared, carrying a silver tray.

'*Ah*, Karabo,' Miss Nan sounded relieved, 'Hand me that tray, and can you take Coral to her sleeping quarters.'

The girl with the body of an athlete looked confused.

'Here, hand it over,' Miss Nan was saying, already grabbing the tray.

Karabo let the tray go.

'Well,' Miss Nan said drily, 'get along now. There's no need to doddle and waste time. I know of skeletons that could jump out of a grave with more gumption than you two.'

As Coral picked up her suitcase again, Miss Nan shook her head. 'Leave it. I cannot watch you tug and heave at that box anymore. I will have it sent over later.'

With that, they scurried off, scolded school children with their heads down, their feet marching along the corridor and not a word passed between them until they emerged into the outdoors. Only then did Karabo speak.

'It's this way,' Karabo pointed towards a lane that wound its way into a thicket of trees. 'You better hurry. An hour is nothing.'

'What's it like?'

Karabo paused, flashing Coral a wide smile, she let her dark eyes roam over the heads of the trees that stood in their way. 'It's better than your maddest dreams.'

Seeing her expression, Karabo laughed, throwing back her head, her dreadlocks wound into a tight bun on the top of her head. She had light skin and high cheekbones, and when she smiled, her oval face reminded Coral of what a fairy must have looked like when silver dust shimmered in the air, and the sun smiled ever so gently, wrapping everything up in a cloud of gold.

'Hey, come back,' Karabo laughed, nudging her in the elbow, 'you better not let that happen when Miss Nan is around. She is an old witch, that one.'

They laughed as they hurried on, and Coral knew she had met a friend.

They entered the forest, for there was no better word that could describe the old trees that grew there. A wind had taken shape, and it shook the life out of the leaves that wriggled and twisted on strong branches, that were clearly not strong enough to hold on to their heavily veined sprouts. She watched as a few leaves tumbled to the ground. The thought occurred to her in a flash that even the poor leaves were not spared the entrapment of life. That it was all a vicious cycle. She had never thought of leaves and branches in that way before. She forgot to focus and tripped.

'Watch out or you will get hurt,' Karabo cautioned, steadying her as she almost kissed the ground, and it was only then that she saw the thick roots creeping out of the ground like fat, bandit carrots that spread everywhere, rogue roots, picking their way through the undergrowth. Her ears boomed into action, the sound of buzzing insects entered them, filling up the qspace. It was a new world, and she tried to adjust, but was very glad when they finally emerged into broad daylight again, only to find a wooden bridge staring back at them. It was a simple structure, with rope on either side for hand bars and wooden sleepers nailed together, stretching across a stream. Dark rocks from the underwater world showed their heads, the water slicing itself on their sharp contours, making a rushing, gushing sound that served it well in its course.

Once they had crossed the bridge and climbed a small grassy bank, the staff quarters confronted them. The rondawels showed themselves, bricked structures of circles, with triangular thatched roofs and a single window each, spread everywhere like field mushrooms, each home lit by its own candle, tucked under the Yellowwood trees. The trees, spectacular in height, leaves ringed in colours of yellowish green, glowed as if hugged by a magical hue.

'It's beautiful,' Coral whispered, 'like a magical forest. Like something from our dreams.'

Karabo giggled, 'Yes, and that one over there is yours.'

Coral stared at the white- coated rondawel sitting under one of the giant Yellowwoods.

It was unreal. She experienced a new feeling of belonging.

Karabo was still talking, 'We must go back now,' she looked at her wristwatch. 'Miss Nan will be needing us.'

They got back just in time for the lunch serving. There were two kitchens in the House, and Miss Nan had put her into Kitchen A.

'Don't worry,' Karabo told her as they parted ways, 'I'm just a few bricks away if you need me. Watch out for the real Lady of the House. We call her The Mistress. She's the one with the fire inside her.'

She winked and was gone, and there was Miss Nan.

'What is wrong with you?' Miss Nan snapped, as she leaned forward. 'Get into gear, girl. Get yourself to the kitchen!'

Miss Nan marched away with her nose tilted to the ceiling, but at the same time, a figure came striding down the corridor, a young woman whose body filled out a dress that looked like it had shrunk three sizes too quickly in the last wash, feet enjoying open air in sandals, the straps of which shone like glass. But it was her hair that made the biggest impression of all. The head carried a massive collection of curls, an aggressive glow of red that bounced as she walked. It took her a while, but she recognised her best friend Matti in the arrangement, and before long she was looking into the made-up face. It had dark peach lips that were set in a permanent pout, and eyes with contoured lines that shot black into her heart faster than a squid. She stared in confusion.

Matti did not smile, but leaned forward in greeting, her eyes grew larger in her done-up face, 'Let me tell you something,' she spoke as if she had gulped down too many shooters. 'You can roll your eyes like a drunk fish, but in a game of survival there are no rules. I didn't make the laws of the jungle,' she snorted. 'I simply follow them.'

How they came to hug each other in the next instant was debatable, but they had breached the awkwardness. The union did not last long as Miss Nan's bark reached them. The girls pulled apart, and Matti hurried past, leaving Coral to take the short leap into the kitchen. A flurry of activity greeted her there, the noise reminding her of the excitement of a Saturday morning market, where the buyers haggled with the vendors, and the white chickens clucked and flurried in their cages.

From behind the long table, the cook shot her an evil eye.

'You are late. Take that tray and get upstairs.'

Coral moved like a puppet, seizing the silver tray handles. She followed the others up a short flight of stairs. The tray held a fat teapot with painted flowers on the sides. The pot was finished with a delicate gold lid. There were several baby imitations arranged on the tea cloth, cute cups with fat tummies and painted flower buds. She lifted her eyes off the tray to find herself in another passage now, and it led into a large room, with a high ceiling. It was like crawling out of a cave and looking at the night sky for the first time. She almost gawked at the sight before her. She was in a room that gave the impression of a grand hall, and in the space that it defined, tall grand candle stick holders stood beside a very long oak table, pouring light into the void. Seated around the table on finely carved chairs were a crowd of people, their faces lit by the flickering flames, their backs covered in a ghostly shade that came from the windows, where parted curtains allowed the night sky domain.

Her eyes sought out the main characters, to fit the description that Matti had painted for her. She found the two brothers. One was thin, with dark hair swept clean off his forehead and a bored expression smothering his lean features. The other was much bigger, with unruly hair and a very healthy moustache. He was occupied for the moment, the young woman on one side of him was busy emptying her food into his plate. He playfully built himself a mound, gathering it to the centre of his plate, then threw half of the lot into his mouth and fed the rest to his moustache. The woman sitting to the other side of him nudged him forcefully, so that he turned his head to her and bellowed, 'Beth, keep your bony elbows to yourself.'

'Rod, there's no need to be rude.'

Coral found herself almost smiling at the drama unfolding before her, but then her eyes drifted, becoming stuck fast on the young man standing behind the young woman. In that dimension with the moon at his back, and the candles on his face, he looked surreal. He stood tall, with his hair reaching just past his collar, the colour of which took her mind to an afternoon in autumn, when the golden bronzed leaves sat on summer fried trees. The leaves, as if dressed in their tanned shade of gold, held the promise of winter's onset, but not before the wind had danced the earth, then returned to colour them with its travels before shaking the last life out of them. That was the colour of his hair, she decided, as if every strand had lifted a pen, and told a story. Her whole being turned on her, so that she was helpless, trapped by an invasion of her senses, of her mind, and of her body. She could feel her legs moving, but her eyes were still stuck on him, so that when he turned his head and met her stare, she saw that his eyes were dark, his face too beautiful for any man to own, the soft paleness of shy youth dappled his cheeks, his fine nose stood over lips that gently curved. His jawline looked strong but did not take away from the delicate fineness of his forehead and cheekbones. His face was bewitching to her. She had forgotten how to breath, felt her body move, legs going somewhere, she knew she had become airborne, her feet lifting off the carpet, and then she landed, crashing almost face first into the carpet. It was a good thing her hands had come out in time, her elbows taking the brunt of the fall. The tray fared a little better than her, landing right side up, its contents quivering in their spot, their insides spilled everywhere.

'You, stupid idiot!' she heard a voice call out, and guessed it had to be the other woman she had seen at the table, the one with the short hair and elfish face. She was still shouting, 'I got tea all over my skirt!'

There was laughter coming from somewhere, and this had to be the big man, Rod, and the young woman. But a pair of large green eyes in a round, kind face had found her own, and the mouth was moving, saying words that came from a distance, 'Are you okay?'

'Beth, get away from her,' she heard the other woman call, 'look at everything, its wet. She should clean up this mess.'

And then Beth was saying in a stern voice, 'Mona, stop being so insensitive.'

'How dare you take a servant's part over mine?'

Into that racket, a voice that held the authority of a ship's captain got Beth back into her seat, and Mona to shut up.

'You, there, get up and tell us your name,' it commanded, and she too, in a single fluid movement, unglued herself from the floor and faced the body from where the voice had come. She had found the Lady of the House. The woman was past middle age, a stern looking creature whose face put the image of a hawk into the mind, the crest on the top of her head taking the form of thick coiled hair with a distinctive peak. The prominent nose sat above a mouth that was set firm and grim, the cheeks slightly pulled into the face so that the older woman gave away some of her age, but it was the devilishly dark eyes that deposited fear into the onlooker. It was as if the night sky, having jumped on the moon and stars, absorbed the chaos into itself and lay tucked inside each one. The darkness of those eyes was nearly overshadowed by the enormous, blinking diamonds sitting in each ear, ears that were too small to carry such a weight. The figure leaned forward, scrunching her eyes, holding up a hand that had rings on every finger.

She should be afraid, but having lost her senses already, she stood there as if she owned the place. Instead of fear, she found herself staring the bird fully in the face as if she did not care, her chin raised higher than ever, as if this were her natural stance, her eyes staring down at the Lady of the House, The Mistress.

'What a strange thing you are,' she heard the woman observe, in her voice of poison, the venom sticking like blobs of jelly to her lips. The picture grew larger in Coral's head until the tickle at the base of her throat, a scratchy ticklish itch that could not be swallowed down, escaped through her lips, breaching the air with a whale's burp. Everyone stared. The young woman laughed and laughed, the sound rippling through the dining room as if it were coming from a possessed doll. The Mistress stood up, kicked her chair back as a horse would kick an idiot standing in its way, as the room went dead still and unfolding herself into a tower, leant her lean frame forward. 'You should ask to be pardoned.'

She knew she had gone too far, that her stance was affecting the woman, but it was beyond her control. This uprising, within herself, gave her strength. She clung fiercely onto it, too afraid now to be abandoned. But then, just like the snap of a twig, the spell broke, and she knew she was back to herself, the silent quiver that stole through her body told her that she was the weak fool once again.

'I am sorry, Ma'am.'

The voice that forced itself out sounded pathetic, even to her ears. She had proved herself to be nothing but a cowardly servant girl, and the woman, whose attention she had earned, rolled her eyes into themselves, and said with disinterest, 'You will address me as Mistress.'

'Yes, Mistress.'

The Mistress waved her off with an impatient hand. She started to move away, when the moustached brother spoke, tilting his head towards her. 'Mother likes to have the waiting staff close, but not too close. So, find a chair, take three steps back, and stay there.' He winked, so that his bushy eyebrows and his moustache became next door neighbours.

'Rod, Mother can speak for herself,' the other brother said with disinterest, 'quit being her mouthpiece.'

'And who wants your opinion Matt?'

'Enough,' the Mistress said quietly, 'and Rod, you are quite correct. The only nose that should be next to my plate, is my own.'

Rod beamed like a nine-year-old who had just caught his first sardine. He sat up straighter in his chair, and roared, '*Eetth* my boy, bring me the pot of cream. I am in the mood for pancakes and cream, with cherries on top.'

'Yes, please do. Give my share to Uncle Rod.'

'Ella,' Rod beamed, 'you are a good seed.'

The autumn haired young man obeyed with a dignity that was unsettling, his stance came from another world. He set the food down in front of Rod, keeping a good distance from the chair that would have been better suited to him. She pictured him in it, leaning forward, his hair draping his face, gently, like a mist drapes the meadow in early morning. Oh, what was she thinking? She brought herself around to find Rod shovelling the food down his throat as if the golden-edged dessert spoon were a spade, and Beth having transformed from the kind angel at his side into something else, giving him the terrible side-eye. The woman popped a lettuce leaf into her mouth, then eyed her husband with open distaste, as the cream piled up on the sides of his mouth, filling his moustache like shaving cream, and sighed, 'Rod, you remember what the doc said. Take it easy on the carbs, or you could have a heart attack. Think about that, all those tubes and things while you lie in a hospital bed, and the heartache I will endure thinking about your chances of making it through.'

Rod paused midway, the spoonful of pancake and creamed cherries sitting just beneath his mouth, while he thought about his fate. He threw the food into his mouth, took his time chewing and then shrugged, 'I'd say worth the risk, all things considered.'

'Oh, come on Rod,' Mona chided him from across the table. 'Don't be so mean to her. She's just worried about you, that's all.'

Rod turned his head to Mona, and an odd look passed between the two. The look did not pass the notice of the Mistress, whose roving eye landed on Coral. Their eyes locked for a second, as if they had both seen something that should never be put into words. The Lady of the House turned her attention to wiping the corners of her mouth tentatively, before saying sternly, 'This empire cannot run on gossip and ants. It needs men of the blood. The chosen ones. Where are my grandsons?'

CHAPTER SEVEN
BETH

Breakfast was done. She was free to wander the gardens, and the extent of the lands that were rightfully hers by marriage. If her true colours were to shine, she knew redemption was off the cards. In the eyes of all things decent, her actions challenged the moral compass. Somebody should have handed her a stonefish, picked straight from the coral reef, and then stepped back to watch the payoff. In her soul, she was not sure about using that term, since the more she thought about it, the more she realised she might be missing one. Still, even if it was there, hidden somewhere deep, her hands would never be able to wipe the dust board clean, certainly not if it had to be done with honesty, a value that seldom surfaced in her repertoire. It came down to the bare fact that even if she had a soul, that part of her would probably be condemned by now. Her very life experience attested to that simple fact. She did not love Rod. She had conspired, cast a fishing line, reeled him in. A simple fact, she cradled her marriage the same way one cradled an ambition, a feat for the accounting books, more so than the chapters of love. She did not believe in such a thing either. Love. What was it, exactly? Perhaps that level of idolization or affection, was meant for beings that occupied another dimension where such values might bring such returns. But in her limited universe, she did an ordinary thing. She grabbed an item off the shelf, a piece of candied sugar, wrapped in opulence, a means to an end, and the extent of that end was vast, and she had taken it and made herself an extension of that candied treat. It brought her vast wealth and a family name that laid siege to an empire, more closely guarded, if she might put her own thoughts into it, than the biblical truth.

Behind the family empire was the face of a single man. She had never seen his picture, though there were rumours that the old dragon kept one hidden in her room. But more to the point, from what she heard, and she always kept her ears open for gossip, especially regarding the family she had married into, it was being said that with every generation that passed, the family legacy grew darker, each new batch taking on strange forces of treachery and other worldly spirits. The latest news turned out to be the juiciest. It was all about her husband's eldest brother, James, dead now of course, who would have been heir to everything. As things stood, with Rod being the eldest surviving brother, he had an advantage over Matt, and Rod should inherit, but the old dragon was leaning more towards placing the eldest grandson into that position. That meant, her Francis would sit on the throne. Either way she scored. She would have to wait and see. But to get back to the story. It was incredulous, sounded more like a folk tale, and it wrapped itself about the girlfriend belonging to James.

She loved thinking about this story, for there could hardly be any truth to it. The way people talked about the girlfriend, saying the woman was a fairy creation, with skin so white that it was whiter than the pale mist that hangs over the small lakes during a morning, when the rain and cold both battle each other out – she had seen such a morning herself. The creature they described must have been ordinary, for Beth dared not think that such a perfect sample of beauty could ever exist outside of the imagination, and with the ribbons of reality tied up into a nice bow, she praised herself for her wit, felt satisfied to leave the girlfriend where she belonged, and hopefully stayed, deep within the well of illusion. Beth needed no competition, not even from the dead. Still, the details were so intricate, so defined, that a part of her latched on, wondering if the strange creature might emerge from the fog one day, where the ghosts of pirate ships stayed hidden, so that her hair, which was said to be as black as that on a bride of the night, might cover them all, under a shade of darkness. Some swore that moment would be darker than the darkest vision one had with both eyes closed, in the dead of night, when one was sitting inside the darkest cave on earth. Beth shuddered. There was more. They said the moon shone in her eyes, that it was as moving as the combined sight of a hundred dead souls coming to life, and that her voice echoed the sound of the morning tide as it gingerly bathed the shore. That her footsteps were as light as fairies dancing in the garden, that her laugh tinkled better than any music they could make, and that in her face one could see the passing of the seasons, depending on her mood. And that she put all of this into the single son she bore. But James, the Father, being selfish with a mind that worked too fast – he got tired of waiting for his brain to catch up, did not see the sense and went and turned his coat inside out, that he got himself married to another woman. . He did this in the quiet. The wife became his true bride, and when his girlfriend found this out, she snuck into the Mansion, holding her infant son, and stood at a window, casting her eyes down to the jagged rocks.

    Those rocks sat crooked and pointed, hump backed goblins under the moonlight, and that she stood there, watching the tide slowly rise, swirling and unfurling, the waves crashing and covering the goblins, then rolling back, leaving them sweating in the moon's gaze. And so it went that she stood at the window watching and waiting, while the servants watched and waited themselves from behind the furniture in the room, shrinking into any space for a better view, wondering what she might do next. And then like one under a spell, baby in hand, she tipped herself into the night air, her white dress clung to her and lit her up like a firefly in twilight and in the blink of an eyelash, they were both gone, swallowed by the goblins, sinking beneath the waves that had become monsters. The witnesses crossed themselves and pledged themselves as true believers of their eyes and ears. For a wind, more like a hurricane was suddenly born in that room. It squeezed itself through the open window, escaping into the moonlit night, calmed the waves down, and then everything went dead.

The witnesses swore they had seen her drop out the window, but her body was never found. To make matters worse, they said James had lost his life that very same night, jumping out of that misfit window, going faster than a pellet from a shooting gun, to meet his end. And they themselves had been sworn into secrecy by the Family, so they could say no more. The story changed depending on which corner of the town it came from. Some said James was never married, that the girl went mad thinking he might be. Others said she hid the baby somewhere, then fell into the ocean, turning into a mermaid, vanishing beneath the waves, waiting to surface again at the end of two decades plus a half, to see for herself, the face of her son, a blood tie of true birth and love. Others said she hit the rocks and dispersed into the wind, being otherworldly it made sense, had gone home to her kind, but that if you stood at the window when the wind was at its worst, you might hear her voice calling out to her son. The problem was that nobody had the nerve to stand at the said window on a full moon night, to count the rocks below, then wait for the tide to slowly build up, and hope that the urge did not possess them at that instant to go flying out the window themselves. The people who spread the story were very happy to keep telling it, and to leave the rest at that.

Beth chuckled as she thought about it. People loved to talk. It was their habit to make life worth living. Being married into the Family, she knew the truth. James had a girlfriend, one that simply vanished the day he died. That was the beginning and the end of the whole length of the story. No baby in the picture, no forms of sea life haunting the Mansion. It was ludicrous, just thinking about it. She put it out of her mind, picking up her chin and letting her nose sample the nicer air as she passed a few others. She was used to thinking of the rest of the world as common, ever since she had married into the Family that everyone feared and respected. When she thought about it, relief washed through her mind and body. It was a good thing, holding herself above everyone else, for it protected her, in a strange way, helped her to keep a dangerous secret close. Nobody suspected, even dared think her capable of the things she had done. It was better that way. If it ever came out, she knew her best chances would be to run. As fast as her lying mouth could put words into a sentence. But she was being reckless this morning, worrying about stuff that was better left behind. In any case, she was beyond reproach, since the Family employed nearly three-quarters of the town, and a few more from the scattered villages, and were known to be fair in their treatment of everyone. The family reputation and regard remained as intact as a circle. That meant her past was safe.

Nobody would dare question that.

She walked without purpose now, past the impressive gardens, threading her way towards the apple orchards. People dropped curtseys. She managed to suffer a nod in return, here and there, when she felt like it. She closed her eyes for a second, recalled her life as it had been. It all came back in an instant. She was born poor, given to parents who were fated like magnets to a piece of ground which they worked like moles, spending time both underground and on top, trying everything from digging for buried treasure to growing potatoes. But their efforts came to nothing, and it was left up to Mona and herself to find small jobs in the nearby homes to scratch out a living. Beth soon learned about the most eligible bachelors in town, and hoping to secure a ticket for herself, set a trap for a certain John. The guy proved to be a boring and lazy idiot, blessed with great looks and a greater fortune, and very little common sense. She had known the catch would be easy to bag and had pulled out a decent number of antics to land him. But then he turned into a toad, took his warts and his croak back into the swamp, leaving her alone and desperate. She was on the edge, pregnant and alone when respite came in the form of part time Christmas jobs offered at the Mansion. Mona and herself, like many other young unmarried women in their neighbourhood, snatched up the offer. She found a new hobby and spent her time studying the younger brother, Rodney.

She let her mind burrow deeper, to the time Mona covered for her, so that she could follow Rod by scrimping off his shadow, following him by keeping her steps inside that shaded patch of moving earth, past the peach and then the apple orchards to the empty clearing. The farm workers were off duty, it being Sunday. She hid inside a thick bush and watched him until the day grew weary, and dusk arrived. The piece of ground on which he lay stretched away into the distance. She knew all about this land. Everyone knew. It was a new puppy project secured by the Family. When word got out about the new project, people rushed from all over to take up their place on the field. Talk ripe like December cherries filled the air, excitement mounting with each new experience. It was said that if a person poked the soil with a finger, and then kept an open eye on the face of the tunnel, barely ten seconds into the counting, their tiny legs carrying them like scuttling popcorn, beetles and bugs would emerge, showing good signs for the future of the ground, giving evidence for the promise of a golden crop.

She watched as Rod lay flat on the famous soil, but in her head, visions of scuttling bugs formed that made her skin crawl. And then, before she could scatter those visions away, Rod had bounced up again, jumping around like a demented rat, he poked holes in the soil, before digging into his bag and bringing out seeds that he dropped into the pockets, sealing each one up with care, he carried on with his task until at last exhausted, he lay back onto the ground, and fixed his eyes up at the sky, where a quarter moon hung amidst some miserly stars. For her part, she screwed up her eyes for a better view, thankful for the light coming off the torch that lay on the ground next to Rodney, the pool of light hanging over the extended figure like an otherworldly coating. She was sure that she caught the moment when a tear slipped down his cheek. Then he was up again, this time taking out a book and pencil from his bag, he let the ground support is lower back, while he worked in an artist's stance, head bobbing between the open book and the night sky. Before long, he had dozed off, and it was the chance she was waiting for. She snapped it up, moving quicker than a fox, she was out of her hiding spot with her nose peaked over the book, her breath squashed in her chest so that the sleeping man would stay so. What she had a glimpse of, was a childish sketch of a night sky with a bright full moon and shining stars all smiling with big eyes. She had seen enough to plan her next move.

The next day brought dull skies and a promise of rain. But there was no time to be wasted. Mona had done the spy work and found out that Rodney was tied up in a business meeting until lunch. This was the perfect opportunity and she seized it. Making an early start, she retraced her steps to the field, sat on the ground where Rod had been before, placed her bag carefully on her lap and waited. It was a long shot, this attempt on her part, to make the gesture of kindness and lower herself to a partnership with the ground. She hated almost every element of it. She did not trust it, especially when she thought about what crawled out of it. There was a reason, she figured, why Humans were designed to move above the ground. She hated trees and flowers and every other deceptive illusion that broke through the soil, looking so fancy on the top, hiding roots that were doomed like scavengers to forage in darkness underneath. With equal measure, she hated the sky. The vast open plain of colour that capped the earth like a giant pot lid. It made her claustrophobic. She loathed the sea too. In her world, water was fine if it came out of taps and shower heads, did not rise above her toes or churn and swirl like an overfull soup pot. There was nothing spectacular about it, except that when the sun shone and the sky lied, the water looked like a big blue heaving pool, reflecting a big fat lie. Perhaps, she hated it so much because she was no different herself.

Her mind brought her back to the moment, to the clumpy clods beneath her skin. She sniffed, got the damp suffocating warmness of wet soil into her nostrils, and wished herself away. But the desire to escape her pathetic fate, to marry into a family where she could live out the rest of her life in luxury, dominated her discomfit, fed her mind with burning inspiration. She knew she was aiming too high, and this thought toughened her resolve so that she let herself lie flat on the ground. The long white dress she had picked gave her a delicate lining, and her hair that she had left loose, lay scattered about her head where the soil held it up like a trophy. This is how Rod found her, barely minutes after she had lain flat. She had seen him coming along from the corner of one green eye and quickly shut both. She sensed he was standing above her, and afraid that he might move away, opened them delicately. She found herself staring up at him, and quickly brought the shyness into her face and body, so that as she blinked, summoning every drop of innocence she could muster into that act, she brought herself up into the sitting position, with her feet together and her dress gently flowing over her knees.

'I'm sorry,' Rod was muttering, obviously confused, 'What are you doing here?'

He was more straightforward than she had anticipated. She made her voice apologetic, 'I come here sometimes, when I need to be alone.'

Still Rod did not move. Nor did he say anything. She felt the moment slipping by, and quickly added, 'There's something about being here, on a field where new life is about to start,' and she forced herself to scoop up a fistful of sand and let it drop with a play of love back onto its bed, 'The soil that bears life also sustains it.'

She glanced up at Rod's mesmerised face, both moustache and beard glittered in the dipping sun, and savoured her triumph silently, while he dropped to the ground beside her, keeping a respectful distance between them.

'I'm Rod,' he extended his hand and with laughter in his voice, boomed, 'But you probably already know that.'

Beth nodded, 'I got a part time job at your house this December, so yes, I know who you are.'

He nodded, seemed relieved at her blatant disregard for him. It was as she had planned, and she cast the bait further, by saying, 'It must be tough, having people want what you have.'

Her words brought his face towards hers, and she was able to watch with hidden pleasure as the look of surprise crossed his features. He wore his brown hair extra short back then, so that his forehead competed with the straight, rather longish nose and generous mouth. His eyes blinked out of his face with gentleness, and it was this single feature that made her job easier. She liked staring into those eyes. They were the eyes of a dreamer. The rest of him was stocky. He lacked the height that his brother had been blessed with. Beth judged the difference to be a good half a ruler's length. Still, he would be a catch dropped from the stars, and she knew that to get him she would have to roll herself into a pastry of honesty and pray that nobody would catch on and push the pastry tray into the oven for a bake.

By now, he had brought out his sketching pad and was chewing on the end of the wood, his eyes already gone to the sky, his thoughts far away. She was losing him and needed a miracle to salvage the wreck that would be their relationship. She took out her drawing pad and opened it, making a fuss over the act so that he would take notice. By now, the sun had done its work, setting in the west, and the night sky was blanketed with dark, heavy clouds. The first splattering of rain fell on their heads, and Rod shot up faster than an arrow, muttering a line of profanities that should never have escaped any mouth. She had never heard anything like it before, nor ever witnessed such a show of temper, brought about by the rain. But she was not to be easily phased, and she sprang up and gave him a slap across the face so that he shut up and stopped his mad tirade. She knew he could just as easily slap her back, but luck was on her side. He seemed to have slipped back into himself, and while the rain went dead, he stood there, looking at her, shocked into silence and wonder.

'I, I'm sorry,' she brought the honesty into her voice, even though she secretly enjoyed the effect that slap was having on him. 'I should never have done that. I don't know what got into me.'

The tears rolled down her face. It was easy to summon that. She had loads of practise in that department. She knew how she must look, her cheeks soft and red at the same time, her eyes wide with regret and taking both hands to her face, she put the finishing touches to the act by wiping madly at her cheeks, the sobs gaining momentum, while she quietly waited for him to do something. Not even she could have predicted her success, but it was swift. The cathartic breath came too early for them. He had already taken her into his arms, but what happened after that, out on the open field where the few drops of heavy rain splashed, it had all changed course, gone another way so that the sky opened into a clearing, chasing away the storm clouds. It was the beginning of the end.

Her mind came back to the present as she quickened her pace, her memories built themselves back into the pages of a children's story book, and that was where she would leave it. Safe from reality. There was no need for anyone to go poking around in her past. She was above that now. Just as soon as she made this resolution, she was back at the site that had been her meeting and mating platform. Those tricks she had played had launched her into a life that she could never have imagined. Yet, her visits to this place sprang from a different source of need. The source of that much required healing stood in front of her now. She raised her eyes to him and took in the finely chiselled features of a wonder creature. Her mind kicked back to the time in her past when the wondrous creature had broken all the rules and transformed itself into a toad. She had been chasing John then, and unknown to her, the man had been chasing someone else. He had gone and ditched her, to marry the other one, while she had gone to their favourite meeting place, a wish in her heart to tell him a truth that would have set them both free. The childish smile he gave her now could have drawn forgiveness from her heart, but the wound was still deep and raw.

'It's a lovely morning, Mrs Rod.'

The words were from his wife, Flora. She had come to stand beside her husband, an ordinary woman in Beth's eyes, one of many in a production line. Her features were even, her built rather chubby and comfortable, and her voice warm and predictable. She could not understand what John had seen in the woman, but he certainly had changed and was still evolving. He put a hand on his wife's shoulder, a sign of affection he had never been known to have and turned his head towards her. The smile on his face was dreamlike, a sign that he was at one with his wife's presence, even respected it. That was far more than she had got in the past. It irked her, made her want to say something to wipe the smile off Flora's face, make her vanish to some distant planet and roost there.

'Yes, Flora, is it?' she heard herself ask in a condescending voice, polished in the new accent of a high marriage, 'I would think about wearing a hat if I were you. I believe it is going to be another scorcher today,' and here she paused so that she could take off her wide brimmed hat and show off her money polished features and cool complexion. 'You know, even with this fine foundation, I worry. And then I think about you, out there on the potato field like laundry under the sun, and I must say, you need always protect the face. The sun can give you freckles, you know.'

Flora had a freckled nose and cheeks, and her complexion glowed from sun and wind exposure, but she was not a dainty scone on anyone's tea tray, and now her laughter swilled into the air, 'Oh no, Mrs Rod, I am very happy having the sun on me and the wind flying past my ears, and the knowledge that John will love me, even if I shrivel up, and by my own standards, end up no better than a raison on an afternoon pudding.'

Beth winced inwardly, cursing the woman for her simplicity. Standing there in her work boots, fitted out in a dress she had clearly outgrown, her arms and legs protruding like a crab, she managed to steal her handsome husband's glance away from Beth. Beth put on her hat once more, and forcing a smile to her lips, she was about to step away when a tall girl came upon them. Beth immediately recognised John in the girl, the dreamy face and slim fairy figure only lacked a pair of wings, but somehow the magic was broken by the girl's ginger coloured head, the long mane lay twisted in a plait down the one shoulder. Beth shuddered inwardly, for this colour infestation came directly from Flora. Both mother and daughter stood before her, glowing in the sun, their hair so bright and feverish that Beth was certain she would be sick.

'This is my daughter, Miriam,' Flora said proudly, pushing

the girl forward in her rough handed way. 'Mare for short.'

Miriam fell into something of a curtsey. It was clear that the girl felt intimidated by Beth's appearance, for she kept her eyes lowered as she made the dip. Her quiet demeanour fuelled Beth's ego so that she felt obliged to reply, 'It is a pleasure Miriam to have met you.'

Then she fell back into herself, remembering the girl's origins. She was nothing more than a potential troublemaker, untried and untested, about as welcome as a potato harvest turned soft and mouldy with the worms crawling out of it, leaving a stench in the air that bred flies like hot underdone pies. She had no appetite for digesting the unpleasant implications that the girl now presented, and chose to remain indifferent, 'So, you have a daughter then?'

'Yes, yes, Mrs Rod,' Flora nodded, her head bobbing up and down like a chicken. 'She was sent to live with John's family before she could crawl,' and she stopped to allow a broad smile to creep up into her fat cheeks, 'You know John's mother is like a grandma cactus, won't hesitate to stick a thorn into anyone that comes near her grandchildren,' and here she paused, drawing breath before continuing. 'Mare is her only grandchild. So, you can imagine. She wanted this one from the time she held her, a little lemon is what she always called her, coming from the way her face always puckered up whenever she wanted to cry. So, her absence would explain why she came as a surprise to you.'

The woman was starting to irritate Beth, 'You let another woman raise your child then?'

Flora shrugged, 'It is what it is. Yes, I did, and the woman turned out to be a far better mother than I could ever hope to be.'

She caught John's attention, her words acted like

firelighters, and he instantly drew her closer to him, while her face caught alight with a blush that rivalled fresh beetroot off the stove. Beth had seen enough. The woman's plain honesty was something she could not go up against, but time would change that. For now, she turned her attention back to Miriam, who was standing with her face cupped in her hands.

'What's wrong girl?'

Miriam dropped her hands to her side, revealing a face wet with tears. Flora moved to her side, and threw her arms about her daughter, as John murmured, 'It's the mention of my mother. We lost her just two months now.'

For a moment, Beth felt the agony of the past slip by, taking with it the desire for revenge. She looked at the man and saw the pain etched into his features, as if there had been an unveiling and it were only now visible. But the moment cracked, and her own pain pushed forward, drying up her compassion and stoking the bitter flames in her soul, resurrecting the desire for vengeance. This man, she reminded herself, was the reason she carried a secret so dangerous that it made itself a cradle in her conscience and would have to rock itself there, until the day arrived when she would take her last breath. It was a terrible secret to keep, and the guilt might have eaten her alive, if she had not stepped up and out of the circle of condemnation and found a reason that justified the cause. Now, the cause for all that suffering stood in front of her, on firm ground, looking as if he had just come out of Sunday service. His miseries, she told herself, if there were any, were far less that hers. And so, she returned to her old self and lifting her chin up, said casually, 'My condolences on your loss. Now I must be on my way, so if you will excuse me.'

She turned around and was gone, even before Rod or his family had a chance to say another word.

CHAPTER EIGHT
CORAL

The morning breakfast was a disaster. She wondered if the day could get any worse, and somehow received the answer to that, as she came face to face with Miss Nan. The lady seemed to be choking on something, her face was contorted, her voice came out on an extra wheeze, as if she had a bone stuck somewhere in her throat.

'You are summoned by the Mistress,' she managed to squeeze the words out, 'immediately.' The last word lay embedded inside a thin whistle, the effort looked as if it would land Miss Nan in hospital.

'Me?'

'Well girl, not only do you seem incapable of understanding a simple instruction,' Miss Nan puffed, 'but you have also proved yourself very incapable of following one. News of your performance in the dining hall is travelling faster than the speed of light, and everyone is suffering from the giggles behind my back.' It was a miracle how the number of words the poor woman had managed to put together still left her standing. She drew breath, launching a new attack, her voice gathering speed and rattling as it came alive again. 'Now the Mistress has requested to see you, and I will be called in to explain. You have cast a slander on my name, and you have put my authority under shame.'

Coral lifted her eyes off the floor to find *Eetth* standing in front of her. That was what Rod had called him so that must be his name. He had been in the act of passing them, standing as they were in the corridor outside the dining hall, but Miss Nan's act of judgement had brought his feet to a halt. Now, he stood there, his face showing signs of compassion, the same kindness he would have shown to an animal in distress. She did not like it, and it did not make sense. She was used to having criticism ladled on her head, and she never cared but absorbed it into her being, and let things be. But somehow, she did not want him looking at her in that way. It made her feel as if she would rather be dead.

'I'll take her to the Mistress, if it will help,' he was saying, giving Miss Nan a slight smile, 'it will give you plenty of time to sort out the morning duties.'

Miss Nan considered his offer for a few seconds, then gave him a brief nod, 'Thank you, Ethan. That, I think, will be a better option, all things considered.' While Coral was left to digest his name, growing to like it, and getting lost in the bubble, she caught the final look of disgust Miss Nan sent her before the lady turned away, shaking her head to the tune of her thoughts. Coral stared after her, blinking and stunned. She was too afraid to shift her gaze, for that meant she would have to look at Ethan again. She was not sure if she could handle being left alone with him. He made her feel strange, uncertain of herself, all the while a drumbeat boomed in her head, lighting the tips of her ears, so that she felt as if she would catch on fire, burst into a flame, sting and burn. It was uncomfortable.

'Come on, you can follow me,' Ethan was saying, and she obeyed like a trained old dog, quietly and with her head hanging down. She was not even aware of the steps they climbed or of the passages they treaded swiftly through, but only realised their mission was at an end when Ethan indicated a door and said, 'This is the room.'

He did not wait for her to lift her eyes to meet his. When she looked, he was gone. She turned to the heavy wooden door and landed a timid knock on its face. She was told to enter, and her feet took her into a magnificently large room, with what looked like an even larger bed holding centre court, hidden under a mountain of bedding, with pillows sharing the same length as sleeping bags and blankets that were white and thick, layered as if a whole farmhouse of geese had come together with their heads tucked under their wings. The phantom light that illuminated the bed came from long windows that were positioned in such a way that even if the sun were exhausting itself outdoors, the room pretended dusk, and the woman sitting at the desk in the corner unfolded herself from the chair like a ghost, gliding towards the door space in which Coral stood, with a grace and dignity that belonged to an era long gone.

'You may shut the door.'

Coral closed the door softly behind her. She stood there idly, not knowing what to say or do. The Mistress moved back to her desk, where she took up her position in the oak chair, a heavy woodwork that told lies because it made the formidable woman look delicate. She should have cut a sombre picture, a tall figure dressed in a black dress of lace, with black shoes and a thick banded black ring that wrapped itself about her middle finger. But she was swallowed up by the grave chair of duty, and now stuffed inside that chair, her devilishly dark eyes flashed like orbs in the pale raven face and Coral felt the shiver run down her body.

'You came highly recommended,' the Mistress observed. 'Miss Nan was very adamant about your abilities.'

Coral would have liked to say that Miss Nan had lied, but then common sense butted in, and her voice crept off somewhere and died like a rodent.

'And I understand you are of Indian descent?'

Coral's head nodded.

'Of Christian faith?'

Again, the head dipped.

'Interesting.'

There was a brief interlude of silence, with the Mistress intent on turning something over in her mind. She narrowed her eyes, put a hand under her chin, a moment that made her look very reachable, then lifted her chin as if confirming a resolve within herself. She settled back into her old composure, fixed Coral with a definite stare, 'There is something about you that begs for an indifference. You are a clumsy sort,' and here she paused, and Coral was sure she had imagined it, but the noble lady seemed for a brief second to smother the desire to laugh. 'But you are sincere. Yes, I see that. I believe you would be the right sort of company for my granddaughter.'

Coral drew breath, but she did not trust herself to speak.

'You will be Ella's lady in waiting, as well as her lady companion, and you will report to me when necessary.'

Coral should have spoken up, told the truth, that she had no experience being either, that she could barely set herself straight for the day. But the time for that passed, as the knock that landed on the door relieved them both from any further discussion. Miss Nan entered the room gravely.

'You asked for me, Mistress?' Miss Nan said in a voice reserved for a funeral. 'And I must say before any words are wasted, that Coral will immediately be sent away. I also ask your forgiveness for my grave sense of misjudgement.'

Mistress waited a full ten seconds before she could speak, leaving Miss Nan to savour the gravity of her apology. The mistress then stunned the head housekeeper by saying, 'Coral has been appointed to Ella. Her possessions will be moved into the House, and she will be given an appropriate room.'

If Miss Nan had fallen onto a bed of snakes, she could not have shown more alarm. Her thin face stretched as her eyes snapped open and shut. She quickly pulled herself together, being the expert that she was, and gave Mistress a single nod. Then, fashioning a smile out of the ashes of her dignity, she turned to Coral and beckoned her out of the room. Once the door had been firmly shut behind them, Miss Nan wiped the smile off her face and let her thin lips curl up into a horrible grimace. 'You are a sneaky thing all right. Snatching that position right out from under Matti's nose, pretending to be stupid and clumsy all the time, with nothing on you to suggest otherwise. Who would have thought, but let me tell you, she won't let you get away with this, you'll see! Very soon, there will be a new power in this house, and your bags will be packed and waiting when that happens.'

CHAPTER NINE
ELLA

Ella stared dismally at her newest chaperone, barely able to fight down the laughter, she let it bubble out of her instead, turning her head away she could feel the crisp morning air as it stung her face. This girl, the one who had tripped over her own feet, was now going to function as her guide. How could Gran think she would be of any use to her? The morning draught chilled her face again, distracting her, leading her towards a new idea for the day. With her spirits lifted, she yawned and casually asked Miss Nan, who was standing beside her chaperone, to pack her a picnic lunch and have Ethan and Mattie join her.

Miss Nan looked delighted at the prospect and rushed off to make the arrangements. One hour later Ella found the lot standing outside her door, though the only one who mattered was the very young and handsome Ethan. The sight of him brought a smile to her face and a redness to her cheeks, that she knew made her look her best. She had put on a light summer dress that was lighter than her blonde hair, and she had left her newly dyed hair loose, so that it hung about her shoulders and halfway down her back for his benefit. She had even put on makeup, choosing a bright red lipstick that enhanced the curves of her lips and inspired the pout she had practised and perfected just so that, he would notice. She had known him all her life, but not once did he make her the object of his attention. For her part, and for the past two months, she had developed a fascination with him that occupied her dreams, and whenever he happened to be around, her heart whipped itself up into ghostly murmurs, so that she was sure she would either faint or die. The feeling was new to her, and it made her go quite mad.

After the morning greetings had been done and dusted, the group turned their feet towards the lower levels of the Mansion, until they had reached the first floor. From here, a spiral stone staircase led them to the basement, which had a single wooden door that opened out onto a stretch of ground which eventually took them to the shoreline. It was wide, a nice stretch of sand, more than enough to set a blanket down, and a picnic basket. The four took their places, Ethan preferring to sit on the sand. Ella stretched out a hand and let the silky cool sand slip through her fingers, but she was not a fan and preferred her blanket.

The sea looked back at them, whipping up a morning frenzy of creamy froth, as the waves curled and stretched, rolling out like a soft tapestry, stirring a light wind that awoke from somewhere and came creeping onto them, so that Ella shivered. Matti was quick to notice and took off her jacket, handing it to Ella, who grabbed it and slipped it on. For the present, she did not mind covering her naked shoulders, but hoped that the dress had caught Ethan's eye. He seemed wrapped up with studying the ocean, and she watched as the wind tossed his hair about his face and shoulders. And when he turned to face her, her eyes slid to his lips and froze there, and she fought off the desire to grab him and kiss those gently curving lips.

'Ella, are you okay?'

He had long stopped addressing them by title, a strange demand that had come from her grandmother of all people. But she liked the familiarity, and now that she had been knocked back into the present, made a quick plan to get rid of the others.

Instead of answering him, she turned around, 'Matti, I need you guys,' she nodded towards the new girl as well, 'to run up to the kitchen and fetch me a nice slice of that morning pie that cook made. I seem to crave it now.'

Instantly Ethan was on his feet, 'I'll get that for you.'

Ella cursed silently beneath her breath, as she watched him hurry back towards the house. She had no craving for that stupid pie and would have liked to smash it into the faces of the two girls who were now looking at her.

'Let's go for a swim, then?' she heard herself say, but a new plan had formed itself in her mind, and it would be a far better one than the first. She felt herself smiling inwardly at her ingenuity, and with a surprise dash of energy, she stood up and got rid of her dress, stepping forward in her bathing costume, she was soon joined by Matti, but Coral had not changed. The girl was smart, knowing that the invite was not for her. Coral stayed where she was, whilst the girls ran down the shoreline to the waves.

Ella had not counted on how cold the water could be, for it was nearly freezing. She hated it, but it was worth the sacrifice. Soon Ethan would be back, making his way down the path, and she would at that precise moment, come staggering out of the water, to collapse in a swoon at his feet. He would ditch the silly pie and scoop her up in his arms, and she would open her eyes, and their eyes would meet. It was the perfect plan, and she kept glancing towards the path, growing more hopeful as her teeth started to chatter from the cold and the salt stung her eyes.

But it was the vision of two figures striding down the path towards the water that made her dreams fade. She watched as her cousins, Chris and Francis, neared the water, each carrying a platter of something which she guessed would be an extra serving of pie. Just then, the sun woke up, shining brightly and fiercely over the heads of her two useless cousins, it beamed nicely on to their carefully styled hair. How she wished it would melt the grease off their hair, so that the two mopheads would get what was coming to them for ruining her day. She was so angry at their terrible timing that she started to sulk. But she was denied even that, for in that slice of time, a high-pitched shriek went off in front of her, and she watched aghast as Matti, in a single fluid movement, lay flat on the sand as if the sky had dropped a coconut onto her head. Ella blinked in wonder, for she knew the moves well enough to have written the autobiography. But in Matti's case, the plot was working, for poor Francis had thrown the pie to the sky, and as it fell, nearly knocking Chris on the side of his ear. Francis was racing to the scene, scooping up Matti, and running with her towards the blanket, where Coral waited, towels in hand, much like a coat hanger. Ella cursed beneath her breath, would have been sick in the water too. But she saw that Chris had a frown on his face, was watching her intently, a wide smile started to crease his elfish face. In this moment, he reminded her so much of his mother, Mona.

'What is this,' he almost sneered, 'the sea threw up a scavenger? I never knew you loved the water.'

'Shut up, you idiot,' Ella shouted through lips that were turning blue. 'Go back to the hole you climbed out of and stay there.'

'Nice welcome back, you little brat.'

Ella pulled herself out of the water and although her body shook with the cold, she kept her head up high and reached the picnic spot to find Matti wrapped up cosy and snug in a blanket that was not hers. Ella could have screeched and tore at the leech, but instead she chose to run her hands through her hair, forgetting the knots that had been put there by sand and water, so that her fingers caught in the twisted strands and pulled, the trigger making her wince hard. She turned around and marched back to the Mansion in her wet clothes, a thundercloud hovering over her head, her mission a disaster.

***

She could hardly believe it. They were headed out, with her Gran's permission, to see the Moonbow. She had dared poach the question after dinner and been given the go ahead. It was a rare thing to have her Gran see things her way. But, seated in the dining hall that night, with the lit candles throwing their centuries old demon glare upon the food, and the floating servants moving eerily like tortured ghosts – shadows that should already be warming their toes in bed, she felt the weight settle on her slim shoulders, and it made her tired. But not too much, so that she still had the passion to put her plan into action. This time, she was adamant that she would have her way. But, she had to endure the charade of dress up and play, Gran's favourite amusement, the reverence of tinkling cutlery, polished and sparkling, so that they twinkled at the table, and men and women in bow ties and aprons, who came and went, fussing without sound, their chins tilted at the same angle, as if some magnetic force united them. A part of her still wanted to belong to the world she had been born into, the lesser part told her that bent rules brought greater gain. She decided to wait her turn. She would be damned if her actions cost her the privilege she had been born into. Her mother, Ann, was the last born and youngest sister to her uncles Rod and Matt. As such, Ella enjoyed her position in the Family, and would hold on to it with her teeth and nails if she had to. But now, her world had grown larger, as if a space had been left behind, by a tooth pulled out much earlier than it needed to go. That gap could only be filled by one person. For him, she would follow the rules, keep her place, keep her comfort and stay out of the crowd. But she would do anything to pull him out of his world and bring him into hers.

Ethan. She wanted them to suffer the ghosts of dinner together, both on equal power, for she knew that he was never made for anything else. One glance and anyone could tell he had more grace and tact in the blink of one eye, than the combined sight of all her family members thrown into a single pit. Except her Gran of course. She was set in a league of her own.

Her mind came back to the present. They were threading their way to the waterfall, to see the Moonbow, and she watched the backs of the others, unknowing victims of her wizardry. Her head still buzzed from the victory of having a late-night pass. She had told a lie, so openly and freely, to her Gran of all people. She had used the waterfall and the idea of a Moonbow to get what she wanted. Yet, she felt no remorse. She would not take it back. It was a simple lie, she told herself, an initiation of her creative side, and the risk she had taken was for a good cause. She had secured a night with Ethan. She had made the whole thing up. She told Gran that this would be the night when a rainbow appeared at the waterfall, when the moon was at its fullest. That the event only rarely ever happened and that if she did not get to see it, she would never be the same now that she had learned about it. That could she take her cousins and Ethan to go see it. Gran did not for once push the issue, but for some unknown reason gave her consent, leaving the room dead still. Matti was added to the list somehow, and Coral was naturally there, going everywhere she went, following Gran's orders, so they were all together now, going in search of the Moonbow. Except, the Moonbow was not scheduled for an appearance tonight. She did not care.

Dinner was over almost two hours ago. The lie she had told was already fried, gone up in crisps during that interval. In any case, she was sure Moonbows appeared elsewhere in the world. She was not sure if there would be one waiting for her tonight. They were almost at the waterfall now, and as if she had a fairy godmother of her own, a full moon greeted her from the sky. It was all meant to be, but she would have to think of something fast to make this night count. She needed to get Ethan to look at her the way he should, and at this rate that would never happen. He was walking behind her, and when she turned to look at him, his sleep dazed face accused her of breaking curfew. She imagined him hating her for being forced out of his bed, made to go through a maze of forest trails, just to protect the sprig, that was her, who moved in front of him. It was not the romantic idea she lusted after. She would have to turn things up a notch, pretended to trip over an unseen stone in her path, hoping that as she tilted backwards, he would catch her in his arms. She pushed the tip of her booted toe into the ground, and let her body waft into the night air, feeling as light as a banana peel, effortless and ever so slight, it was an action that needed a strong and determined arm. But she had no support as she went down, almost flat to the ground, her hands went out in the last nick of time, and cat instincts she never thought she had, broke free, securing her fall. Only then, did she see that Ethan had stopped some way down the path, to examine the path to the left and right, as he was doing now, the beam of the torch pointed away to some untrodden path that should have been left alone. She heard Coral's voice break into the silence, as the girl came rushing towards her, calling out her name in that soft mouse voice, which born of a new breed, carried into the night air and reached the ears of Ethan, that he hurried forward to check on her. She was sitting on the ground, clutching her elbow and looking worse for the wear. When he knelt beside her, and turned his dark eyes towards her, she could have reached out and squashed him, pressing her face into his, searching for his thin lips that curved like a musical bow, winding her fingers through his soft hair. She was sure she would go stark raving mad, if she did not act now, but then his face was pulled away from hers and Francis stared back at her, his hand shooting out to drag her back onto her feet, his angelic features sharpened with sleep deprivation and irritation, he growled as he said. 'This is the dumbest thing you have ever come up with.

They carried on, with Francis and Matti leading the way, Chris following, then Ella, Coral and Ethan tying up the procession. At long last, they reached the waterfall. They stood on the carpet edge of the forest, watching the ghostly falls as it rushed over the mountain face, the sound of thunder filling their ears, as if the sky had swallowed gallons of water and was now dumping it onto the rough bony edges of the mountain. Water bashed against the rock, plunging down a towering length, into a churning basin, to hit the surface hard, sending white spray and making waves that rolled to the sandy edges. The water from the base pool flowed into another ghastly crevice, where the dark jagged rock fitted like broken teeth into each other, until the gushing force finally choked itself into a smooth-flowing stream that meandered through the forest and ended up somewhere else.

Ella saw the entire picture in her head, having seen the enormity of the falls in the day, and now at night it did not disappoint, with the sights and sounds of a spitting monster, and somewhere inside her there awoke a tiny creeping fear. She ought to put an end to this madness, but somehow did not possess the nerve for that. She would not leave until Ethan was hers.

Settling down on the bank, with her shoes pointing towards the edge of the flowing water as it coursed on a raggedy path towards the next rocky crevice, she laughed. 'Okay, now we wait for the natural sighting.'

'Of what exactly?' Chris asked. 'Don't you think this is dangerous?'

'Well,' Ella shrugged, 'if you sit here and shut up, I don't see how the waterfall can move and get you.'

Chris sat down, irritated, and shook his head, but said nothing more. He was the stern one, the one with the thinking cap on, and his logic irked her. But seeing him subside into himself, with his sulking face and quiet demeanour all wrapped up for the night, Ella smiled triumphantly as she turned towards the others. Francis and Matti were missing. Her temper rose as it came to her that they were benefitting from her hard work, and she was stuck with Chris and Coral.

'Okay guys,' she sprang to her feet once more. 'You two just stay,' she nodded towards Coral, 'keep my place until I get back, *Eetth* will help me up to the viewing deck for a close up.'

'There's no viewing deck,' Chris muttered.

'Oh yes, there is,' Ella insisted, 'I found one this morning.'

She turned around abruptly, started walking back into the trees. She heard Chris shouting for Ethan, so she took her time. Her aim was to head straight up the mountain, to take the footpath to the top of the waterfall. Of course, she would not dare think of stepping across the narrow opening, but it would give her time alone with Ethan. She could hear him calling out her name as she picked up her pace and made a blind dash for the path ahead. She was sure that he would drag her back to the others if he had a chance. She picked up her pace.

The path that led upwards was primitive, a rough imprint that was maintained only for the family since the falls was not open to the public. It was a decision that had stayed its course over generations. And the family itself never cared much about the waterfall. She did not know which of them, if any, tried the uphill slog, except herself, every now and then, and she liked to think of Gran sending people out here to look after the place just for her. In any case, she made a mental note to complain about their clumsy efforts, having to dodge overhanging branches and upturned roots in her path, she knew it was not a place to let her guard down. With outstretched hands, she moved forward, glad at last to lean into the pool of light coming from Ethan's torch. She relaxed. They were alone at last.

The night had been still, quietly behaved, and uninteresting so far. But then, out of nowhere, a strong blast of wind pummelled past them, as if a night monster had burped in its sleep. Ethan's hand was suddenly on her elbow, bringing her around rather roughly. Only then did she realise just how close she had come to stepping off the edge of the path. She knew what lay over the edge in the dark. It was a sheer drop to the bottom, a steep downhill plunge of trees and bush studded with sharp spiky needles and whatever else these parts hid.

'Why are you in such a hurry?' Ethan demanded, his voice urgent and unfriendly in its concern. 'You were nearly off the path!'

Ella bit on her lip, but she would not give in. Instead, she brushed off his hand and making new footprints in the light of his torch, she carried on with defiance.

'We should turn around. There is nothing good that waits for us on this path.'

'Don't be so childish,' Ella stopped and shouted into his face. 'You forget, I am on a mission, and I am not leaving until I get what I came here for.'

'You could just as well see the natural sighting from the foot of the waterfall, like the others,' Ethan said calmly. 'There is no reason for you to be up here.'

She could have slapped him in the face. She could not understand how he did not see that she only wanted to be alone with him. She was losing her patience in this game of affection, a trait she had never truly possessed, and with the thought ramming her insides she unzipped her jacket and casually tossed it into the air and over the edge of the cliff. The idea of her jacket making a parachute landing filled her up with a sense of something achieved. At least she had made her mark on the night, and she did not care if it made her look insane.

'What are you doing?' Ethan sounded desperate, not knowing what to think as he pointed the light towards the space that had swallowed the jacket. 'What did you do that for?'

Just then, a shot of icy wind rippled past, carrying the sound of swaying leaves like an ocean current that threatened to lift them off their feet. The wind churned again and again, as Ella shivered, the spaghetti straps binding her thin top to her body quivered as the piece of cheese cloth drew the wind's wrath, fluttering and flapping, it looked like a rag pegged on a clothesline. She was so cold, and the wind cut at her chest like a blade of ice. She clutched at her chest as the coughing started, followed by a painful bout of wheezing.

Ethan's jacket came off in a flash and he pushed it into her hands, urging her to wrap herself up. She was, by now, delirious with anger. The plan was not working; instead, she was doubled up with agony, and the stupid wind had taken away her chance for the start of something romantic. Ethan's compassion, the pathetic pity he must feel for her, plunged her mood into overdrive. She tossed his jacket overboard so that it too took the plunge and landed somewhere in the pitted darkness.

'WHAT's wrong with you?' Ethan shouted above the wind.

The desperation in his voice sobered her up. She realised she was freezing, that her breath was coming in sharp gasps. She saw the worry etched into his face, and her mind took her back five years ago, when she had snuck out into a storm drenched night, to dance around a wildfire and camp out with her friends. Well, she partied hard that night as if it was her last day on earth, and the next day almost took her there. Wracked with pneumonia, her body took a few days to choose between life and death. She had emerged from the ordeal, bitter and bent on exacting revenge for her sufferings. She had earned the right to get what she wanted from life. That would come on her terms, and she would bend her will to nobody. She straightened now, forcing her breath to take refuge in the might of her pact, and said calmly, 'I want *you* to hold me and keep me warm.'

As her hands went out to him in that torch lit space, she looked into his eyes and saw something in their depths that unsettled her. She had seen it in the bathroom mirror once before, staring back at her, an orange glow that sparked in the depths of each iris, a faint light that grew from the inside out, that like a falling star, vanished before she knew what it was. She saw it now, in Ethan's eyes, but before she could make sense of it, she felt herself given the boot from behind as the wind sent her reeling forward, and as she flew, her toe struck something hard. It stirred up a searing pain that travelled to her ankle and nested there. Her lips opened and she gave a loud yelp as she tumbled to the ground. She hated the wind, that demonic gust from nowhere had ruined her plans and come back to torment her and extract revenge for every nasty thing she had ever said or planned. She would get her back on that force of nature somehow. But now, the ankle proved to be a major distraction. She saw Ethan bending over her ankle, so she could not read his expression. The torch lay on the ground, the round light moving like a carousel as the silver handle danced. She let her eyes focus on that spinning metal, and as the first drops of rain found them, she passed out.

CHAPTER TEN
ETHAN

The rain had turned spiteful. It came down like spitting cobras, hitting everything with a wind driven force that sent the trees heaving for cover and the sand melting into slippery eels. Thunder cracked the darkened sky, dropping a lightning bolt that sizzled and spat a magnified glow onto them. He had gathered an unconscious Ella into his arms and now faced the daunting mission of getting them both downhill.

He staggered and almost lost his footing as a new gust of wind threatened to knock them both over. It was impossible to get any further. He would have to find a shelter of some sort and wait the storm out. But the footpath was narrow, with fallen boulders that littered the path, some needing to be negotiated with hands and feet. A misplaced hand or foot, he reasoned, could send the adventurer rolling off into the depths of the forest. Then came the twists and turns that waited ahead and here a person would be at the mercy of either a steep uphill climb or a downward tumble. The options made him feel numb.

The feeling of hopelessness was new. He felt it bite deeper than the lashing rain that beat into his body. Hardening his resolve, he took another step. That step might have been his last had he stepped forward in shoes a size bigger. The head of branches that smashed into the ground lay quivering before him, just missing him by a toe's length. The tree that had been knocked down was massive as the flashes of lightning kept showing him, and in that concentrated light show, like peeping Halloween monsters, sharp tipped needles, longer than most adult palms, stuck out their pointy tips from between the leaves. He would have to get over that bed of thorns, but there was no telling what lay on the other side of the fallen tree.

What came from the other side was a voice, a thin sound that at first sounded as if it were catching a ride on the fringes of the wind. But then, he heard it again, louder this time. It was that girl, and for the life of him he could not remember her name.

He shouted back, noting that the rain had stopped at some point, taking with it the freak show of thunder and lighting. He was glad for it. If the others had made it up this far, then all they needed to do was get over a fallen tree and be on their way back home.

He saw that Ella was stirring back to life. Things were looking up and they would soon be with the others.

'It's going to be okay,' he told her reassuringly, as she clung to his neck. *'We* will be okay.'

She nodded weakly. He smiled into the face of someone he loved as a younger sister. That was the full extent of his affection for Ella, and he knew it could never be anything else. He would have to put things right with her when they were back at the House, and comfortable again. For now, he must concentrate on getting them both to safety. He gently placed Ella on the ground, with her back up against the mountain, and her knees propped up under her chin so that her feet lay short of the edge of the path that fell away into the deep forested pit.

'I'll be quick,' he said comfortingly, 'just rest.'

He was about to make the climb over the fallen tree when desperate shouting from the other side stopped him. The face that appeared had thin arms that clutched precariously onto the partially uprooted, splintered trunk, a slight figure whose body weight should not, but actually was, putting pressure on the broken structure, making it look as if the roots that tilted into the air like a fibrous onion bulb might roll back and swing the stick figure into the air.

'Don't!' she screamed hoarsely. 'there's flat rock on this side. It's wet and you'll slip.'

He could picture her balancing on the narrow muddy bank, her feet slipping and sliding.

'No!' he gestured wildly with his arms, afraid of what would happen.

'I'll come back,' she yelled, and then disappeared.

It was stifling, a feeling he was not familiar with, this inoculation of helplessness. If it were up to him, he would take his chances and jump off the mountain. But he turned around and knew that he was bound. Ella lay fast asleep. For her sake, he would take the unfamiliar path and wait. Looking up at the night sky, he saw the clouds had shrunk, but hanging like the single eye of a mad dragon, the reddish orange moon sucked up the night vapours, and poured its devouring gaze upon him. Reeled in and hypnotised, he could not look away. The natural phenomenon of which he had only read about was now in his face, breathing into the pages of his life, sheets of water that lay frozen like ice pops, stowed deep in his mind. He could feel the ice melting, flowing off the tips of the pages. He could see the writing uncovered, every stroke fashioned by the pen of life, in ink of oil, setting out a life lived. The sheets of water covered by the pen of oil shimmered and floated under the moon of colour, and for a small speck of time the memories awoke, flowing through his mind. They showed their faces, and he felt every muscle stiffen.

He was back to his childhood days. It was an awkward space that he fell into, for he had always lived at the House, in the staff quarters. He remembered Miss Nan's visits, every night she would appear, just before bed, quizzing him on his homework. And during those long afternoons, when he came home early from school, he spent his spare time in the kitchens or helping to tend the gardens or playing with the children of the House – Francis, Chris and Ella, but those occasions were rare, and only came around once in a long while when they were home on school vacation. The hours of his usual day interlocked like the weaving of a basket of sweet grass, and no matter which direction the threads took, he always put himself to bed. He dreamed of his parents and of a family with no faces. His story led straight back to the House, and to the Mistress. There were whispers filling up most corners, like spider webs the hushed voices stayed trapped in the silky catch, and their words stayed long after the bodies had gone, but when he turned seventeen, Miss Nan told him an official version of the story in her cold and detached way. He learned with accuracy that the Mistress, in her younger days, had one dusky evening gone out for a walk on the beach, to clear her mind. And in her mission to reorganise her thoughts, almost stumbled over the screaming bundle wrapped tightly and placed in the direct pathway of herself and the rolling waves. She picked the infant up and went straight indoors, to give instructions that if the family could not be found, the baby was to be raised in the Mansion.

He preferred to think of it as the House. He barely had any interaction with the Lady growing up, and it seemed safe to say she went to great lengths to avoid him. Miss Nan became her mouthpiece, and everything that passed between them, passed through her. The Mistress took care not to bump into him in the corridors, but then their paths seldom crossed, as it did of recent, when he went into the dining hall, but even so, she never addressed him directly, and when he was younger, if their paths did cross, she would nod to the wall and move on as if a hundred rats were after her. Yet, in his earliest memories, when his pillow sheet held more tears than thread, it was her face that drifted into his mind, her smile that assured him the nightmare had flown back to the sky and was held there by the stars, and that the moon smiled upon him, shedding its light and winking at the night wind to softly rattle past his window, a goodnight kiss that filtered in through the tiny cracks and bade him goodnight. Later, when he was older, he knew he had never seen the Mistress smile, nor ever looked into her eyes, but she had become the grandmother he cherished in his mind. The woman herself wanted no part in what followed, he knew that plainly. Yet, he was proud to have her written into his history, and the strangest thing of all, he felt a sense of belonging when she came into sight. It was different for the other members of the family. He kept to himself, not wanting to be drawn into their drama. He had made himself into a hard knot, he knew that, and was happy to stay tangled in his own world. But he found a smile coming to his face when he spotted the Mistress walking through the house, for her presence was like a fumigation in progress. She had a way of getting lazy bottoms up faster than hot coals, and feet scurrying across floors as if a bear were on the hunt. When he listened to the staff talking, it took effort on his part to keep a straight face, especially when the talk got around to her gaze, that was likened to a flaming dragon's curse, and that if she stared hard into the eyes of the offender that person would see an orange spark appear in the depths of those coal eyes, and then that person's fate was sealed, as tightly as the lid of an old jam jar that had not been opened for years. That person was sure to spend a night rolling in nightmares, and it was a better thing to pass the time sitting wide awake, being outdoors, under the forgiving night sky. He did not tell them then, but he had seen that light secretly, when he stared into the bathroom mirror, an orange spark that lit up the centre of each pupil, only on days when he was moved beyond the normal threshold, and it would appear for a second, then shrink into nothing. He pretended as if what they told him was impossible, by pointing them towards the logic behind such talk. And that was another reason he kept his distance from everybody. He did not want them to know what he had seen in his own reflection.

It had been a while since he had thought back to those years, but the fiery moon summoned another vison before him. It happened when he was no more than eight and fresh home to the House from a sports day at school. He had come first in the athletics and felt obliged to treat himself to something. But there was nobody in the second kitchen. It was as if time had frozen still, and he was free to do as he pleased. It suited him perfectly. He climbed up a kitchen stool, in his sports shorts and shirt. He reached for a glossy faced red apple, and his eyes went to the shiny knives that cook used in her daily chopping and slicing. He had always wondered about that. He managed to secure one for himself and tried to pierce the giant red apple. The knife slipped. He saw the red bubble of blood appear on the end of his thumb, watch it grow fatter until it spilled over like a volcano and slid down the side of his palm, splashing onto the white table. His thumb started to throb, and just when he opened his mouth to wail, cook and the ladies came into the kitchen. Cook slapped him on the back of his head, then quickly put a plaster on the offending thumb and got one of the kitchen ladies to take him back to his room. He lay there on his bed for hours, looking in awe at the wrapped thumb, feeling it throb. Cook and the others had forgotten about his supper. Perhaps, they were still scrubbing that ancient oak table. He felt bad about that, but was still annoyed at Cook for taking a swipe at him. Anyway, there was nothing for it, but to forget the hunger and focus elsewhere. He looked at his thumb, pretended to see it take on a life of its own. He ripped off the plaster and stared at the red line. He tried to wipe it off, then realised he had opened the cut again, the jagged line oozed fresh blood. He got his old stuffed bear from its resting place at the foot of the bed, found the side where the stitches had come undone, and stuck his finger into it, felt the comfort of the old sponge bits and closed his eyes. He saw her face again, draped in youth. He watched as she walked in the moonlight and picked up a bundle, then cradled it to her face and kissed the baby with tears flowing down her cheeks. He fell asleep and by morning, the gaping cut had closed into a blackish red angry line, and somewhere deep inside him, a hollow formed. He had survived the night, healed himself, fought off the hunger, the old teddy was still by his side.

Time nourished the new independence that was becoming his shadow so that even at school, he kept others outside his world. They were bodies that existed, and he exchanged words and expressions with them, but at the end of the day when he lay down in bed, he knew the drawing board would be wiped clean and the whole cycle would repeat itself the next morning and the one after; the charade that was only lacking a stage and costume. Then one day, when he turned fifteen, he decided to take his independence to a new level. He made the decision to run off, encouraged by the notion that nobody would notice. He was wrong, and before the sun set on that auspicious day of free will, he had been found and returned to his room. Strangest of all, the whispers told him that Mistress had gone nearly mad from fright and horror, shouting out orders and running out the House ahead of her driver to raid the streets with her hawk's talent. He knew this could never be true. Such a Lady would never lose her countenance. But she had been the one to spot him that day, as he stood casually with his back to the wall of a village cottage, chewing on a blade of grass, mapping out his plan of exile. She had sent the driver out to box his ears and bundle him into the car. But as he got in, she stepped out, turning her back to him. He had been returned to the House swiftly, the while another driver hastily sped past them to fetch the Mistress.

    He looked at Ella now, still sheathed by the draught of sleep. Growing up, he was lucky enough to have some personal contact with the children from the House. He was there with them, during the afternoons when their school holidays threw them up, fleeting images of the time he spent with them, although they rarely ever took the time to know him. He was their companion, a fetch and carry sort, so they never paid any close attention, and it suited him that way. They were the closest connection he had to family, yet they belonged to another world, where their ties of blood kept them bound to each other. Their attachment was like an oak tree, with rings on the bark, the years that had gone by counted would make an impressive number, spanning a circle of life, wide enough to have its own fairy tale branding. He thought of the rumours that spread like stinging wasps in the village, and this added another dimension to the family saga, the gossip of a young woman dropping from one of the windows of the House. It left the listener's ears sizzling for more, and the air charged with suspense. In his eyes, it fed the family history, made the cocoon silvery and delicate, it added intrigue to the lineage, even though the story had been spun from the imagination, still, it made an impression. He wished he had a family tale of his own to spin, but that kind of thinking was better kept under the latch of a nightmare. Now that he got onto that topic, his gut reminded him yet again, that he was being watched, by the shadow of something unknown, that when he walked the corridors during late evening, he felt a presence tripping along with him. If his heart could speak, it would say that his soul had reached out and awoken another one in his likeness, brought it out of the grave to walk alongside his troubled self. He knew he was being reckless with his thoughts, but if he had indeed fetched a fellow soulmate from slumber, he had no qualms about it, for he was not afraid. He had asked for it, with his constant mistrust of Human company.

He heard the voices coming from the other side of the massacred tree. The rescue party had arrived. It was time to put this night to bed.

CHAPTER ELEVEN
BETH

She walked into the room to find the young crowd gathered around Ella. With a single sweep of her long lashes, she counted red-haired Miriam, then Matti, her Francis, plus Mona's Chris. She could understand Matti being at the bedside, but she had not counted on Miriam being on such familiar terms with Ella. A cold slice of ice chilled her to the core as the thought struck her with horror. Was Miriam there for Ella or did the new arrival already set her sights on Francis? Beth felt the bitter taste in her mouth, and filled with panic, rushed forward, pushing the two girls aside as if they were props. She was in time to catch the look of admiration pass across her son's face. It was a look that had been directed at Matti, and even though she had no preference for the gold digger, having seen too much of herself reflected in the girl's wayward manner, she could breathe again.

She turned her gaze to Ella now, who looked miserable.

'You need anything, my honey' Beth coaxed, even though she did not really care, 'just tell me. I will get it for you.'

Ella smiled weakly, showing an upside-down smile, but then it floated up into her cheeks, dissolving her eyes so that Beth stared at a face that was desperate. She put it down to excess medication.

'I called for Miriam,' Ella managed to gesture towards the girl, 'but it's not working. No friend is going to help me, when it is Ethan I want. Get him for me, I need to see him.'

It was that simple. A straightforward confession that knocked even Beth sidewards. Quickly pulling herself together, she covered her surprise. So, the rumours were true, their song had not been far off the mark, when the news broke and everyone was talking about Miss Ella suffering from a broken foot, that went together with a broken heart, but that nobody knew who the heartbreaker might be. She was spared any further thought by the rare sighting of the old dragon, followed closely by all the offspring. Ella's mother, Ann, had obviously been summoned back from wherever her latest whims had taken her, and now, like a spoilt child herself, all glum and sullen, she walked just inches behind her mother, who, leading the pack, dressed in her black clothes and jewels, with the diamonds twinkling from her earlobes like fallen stars that were too big for the sky to hold, approached the bed with a deathly flourish, sending the young crowd scattering. But the effect was lost on Ella. Ella, a spoilt grandchild, had never been denied anything before. Being the only granddaughter, she was brought up to believe that her feet would never test wet grass, that even if they did and she slipped, her Gran would reset the clock, get a carpet over the wicked host, and put Ella back on top as if nothing had ever happened. All dry and snug, like a bug in a decaying hollow tree. Beth shivered at her thoughts as Ella sat up straight in her bed, her pale cheeks took on colour and she gave her most adoring smile.

Beth felt sorry for the child. If it had been her daughter, she would never have let things progress to this level – having the dragon come in herself to deal with an issue of this nature was to awaken the true nature of the creature and then expect to feed it rabbit food. It was a different matter to have her play the doting granny, but the woman was no fool and Beth herself sensed something was about to happen that would bring dire consequences for all of them. If Ann had been dragged back so quickly, things had gotten messy already, and would certainly get worse. Naturally, both Ella and her mother lacked the advantage of inner intuition in these matters and had not seen the signs. Beth, on the other hand, was born with the knack for a third sense which put her a jump ahead and a sprint across from others. It made her think of how she had fought like a wild animal to grab onto what she wanted, and once she had her sights set on Rod, he was spoken for. She had clawed her way into the family, why, she had taken a bubble bath in the tub of decaying morals for it, gone the extra mile and sealed her soul off from anything good. She patted her hair now, thinking herself above reproach or consequence, feeling the luxury satin of the glove on her fingers. She thought about how she was now a senior member of the family, and that when she presented herself as such, sitting in the front row dressed in her expensive clothes and treasures on her ears and fingers, that if she chose to purchase half her town from where she had come, there would still be change left over. She was no longer that poor girl from the patched house. She had come far and brought her sister Mona along for the joy ride too. Mona owed her everything, for she had everything now only because of Beth's help. Her parents too, having crawled off their potato patch, having gone bump thud in the darkness for most of their lives, had landed in two separate pieces down a gold mine, thanks to her. They were wealthy now, and the greedier they got, the happier they stayed. Beth smiled to herself as the irony hit her. She had done well with the talents she had been given. Nobody could argue on that point.

Beth stayed where she was on the bed, enjoying the thrill of her status and of watching her mother-in-law dip her chin towards her. It was the respect she had earned as both wife and mother to the future heir of the Mansion. She turned to see her husband and Matt take up their positions as guard dogs, with Ann standing between them.

The Mistress took the armchair, arranging her skirts before lifting her face. It was directed towards her spoiled favourite. She took her time to speak, and when she did, her voice was firm. 'You had quite an experience last night. But it was careless of you to ignore the others when they warned you of the impending danger.'

'Was it Chris who complained?' Ella, the favourite asked, twisting the bedclothes around her finger. 'He always complains.'

'This is not about Chris. This is about your bad behaviour,' the Mistress said plainly, 'and the fact that your actions put others in the way of harm.'

'I did not do anything to them,' Ella's voice was rising, 'they *left* us.'

'Yes,' the Mistress said slowly. 'I believe that was after you ignored their warnings and chose to wander off with Ethan. You put his life in danger as well.'

'*Eteth* doesn't mind,' Ella chirped brightly. 'In fact, he will tell you himself,' she stopped to look out the open window nearest to her, 'but he hasn't come to see me, not yet. I don't know why.'

She turned her gaze upon her grandmother fully now, her eyes begging, 'Please grandmama, please bring him here. I want to see him, and then we can tell you the good news together.'

Silence swallowed the room, like the quiet, before the

burgeoning storm wreaks havoc, devasting and merciless. Beth sensed it, and for a quick fallen second, felt pain again for this child who would soon learn the misery of a broken heart. But even she had misjudged the storm.

The Mistress jumped up from her chair, something they had never seen before, her eyes burning with fury. She looked fierce in that moment, nothing like an old dragon, more like a vulture on the scavenge, in that black dress with the ruthless skirts. Her black hat shook as her head seemed to move into her shoulders. They had never seen this much movement from such a refined Lady, nor such emotion. When she spoke, her voice seemed to belong to something dead, then it remade itself and lashed out, burning every ear, as the cheery sunlight flowed in through the open windows, and a fairy wind trailed its magical sweet air into the room. All that magic vanished with the outburst, for she had never gone mad like this before, and Beth had never seen such a performance, and judging by the frozen looks on the faces of the siblings, neither had they.

'Find the boy!'

Her guard dogs stood like ice pops in a row. She howled again, and this time Matt went out running and came running back into the room, the time in between lapsed like a broken day. When he returned, Ethan was walking beside him, and when they took their places, Matt beside his siblings, and Ethan further apart, but with the sun in his hair, mapping out his shoulders, and a golden flush lighting up his face, he looked magnificent. Beth was taken aback at this young boy, for she had seldom paid him any attention. But she saw he was both handsome in face as well as deeply captivating. There was something about him, the way he fitted into the picture, the way he stood, with his head held high, those dark eyes so guarded, so like… She stopped herself in time and brought her attention back to the drama enfolding before the small group. Ella had managed to hurl herself out of the bed, so fast, so effortlessly, almost as if she had flown, straight onto the carpet, and was now kissing it, unable to move, her lips were locked onto the soft surface, whilst the rest of her body writhed in pain. Ethan was the first to rush to her side, quickly gathering her up and placing her once more on the bed, in the time it took Ann, Matt and Rod to move. They stood helpless, watching the scene unfold in front of them, as Ella, in a state of passion and desperation, roped her fingers about Ethan's neck.

She clung to him so that his dark hair hung like a black curtain about their faces. Her voice came in gasps, sobbing, her words might have moved mountains, 'Please don't leave me, *Eetth*. Tell them, tell them, we love each other.'

Whatever Ethan said to her was muffled, not meant for any ears except those belonging to them. Beth, who had during this time abandoned her position at the foothold of the bed, now eyed that space with disdain. But she could not in all modesty, claim it again, and watched with the others, as Ella allowed herself to be laid back onto the bank of pillows. Once she was settled, Ethan turned to face the Mistress. The woman, who was rumoured to be more invincible than the foundation upon which the Mansion itself was set, had piled herself into the armchair, and staring from that point, seemed to be fighting off vampires in her head. Shrinking as far back into the chair, her face turned away from the sun, she did not look up again until Ethan took up a position in front of her and boldly said, 'May we talk in private?' The calm dignity of his voice reached into the depths, somewhere in the tormented woman's mind, shaking the ruins of what must have once been her fortitude, somehow, his voice managed to resurrect all of that, to bring the Mistress back, as she stood up, straight with a liquid grace that settled things back into place. Moving like a queen in mourning, her every movement so defined, so precise, as if she walked the halls of a museum, where only the dead got to tell their tales, but none were in the habit of spilling the beans except straight into the ears of their queen, she left the room with that grace. Ethan followed her. Beth realised, in the aftermath, that nobody seemed to have picked up the strange fact that Ethan, in that moment of disharmony, when so much could have gone so bad, he had forgotten his place, and when he spoke, it had been with a quiet, firm authority. It was unnatural. Something was unbalanced.

For her part she was aggravated, silently cursing the turn of events, and more irritated that she could not follow the duo to find out what was being said. She was prepared to eavesdrop from whatever perch she could find, but again, she would be risking too much. Besides, she could not ignore Rod's neck any longer, as it jerked like a chicken. She followed his bobbing head and realised what he was so desperately trying to point out. His sister Ann needed help, for she had lost all self-control, and was now kneeling on the carpet, swaying back and forth, and muttering to herself, with her brothers standing by, confused and uncomfortable. The daughter was in no better shape either, having realised that Ethan was no longer in the room. Beth cursed Mona for having chosen this morning to go away into town, for some scheduled appointment. She was always going to secret appointments, the details of which nobody knew anything about. It was left to her to sort out this mess now. She rose to her feet, and with new boredom in her eyes, took herself to the unfortunate pair.

CHAPTER TWELVE
MONA

She hurried indoors, having cut her trip short. She was expected to arrive after lunch, but Beth had called her up very early with news of family drama, Ella. Why was she not surprised? The girl behaved badly, was never put in her place. But worse, falling in love with a servant of the Mansion. No matter how charming he might be, he was still far beneath her station. She should have been in that room when things had come out into the open, but it was just like her sister to think about herself first. She possessed no mind, only a candy-floss zone, all sugary sweet and fluffed up. It was being preserved better than any pickle, Beth worked at only looking after herself and her own interests. She was as shallow as a puddle.

The Mansion lay sleeping as she threaded her way in, but she knew better. She picked up her pace, hoping to find Beth and get a rundown before meeting anyone else. She was not so lucky and came face to face with her mother-in-law.

'Good morning mum,' she said softly, as she dipped her chin gently. They were not allowed near the sacred body of the woman. They were only to demonstrate emotions from a distance. It was a strange thing, as if the monster that ruled them, could be afraid of anything. Sentiment, perhaps, or the Human touch. That was the problem at the heart of it all. The search for emotion. It was far safer to keep distance, so she had copied Beth and everyone else in the inner family circle by imitating the gentle dip of the chin, with eyes downcast, to show respect and familiarity. To show distance.

'Good morning. Might I ask why you found the need to stay out last night, since my son seems to have no idea under which roof his wife spent the night?'

Stupid Matt, she thought to herself. The quiet idiot could not even come up with an excuse. Why, when he went off on his golfing excursions, nobody raised a single eyebrow. Not even the Queen of the brood, standing in front of her now, with her features showing open disdain, put up a fuss at his frequent disappearances. Instead, she would cluck like a good mother hen, saying without feeling. 'Ah, golfing runs in the family genes.'

Mona put on her best face, 'I had a doctor's appointment in town, Mum,' she lied earnestly, 'and then went to visit a friend whose mother had passed on, and it got late, so I stayed rather than drive.' She was quietly hoping that she had said enough to put the matter to rest.

Her mother-in-law was not one to put words through the juicer. She met her gaze fully, 'Are you ill?' to which Mona replied quickly. 'No, no. It was a routine visit, just a check up to make sure I have nothing to worry about.'

'In that case, I suggest you remember to inform your husband of your whereabouts the next time you run out.'

Mona managed a nod, as the dignified Lady walked away. She could not help but marvel at the woman, and it was easier to think of her as being a rare kind of fruit from a tree that had ended up as firewood. She had never met anyone with such a disposition. It was as if the grand old lady had been brought up on a different planet, then stepped in to rule over this one, yet none of her children showed that unique trait. They were quite ordinary. All three lacked everything that should have mattered. For instance, top of the charts, there was Matt her husband, youngest of the brothers and the most insufferable. She should have never married him. She should have known from the start. She could start top of the page with his erratic movements, where he would sometimes come to a dead stop, right in the middle of an errand with purpose, to turn something over in his mind, his tall, thin frame poised perfectly, with his feet pointing off in whatever direction they had stopped, his hand going up under his chin, as if the debris that had gathered in his mind might be cleared with this frozen stance. She hated to admit it. But she loved him, despite the odds.

If only he could see that.

Yet, she had secrets of her own. From the start, she much preferred Rod's character, from a friendly point of view. He was at least interesting. It was not his fault he had been made so different. She smiled just thinking of it. He sometimes walked into the dining hall with the candour of a fisherman straight off the docks, with a large net full of the dancing silvers stashed somewhere on his boat, his round cheeks puffed up from the fresh air and sun from a day out, his smile broad, his eyes already scanning the table for the spread. He did not care about the grace of anything, and focused on doing exactly as he pleased, completely oblivious to everything else. He just sat there, putting food down his throat, making silly conversation that most times nobody ever bothered to listen to, but she always did, even if she could not let anybody know how she hung on to his words for survival. Because she spent so much time secretly studying him, she knew how much he annoyed Beth. She knew her sister, better than anybody else ever could, and she saw how Rod's carefree manner put Beth out. Poor

Beth. She imagined the permanent sound in her head must be that of a chalk dragged backwards over a blackboard. She knew that irritation very well, from her school days, a screech that set your teeth on edge. She liked to think that in Beth's case, that was the sound she heard in her head whenever her husband was around. She knew she was being horrid, but she had seen how her sister's fingers had started to quake recently at the dining table. It was as if they were filled with a nervous energy that ached from wanting to reach over and strangle the man. Oh, she knew her sister well enough, so much that she hated her, and loved everything that her sister despised.

She was no angel herself. Not counting the days from her marriage, especially. She was happy in the days before. But Beth made sure there was enough misery to go around for them both. In truth, Beth had only pushed for the match between Matt and herself, to secure the money pie, she wanted no holes in it. She wanted to keep it in the family. But that was a topic for another time. For now, her mind dwelt on the days after the marriage, on how unhappy she had become. Matt was a man set in his ways. He did not care about anyone, except himself. He had no intent to alter a single old habit to accommodate anybody, much less a wife. He had copied one trait straight off his mother, and thought himself untouchable and unreachable, but he lacked the finesse to pull that off. He preferred to make a show instead, by blowing his nose into his handkerchief, every single time she called him out on anything. At first, she had been concerned. But she learned quickly there was nothing wrong with his nose. It sat perfectly straight, a prominent feature, on his handsome face, and it was a nice sort of nose, and that he could go for days without any trigger. Later, after Chris was born, she got to know that he resorted to the action when he wished to be left alone with his thoughts. Over the years, Matt disappeared more often into his bed with his back to her. And those times were scarce, counting the times he was actually under the same roof as herself.

She was not like Beth. She had not remade herself into a painted doll, a caricature of wealth and status. All that Beth was missing was a crown to finish off her transformation, and no doubt Rod would buy her one soon enough. For her part, she tried to stay true to herself, but that was a joke. She failed dismally. If blame was to be attached, there would be a nice sized portion coming her way. She thought back to the night when Rod came knocking on her door, looking for Matt. She was about to jump from the window, having one foot on the window-sill, perched and ready, but not having enough courage to bring the other one up. Rod pushed open the door in that moment when the sky was raining wheelbarrows that smashed onto the roof, for she had never heard it rain like that before. The fire danced and shed its warmth and heat in the room that was hers, and Rod came in, talked her out of her ridiculous position. She found out that Beth was away and did not ask where. Before the night was up, Rod and herself found their way into bed. It was something that lay between them, an unspeakable thing that hovered over their heads, like an ugly rainbow. She had been a wreck after that, worrying about what would happen if Beth found out, knowing that her sister, for all her twisted and conniving ways, would never have betrayed her trust in that way. She had done the worst imaginable thing, not just to her sister, but to herself. Yet, the hatred she had for Beth simmered, carried on brewing like a stew in a bottomless pot. There was nothing she could do about that.

Matt. That was a different story. She had corrupted that

love, and it filled her with pain and guilt. She spent a month hiding behind an ordinary face. Her mind suffered, her spirit died but she could not confess either to her sister or her husband. She avoided them both which proved very easy, since Beth was always busy, and Matt was always absent, and when he chose to be at the Mansion, it was never to spend time with her. But she found out that she was too tough to lay down and die. She started taking walks through the estate, and the constant roaming about brough Philip to her. That was the beginning of something different. They went from being friends to part time tenants in a small flat on the outskirts of a nearby town. She knew she was playing a dangerous game. There was no way she could remember how many times she had pressed the lie to avoid dinner, saying she would be spending the weekend at her parents. Nobody went to visit her parents, hardly Beth either, so it was a safe anchor for the lies that built themselves into a hive.

As Mona climbed the stairs to her room, she ran into Matt who was hurrying down. He stopped short, gave her one of his half smiles, then informed her that both Ann and Ella had been sent off that morning, before sunrise, to the country house, a good three-hour drive away into a more remote part of the landscape than they already occupied. Mona shuddered. She knew the house and pictured it now, lying boxed in by a forest. She had been there once with Matt, just when the house had been newly built. The first night produced a sky of stars and a friendly moon. They sat outside in their chairs, with their blankets. The house did not have any staff, so she had made them cups of hot chocolate and they sat and sipped silently, until it grew darker, and then went indoors to a cold bed, since there was a problem getting heating into the house. But she had not minded, and quite enjoyed the treat of having Matt hold her in his arms, and they had fallen asleep like that. The next night brought the wind to them, the trees mimicking the waves, which was not so bad. But the following night delivered a nightmare. First, she woke up to something thumping the roof, as if whatever was jumping on it was trying to get in. Then the wind started up, roaring and tearing through the trees, it came at them with the cries of a hundred cats. The rain put in a performance too, pelting the roof and smacking the walls, raising a groaning and moaning, the kind she had never heard before, and that fiasco got the leaks activated in the ceiling so that she had water trickling onto her head. Thunder banged and clanged as if it were biting at her earlobes, whilst its mate shot lightning bolts into the room, in terrifying beams, as if it would set the house on fire. The room door moved, gliding silently open. That door had been firmly shut – she was sure about that. And to top matters off, the new, fat candles shot flames that swayed as if someone were standing there, fanning them with a roll of newspaper. She sat up straight in the cold bed, and shook her husband awake. Agitated and scared, she flipped out, went crazy and nagged and ranted about how miserable she was, until Matt finally unable to take any more, yelled at her to shut up, then pulled the pillow over his head and was soon comfortably fast asleep. She had rocked herself on the bed and finally drifted off sometime towards early morning, when the wind had died away, and it was quiet again. When she woke at nine, the car was packed and ready to go. Matt had nothing to say. Her nagging had been enough for him. He was eager to cut their week-long stay short, so long as he was not stuck in with her. She found no reason to deny him that, and it was done.

But Matt told her afterwards that a visit to his mother had

secured a change in the property, with the house now being fully and permanently staffed, with new heating arrangements and that a separation between forest and house had seen a landscaped garden put into place. Still, she felt sorry for the two who were banished to that country hideaway. She would not spend a night in that house ever again, no matter how fancy they made it up. Matt told her he was on his way there now, together with Rod, to check up on them. He did not ask her if she wanted to join them but said he would see her later in the afternoon, or perhaps in the morning. He would let her know. He rushed off, and she knew she was not going to see him anytime soon. She continued, on her way, to the sanctity of that space, her room, that lay just around the corner. But, instead, came face to face with her sister. Beth pecked her on the cheek, then drew her aside and whispered, 'I am going to our parents for a bit. Want to come with?'

CHAPTER THIRTEEN
THE PARENTS

Two hours later they were riding through the massive, polished brass gates and up the short driveway to the square brick house. The large, double- storey feature sat like a proud mantis shrimp, the rows of blinking windows and walls of flamboyant colour watching the driveway, as if a thousand eyes were staring. But as their mother always said, windows were a touch of high class, and she would have as many as she liked, the smaller the better, so as not to give the impression of taking a shortcut and cutting costs, now that her daughters were flying high. And their father, who lived to keep the promise he made himself that he would never go back to where he came from, worked hard to prove this to himself and everyone else. So, he went out of his way to do what was necessary to keep his status. The result was a house, both inside and out, that was a spectacle.

The girls passed under the porch, their heads narrowly missed being spiked by the hanging, overweight chandelier. The interior was alive, with the dark velvet curtains being drawn, and the light coming in from the dozens of small windows, casting miniature stage spotlights throughout. The furniture and ornaments glowed under the sun's pouring of fat pools of hot light. The owners of the building, dressed in their Sunday best, and sweating from the heat and light, rushed to greet their daughters.

'Oh, it's hot, hot every day,' Moira said, her thin high-pitched voice coming across as a shout, patting her red face, shaking her head, 'but I hear sunlight kills bacteria, so that must mean it's a good thing to have a hot house.'

'What do you mean it's a good thing? Pat spat back, mopping his face, 'it's so hot even the mosquitoes don't bite any more. I haven't even seen a fly in weeks, gets toasted soon as it comes in.'

'Then why are you complaining?' Moira returned irritably, 'Go back to where you came from, and live with the mosquitoes and flies, see if I care.'

Pat breathed in deeply, as he broke out into a new sweat. He rolled up his shirt sleeves and wiped down his face with the back of them. The purple tie that held up his white shirt collar took on another smudge as a new drop inched off his chin, and he used his shirt sleeve again to soak up the offending brow.

'Don't do that,' Moira growled, her own face starting to melt, the layers of make-up that covered it dissolving into a greasy mess. 'it's bad manners. Use the handkerchief that I put into your pocket.'

Pat took out the white handkerchief from his pocket and wiped his round face as if he were shining the bonnet of his car. When he was done, he threw the wet piece of material onto the floor and dug the heel of his expensive shoe into it, twisting his foot around as if he wanted to dance.

'That will be the day I get told what to do,' he said through grated teeth. 'You are taking things too far, woman. Stop telling me what to do.'

'And no suit and tie will ever fix what's wrong with you,' Moira squealed. 'Not when you look and sound like a goat. Good for nothing.'

At that point, Beth chose to flounce past the two of them,

throwing her lean frame onto the cushions, she cleared her throat loudly and brought all eyes onto her, 'Mummy, I feel for a bit of your tea, the way you used to make it when we were little.'

'Oh,' Moira chuckled, as she rushed from the room, with Pat following her closely, leaving the girls to themselves. Beth shrugged as she settled back into the soft cushion. 'You are making me nervous. Come sit.'

Mona found herself propped onto the couch next to Beth. She was not as tall as Beth, and in her dainty state, probably weighed half of what Beth put onto the scale. Beth leaned forward, her round eyes became serious, and she pursed her lips tightly, before saying. 'I never got to say but something strange happened that day, between our mother-in-law and Ethan. Nobody knows what they spoke about, but she came back alone, all hushed up and ever since then, he keeps out of sight, never comes to table service. Odd, don't you think?'

Mona shrugged, 'She could have asked him to stay away from Ella. You told me they had something between them?'

'But that's it,' Beth frowned, 'The old dragon doesn't have a thing about marrying out of your class. Look at us, we're chilling in the Mansion, and where did we get pulled out of? It was never an issue. They have enough stashed everywhere, there's no need for more. And if you saw Ella that day,' she stopped as her green eyes went wide, 'she looked mad enough to crawl up the walls if it gave her half a chance to jump on Ethan.' she paused, shuddering at the memory. 'She was at the edge, that girl. I can tell you that. I was there.'

Mona was intrigued and nodded for Beth to go on.

'But when they came back, from that talk, we were asked to leave the room. And those stupid doors are so thick, I could hear nothing from the other side. Do you think Ethan turned her down?'

'Well, not everybody is in for the money.'

Beth ignored her, 'We're missing something.'

Just then the doorbell rang, and Pat came rushing from the inside of the house, his short frame whizzed past as his voice followed it, saying. 'Hang on, hang on.'

A few seconds later and Pat reappeared, followed by a tall young man with light hair. When Mona saw him, she stiffened, and Beth might have noticed the look that passed between them if she had not been so engrossed in staring at her father, whose chubby face had taken on a whole new look of joy.

'Philip's here, and what a saving it has earned me.'

'Saving?' Beth asked, confused, dipping her head in acknowledgement of the visitor.

Pat's head bobbed like a duck out at sea, 'Yes. But your mother can fill you in. Come on Phil, time is everything.'

With that, they were gone, and not long after, Moira entered followed by a lady in her mid-forties, carrying a silver tray with a tea cloth. A tea set with a very large teapot was lifted off the tray and set on the antique coffee table.

'Come Tan,' Moira sang, 'pour the tea quick, quick for my girls.'

Moira turned to Beth and said, 'Tan comes from the village. The ladies from our tea club told me about her. I hear she's worked at the Mansion before.'

'When was that?' Beth inquired, looking at Tan, as she poured the tea out, but it was her mother who answered her. 'I believe some time ago, but Tan comes highly decorated. This tea for instance,' Moira said, as she picked up a cup and took a sip. 'It's high class.'

Beth took a sip of her own, and squeezed her eyes in agony, 'What tea is this mother?'

'Oh,' Moira nodded sagely, 'Tan makes it herself. She has friends in high places. They gave her the secret. I hear only the pedigree bloodline can taste the delicate fineness of it,' and here she paused and took another sip, 'I must say I can taste it myself. It must mean we have that noble blood in us.'

Beth put down her cup and saucer. She could not believe such nonsense. She had never tasted anything so horrendous before. She could not resist and turned to Tan, who was in the act of handing Mona her teacup, 'So Tan, what filth went into this brew, huh?'

Moira choked and spluttered on her first sip, as Tan squared her shoulders and set her broad chin up into the air. She was a large woman, with a round face and a wide mouth. She smiled broadly now, an ugly smile that filled up her face, 'Maam, since you asked, judging by the size of the gulp you just took, enough went in to make your fancy insides fill up like a tank of gutter water. As for your mother, enough went down over the past few days to fill a bathtub, so there's something for you to think about.'

Beth shot to her feet, her face was ablaze, 'How dare you!' she screamed, forgetting her new breeding, 'Get out of here, you ugly stupid thing.'

'Oh ma'am,' Tan smiled that awful smile again. 'Seems like you can take the rat out of the neighbourhood, but never the other way around.'

With that, Tan placed the tea tray on the coffee table and left the room with a haughtiness that astonished everyone. The silence went unchecked for a while, until Mona stood up and went to her sister who had remained standing, her head turned towards the door.

'People are still jealous,' Mona said simply. 'They will always be jealous.'

Those words seemed to put things back into perspective for Beth, who as if waking up from her sleep, was instantly back to herself, bustling about the room, she picked up the teacups and the large teapot. She went towards the open window, tossed them out as if they were empty bottles. She dusted her hands together, then said sweetly to the figure below, upon whose head she had nearly thrown the tea things. 'Go tell everybody, we don't keep trash in this house.'

Turning away from the window, she said, 'I will have a new, fancier set sent up to you by this evening, mother.'

Moira looked uncertain, 'They will talk about me behind my back, at the ladies club,' she looked worried. 'And Tan must be already knocking at doors, telling them how badly we treated her.'

'Mother!' Beth almost yelled in exasperation, 'Don't you see, they were laughing behind your back a long time already. Really, I don't understand why you are not head of that club by now, since you have two daughters in the Mansion. I will get Miss Nan to sort things out for us. I should have done it years ago. Then we will see who laughs last.'

The other daughter watched as the two of them transformed into themselves once more, the drama from the last five minutes proved to be a springboard for the duo, from which they could launch themselves into a new future, wiping the slate clean with plans for revenge. They were, at a quick glance, very much alike. It was a scary deduction, and Mona brought her mind back to the matter that was secretly distressing her. As she followed Beth to the door, she turned to Moira and made her voice sound as plaintive as she could, 'Who was that with Dad?'

'Oh,' Moira flapped her hands in the air. 'It's Philip. He is helping your father with the roof. The one for the garden hut. The storm from last week blew it away. Now, Philip is putting a new one together out of the branches of the other trees. It will cost nothing, almost nothing to finish.'

'But how did you meet Philip?'

'Oh,' Moira nodded her head, as if she had just remembered something. 'We came across him last Monday. I forgot to tell you that we dropped by, your father and I, for a visit at the Mansion. I know,' she said, seeing the shock enter Mona's eyes. 'We should have called first. But it was a last minute decision. In any case, Miss Nan told us nobody was available, so we took the chance for some exercise and went walking. We ended up by the fields, and he came running after us with this,' and she turned around and went to a small writing desk that stood in the corner of the room, from which she took out a ring. Holding it up as if it were a lantern, she approached them once again, and said, 'See, it's a ring, a ring that was found on the potato fields,' and she gave it to Beth to inspect. 'Philip said since we are family of the Mansion, we would know what to do with it. And that is how your father came to know of him and that he is an expert handyman.'

Beth turned the ring over in her hands, whilst Mona fought back the urge to grab it herself to get a better look. Beth slipped it onto a finger, where it stayed midway, refusing to budge. She tried the ring on every finger, but it did not sit well on any of them. Mona snatched the ring from her sister, unable to contain her curiosity any longer. The ring did not sit well on her fingers either, even though they were so delicately fashioned. It swung loosely on every one of them, until she gave up trying. Instead, she held the ring up, peering closely at the unusual piece.

'It's so strange,' Mona declared. 'Look at the design. It seems to be some sort of fish, there's two of them.'

'Fish?' Moira snorted, 'I knew it was worthless. I thought so, it's a thick black ring, no hidden gold, or diamonds to see, with that funny pattern on the top. Probably came out of a party lucky packet like the ones I used to make you girls. And even when I turned the ring upside down, and the scribbling, that scribbling means it has no value. What a waste of time. It must have been dropped by one of the field workers, yes, no other way, but by one of them.'

Mona looked at the engraving on the inside of the band and squinted hard but could not make any sense of it.

'It's not very clear,' she said, 'but I bet this ring is an expensive piece. Look here,' and she pointed to the pair of fish. 'It might be diamonds, I can't say, but there's fine black stones worked all around the sea creatures. It's so unique. I've never seen anything like this before.'

'So, it's expensive then?' Moira suddenly perked up, her shrill voice getting higher.

'Yes, it must be,' Mona confirmed, 'And very exclusive.'

Mona walked to the writing table and switched on the lamp. She held the ring under the yellow light, and the black ring blazed. It brought Beth and Moira rushing to the lamp.

'Oh,' Moira squealed. 'I nearly put it away and forgot about it. What should we do with it?'

'Well,' Beth replied quickly, snatching it from Mona. 'Since it was found on family ground, I think I will keep it.'

'But it doesn't fit you,' Mona reminded her. 'How will you wear it?'

Beth considered this for a moment, then gave it back to

Mona, 'Fine. You decide then.'

'No, it's not my place.'

Beth thought about it for a second, then lightened up. 'I think I will give it to Mummy dragon,' she chuckled mischievously, remembering the thick black ring on the old woman's finger. 'Yep, something tells me this ring brings trouble. It's going home.'

CHAPTER FOURTEEN
CORAL

The past three months had whizzed by, bringing changes that were both strange and unexpected. The most startling of these was the announcement of Matti's upcoming wedding to Francis. It was great news, delivered on the winds of surprise, and it blew through everyone like a gale force. Theories on the matter were exchanged in the halls of the Mansion, and like the aroma of a good baking pie, it floated out onto the streets and beyond for some time, as everyone digested the news of Matti; the unknown girl from somewhere, soon to join the ranks of those they respected and gossiped about the most. Matti, for her part, could care less about their gaping stares, as she sailed past them, smacking everyone in the face, with the fact that she had already portioned the offenders into a new precinct of her brain, the site for garbage removal. Everybody agreed, she was like a pangolin, keeping her secret ways to herself. They decided to look past that, and in return for her extraordinary treatment of themselves, they pardoned her and took her into their fold. Matti was fast becoming a favourite at the Mansion, her fan base multiplied, the fever mounted, and on the other side of the delirium, Coral had become the outcast. She knew Matti was the cause for the shift in the general mindset. Ever since she had moved into the Mansion, Matti had moved out of her life. And now with Ella gone, she was back at the staff quarters, still Matti snubbed her. The fans played copycat, and everything was becoming almost too much to bear. But she had been granted a small act of mercy in all of this. She was back at the rondawel. Coral liked it better that way. She had never wanted to move into the Mansion. She could not understand why Matti was being so unkind, treating her with such distaste. She could not help it, but if she had to describe the look that passed across Matti's face when they did lock eyes, it was worse than the face of a guest receiving a bowl of soup, that had been left out too long, the coagulated fat and trimmings reeking of rotten decay. It made her feel ill.

The morning of the wedding arrived. Coral finished dressing in the wardrobe of black shirt and pants, with the starched white apron and cap and black soft takkies. Matti had put in an additional request about the dress code, asking for staff to keep their hair tied back and that, no makeup was to be worn on her wedding day. Now, she finished doing her hair into a tight coil at the back of her head, as was her custom, and since she never had a habit of wearing makeup anyway, the request did not upset her, as it did the others. Thinking back to the only time she had put on makeup, she remembered Dinesh's visit and his parents. Something inside her had broken that day, much like the nagging pain of a wood splinter that burrows into the thumb and makes a home in it. She brushed the thought aside now, as her mind went back to the events of the night before.

Karabo had come to visit her, standing at the doorway, she gave her the news, expressly delivered straight from Matti's mouth. Coral's parents and sisters were invited to the wedding. Matti also wanted her to know that a last minute change brought two more surprise guests. Karabo looked at Coral with compassion in her eyes, and Coral knew for a second what it felt like to have a friend again. Karabo was one of the few people who stayed outside the circle of drama, but she also kept a distance from Coral. She never asked any questions during her visit, only shook her head, mumbled something about Matti not being right in the head, and then vanished faster than she had appeared. Coral returned to the moment, and to the knock that landed on her door. She did not move, as her mind gave her peace. If only briefly, she looked around at her home. As if for the first time, she saw the single bed, adequate for one, with the large window next to it. She looked at the brick wall that sectioned off the portion of the interior, dividing the bathroom with shower and toilet from the kitchen, a bite sized portion with a small counter, fitted snugly into the wall, holding a tiny hotplate and kettle. The tray on which a single plate and mug sat, together with a short glass and cutlery for one looked neat and tidy. For the first time, she knew what tranquillity must feel like. The gentle flutter of the pale beige curtains at the large window caught the corner of her eye, and it nudged her into action, as the door received a series of impatient bangs. She rushed forward and opened it, to find her sisters staring back at her.

They pecked her on each cheek, floated into the room and gingerly placed themselves on the edge of the bed. Arya crossed her legs, picked up her chin, to better survey the room. 'It's tiny,' she concluded, 'And claustrophobic.'

Veru nodded, 'Yes, it is, but I think it is better than having no roof over your head at all.'

'You think?' Arya asked 'But where does she keep her clothes? There's no closet here.'

Coral went to the single wall facing the bed and pulled open a door that was part of the white wall. The action revealed a cave like space that held four hangers and four shelves.

'Very clever,' Arya laughed. 'But Mummy pegs more washing onto her line than you have in there. Don't tell me that's all the clothes you have?'

Coral could not tell them that since they had shared their clothes from childhood, she had taken very little with her when she left. She smiled instead, 'You both look beautiful.'

They were dressed for a ball. Veru shone in a silver dress that sparkled and hugged her chest, flowing out from the waist towards her ankles. Around her neck she wore a thick roped piece of sliver, the earrings that matched dropped to the tip of her shoulders. Veru's hair had been trimmed, rather she was missing half of it. She was beginning to slip into her own identity, Coral thought silently, since the three of them had always kept their hair long, so that it went past the small of their backs. The new hair style gave Veru a more worldly look, as if the young girl she had known had traded places with the grown up facing her. It suited Veru, she decided, especially the way her hair framed her face, cut to mimic the feathers of a bird. While she was absorbed in this assessment, her sisters were talking, and during this interlude, Veru's hand was doing something strange – it moved in front of her face, as if she were twirling a hoola hoop, her wrist worked itself, fingers convulsed like a thrashing octopus. Coral saw the reason for the display. A gold band with a single diamond occupied Veru's finger. It must be the engagement ring. Veru was going to great lengths to make the ring stand out, her gestures were growing more frantic. Coral held her breath. One of two things were going to happen soon – either the ring was going to fly off her finger, or that hand was going to land a hot slap on Arya's face. Thankfully, the girls stopped talking, and Veru placed the performing hand on her thigh, where it rested for now. The ring however was no match for Arya's dress. As Arya shifted closer to Veru, the sheet of gold sequence that she was wrapped in caught the light, as it streamed through the window. The effect was mesmerizing. Arya transformed into a bar of gold. The gold brick ended way above her knees, but the high heeled sandals, with their open toes showing polished glitter that glowed like nuggets, fed the illusion, so that the gold straps that looped each ankle took on fashion's pledge, drawing focus on the perfectly shaped legs. And when Arya leaned towards Veru, feeding words into her ear, Coral found their bright red lips, blush polished cheekbones and heavily shaded eyes took her mind away, to a puppet show she had once seen at school. She swept the thought out of her mind quickly.

'I am so happy for you and Dinesh,' she told Veru.

She had caught Veru's attention, and her sister gushed about her happiness, throwing her hand out, raising the finger with the ring, almost into Corals' face, 'It is stunning, isn't it? And it is just as mummy said, a diamond this size is worth almost anything.'

The two sisters nudged each other, and Arya laughed. 'Well, that's what I tell myself every night. If this guy I am seeing manages to live long enough to get the question out, I don't know. The second most annoying factor is the company he keeps – that hyena, his mother, is always by his side,' she shook her head whilst pulling a face. 'I see all thirty- four teeth at once when she smiles. Still healthy as a horse and going strong at eighty. As if dealing with the mother is not enough, he has two sisters… both nutshells, no brain, all talk. But if he asks, I'll accept,' she rolled her eyes to the thatched roof and back, before shrugging. 'There's no such thing as love. So, who cares anyway?' Besides,' she looked Coral in the face, 'least you can be sure to get an invite to my engagement.'

Coral hung her head, not sure of what to say.

Veru jumped off the bed as if the bed had poked her with a cactus spine, 'You're only saying that to look good. You know that I had no choice, not after what she did.'

'You could have insisted,' Arya said calmly, 'But you didn't.'

'Well,' Veru shook her head, 'It looks like it turned out okay for her. She found the guts to tell them at home she has a job and is not coming back, she has a place to live, and I think it's all because of me.'

Coral took the brief second of silence to intervene, 'I really didn't mind. Besides, Matti filled me in on all the details, so it was like I was there.'

She was rolling out the lies like a trusted pie maker. Matti had told her nothing, and somewhere deep inside, she held on to something dark and twisted, and she could not understand what it was, only that it was growing.

But her words had warmed the air between the two sisters, who were swiftly moving on to more relevant details. They had started an inspection of the place, and Arya sighed deeply. 'It's very simple. Veru, what do you think, would you be able to live here?'

'No,' Veru said quickly, picking up the teaspoon and looking into it, 'But her things are clean. Look, I can see my face in this spoon.'

'I could make us some tea?' Coral said brightly, 'We could talk and catch up.'

Arya chuckled, 'No, that's okay. Besides, you only have one cup. We don't want to put you out.'

'But I have these,' and Coral reached into the tiny cupboard beneath the sink and took out a pack of six plastic cups.

'No, no,' Veru chimed in, 'You can't put hot tea into that. And besides, I want to go now. Dinesh is waiting for me.'

Silently, Coral counted Dinesh off the surprise guest list Karabo had told her about. She wondered about the other guest.

They left the rondawel behind, making their way across the bridge and back through the densely forested path, the old trees standing still on either side of the cobbled pathway, their branches leaning lightly into the passing faces, still as stone knights. Arya and Veru took off their shoes, ducking the branches, picking up their speed, eager to get to the Mansion, and to the gardens where the wedding was set to take place. As they got closer, both sisters put on their shoes, the sounds of the guitar and piano called out, infused in perfect harmony. They spotted the white pitch of the tent, the side flaps rolled up, so they had a good view of the chairs, dressed up in giant bows, the tables heavy with décor and food, and the rows of heads already arranged in lines. The music changed, bringing out the sounds of the jungle, the roar of the lion stung every other note, and to this music of power, the jungle beast serenaded the bride and groom. They appeared as if they had dropped from the sky, cloaked in white, as if to wash away every bad sight.

Arya and Veru dashed towards the tent. Coral for her part, stood briefly, looking at the beautiful couple, and was secretly overjoyed for Matti. But then she put her own feet into action and rushed to the first of the two kitchens, where she filed into line. The staff were adequately prepped, arranged in rows, holding trays of glittering glass on which dozens of tall, thin stemmed glasses with slim bellies stood. Gloved pairs of hands held the trays stable while every head stayed pitched at the right angle. When the call came, the feet started their practised march towards the garden, a sign that the vows had already been exchanged, and that the time for a celebration was at hand. When the procession reached the place of gathering, the bride and groom stood as husband and wife, flanked by their closest family, watched over by the Mistress. It was an impressive display of power, Coral saw that Matti's parents were there, and that whatever briefing Matti had given them prior to the event, the mother was visibly holding herself back from bounding across the room and putting Coral into a coma. She prayed for the woman, that she would restrain herself, for the sake of her daughter, that the day not become marred by madness. The Father for his part, looked out of place, staring at his daughter as if someone had dragged her out of the deepest, darkest cave. He looked bewildered, as if he could not believe his eyes would take such a gamble, that Matti had secured for herself a husband and a future that he could never have prophesied. Coral was stuck in her thoughts, observing, when the glasses were yanked from her tray, hands reaching out, snatching them away faster than any flytrap might, her tray started to empty often, and in a numbed state, she made the many trips to the kitchen for refills, coming back to the eager hands and loud talk. As she got deeper into the mingling crowd, a set of familiar faces looked back. The second surprise guest was amongst them. It was Kesh, dressed in a roll of pink satin, her blushed cheekbones and bright red lips stood out, her hair coiled at the top of her head to resemble a giant burger bun, dotted with pink and silver beads, looked ready to knock her off balance. She had gone all out, the bangles on her arms reached almost up her to elbows, and the grand centre piece, earrings designed for battle, held their stature, in a heavy artificial gold base, with pieces of glass hammered in, a shimmering duo of art. It was impressive, and as she moved her head, the sparkle caught many pairs of inquisitive eyes.

'Coral, my darling,' Kesh crooned, as she stepped out to give her a peck on the cheek, her one hand holding onto the empty glass of champagne and the other raised in mid-air, a perfect poise for an art lesson. 'How nice it is to see you sweetheart.'

Coral smiled, and her parents came forward, greeting her in the same manner too. Dinesh tilted his head towards her, as her sisters reached out and took their drinks. She was a glass short, and the parched victim was none other than Kesh. 'Girl,' Kesh sang, 'where's my drink?'

'I'll be back now, Aunty Kesh,' Coral assured her, but was checked from leaving by her mother's voice.

'Seems like you are no different than before,' Nancy shook her head, 'worse now. What will the people say, when they find out that your father and I let you work as a servant? And a bad one who can't even do her work properly.'

'And you should see how small her place is,' Veru broke in, giggling. 'Dinesh's guest bathroom is bigger.'

'I told you,' Nancy turned to her unfortunate husband, in anguish. 'You see what happens when you don't listen to your wife? Look at her, a disgrace to the family. And such filthy lies she spoke, telling us she was coming here to visit. My foot. She already had a job planned, and never said a word. It's the ones who look quiet, like a cat that you must worry about.'

'Oh, she is trying,' Kesh said, winking at Coral, 'Go get me something to drink, honey.'

Coral was about to turn around, when Ethan appeared, a tray full of drinks in hand.

'At your service,' he called out, in his dignified way as he bowed his head charmingly towards Kesh, who flashed him a wide smile, that stayed in place, as was her custom when meeting someone for the first time, whilst she turned on her surveillance radar and scrutinised the young man. She took her drink in that time too. It was Arya's turn next. She took her drink, held it elegantly to her lips and downed the contents in one go.

'What are you doing?' her mother beeped instantly. 'That's not how I brought you girls up.'

'Relax,' Kesh comforted her sister -in- law. 'It tastes like juice. Maybe that's what they put in the glasses, trying to bluff us. Imagine, giving all of this for free,' and she took a generous gulp from her crystal glass. 'It would cost too much.'

Whatever should have been said next was drowned in the sounds of the jungle, having reached a new peak, the drums and animal sounds peaked, the crescendo was almost hilarious. Ethan left the group to themselves. Arya stared as he disappeared into the crowd, blinking like a doll looking down from a shelf, she turned to Coral and spoke in a voice from far away. 'Who was that?'

'It's Ethan,' Coral replied quietly, as she said her goodbyes and left the group, to take up her work once again. Thinking of Ethan made her uncomfortable. He had not said a word to her after the incident at the waterfall. He had not thanked her for her part in it, instead he had gone out of his way to avoid her, and she could not make sense of it. But it did not bother her, just made things awkward in case she needed to come face to face with him again.

CHAPTER FIFTEEN
ETHAN

It was late. The note had come for him and for the girl, as he thought of her. For his part, he was to accompany the small group as a fellow comrade, to join in the celebrations of the wedding that was to be extended into a camping spree. For her part, he had heard, she was to see to their needs.

As he took his place in the winding train of nine, single file under the moon torched skies, made for a night in Halloween, he thought about the House, and felt a twitch of guilt. He ought to be helping, making sure that everything taken out, got put back into one piece. Yet, Francis had sent for him and asked if he would join the small wedding party on the beach for a night out camping. It was a strange idea, the fact that the bridal couple had decided to stay put, but news had spread that they were to leave on their honeymoon the next day.

He had showered and changed into denim shorts and a white shirt. It was a warm night, with no wind and a moon that spied on them with reddish-yellow eyes as they finally spilled out onto the shore. The waves were behaving too, and like a soft wind rustling the tops of pine trees, the whispering waves caressed the night sand as lovers might. He looked around at the group and was surprised to find the girl still dressed in her clothes of before, looking tired and hanging onto a picnic basket that she had dragged down the winding cliff. He knew he should offer to help but could not bring himself to. Just as he would never bring himself to thank her, that night at the waterfall, he owed her so much. He did not know why but the sight of her upset him, somewhere deep inside, it put him on alert as if he were about to be stung by wasps. He wanted to run when he saw her, and now it seemed as if he was going to spend the night forcing himself not to.

He saw that a few camping tents had been set up on the shore, around a large iron chest, and to the side a nice fire thrived, a growing mascot of colour that invited the group to sit around it, and they formed a circle, the couples attaching themselves to each other, leaving him in the middle of Arya and Coral. He edged further away from Coral, driven by natural compulsion, and realised too late that he was almost sitting on top of Arya. He was saved any embarrassment by Matti jumping up and wobbling towards the treasure chest that sat under the moonlight. She threw open the lid, and almost fell in, managed to dig deep, and handed out bottle after bottle, shouting at the same time, 'Coral, keep watch.'

The girl stood up and went to the chest, started dipping into it and taking out two bottles at a time, the glass chinked against the other cold side. The mechanical gesture and sound irritated him for some reason. She did not take one for herself. They sat around the fire, gulping out the insides of the glass bottles faster than a thirsty dog, and somewhere in that passage of time, Matti shot to her unsteady feet, and swaying in the still night, she yelled, 'treasure hunt!'

They were all on their feet. Arya had attached herself to him. Together they stumbled on, until they reached the huddle of rock in their way. The shoreline had narrowed out at this point. The bedrock sat there, with the water gently lapping against its sides. They needed to inch past it, but the effort of doing that made no sense. Instead, they stepped onto the rocky outcrop. One of Arya's heels wedged itself inside a tiny crevice of rock, and she grabbed Ethan by the neck, the bottle from her hand flew into the air over her head, as he managed to grab it in time, not wanting it to smash onto the rocks. He threw both their bottles onto the soft sand, thinking more of cleaning up than of the awkward moment he had walked into. Arya wobbled, and he instinctively grabbed her around the waist, looking down into her face.

'We planned this,' she sang in an oddly pitched voice, 'So that you would come.'

'Oh?' he smiled, trying his best to keep them both steady.

'Yah,' she put her head back, taking them both for a ride, then came up again and blinked hard. 'You are gorgeous, you know,' she yelled, then tracing his lips with a finger she suddenly spoke softly, giggling. 'I love the way it curls, your lips. You are yummy.'

Ethan pulled her closer. They kissed, but it was a dream that held him. In that dream he felt her lips, warm and soft, as they pushed against his own. His lips were numb. The loss of feeling in his body remained, yet his eyes stayed tuned, for something else. He watched himself from an eagle's perch, standing on the bed of rocks, holding Arya in his arms, and called out from somewhere for help. When the water stung him on the face, the slap woke him up a little too fast, so that the vision evaporated, and for a while, he could think again. His eyes tuned into the scene now, burning from the saltiness and he saw the tide had risen. He saw the waves thwack the rocks, smacking the hard faces with fury, sending spurring spray onto their legs and ankles. Arya woke up in time to sample the beating, and with this recognition she moved too quickly. The heel of her shoes was still pinned in the rock crevice. He would have to do something about her shoes. Crouching, he tried to get the straps off her feet, but Arya was making it difficult, squealing and wriggling, she yelled that she would never give up her shoes. In the end, he managed to pull the sandal free, just as a great wave smashed the rocks, sending spray into their faces. Arya shrieked like a cat, bounding off the bedrock, clutching her sandals in one hand, pulling Ethan with her, so that they landed tied up in a knot at the feet of Matti, who, supported by Francis, was hardly aware of their plight, bent as she was on feeding them more spirits. They got to their feet, reached for the glass bottles, and tipped them straight into their throats.

Later, he did not know how far that stretch of time went, they were back at the campfire. The night was fading, staggering into the morning. He saw Francis sitting opposite him. Francis rocked himself, then picked up something from the ground.

'Look,' he yelled, amazed, 'It's a crab.'

'It's a ghost crab,' Ethan heard himself making the correction in a strange voice.

'Ah,' Francis held up the little creature of claws.

'They make a screeching sound when annoyed,' Ethan drawled, finding it hard to hang on to each word and thinking of two when he should be using only one. 'I read some place.'

'They make sounds?' Francis made his eyes wide. 'Always thought ghosts worked silently.

Everyone laughed, and Ethan found himself joining in.

'*Ghost* crab,' Francis repeated, as if locked in a conversation with the sandy struggling creature. 'You will soon be a…' and he threw it onto the ground, raising his foot high he continued, 'A *dead* crab.' His laughter split the air, and something in it made everyone uneasy. Ethan found himself locked in a battle with his senses, forcing them to work, but was numb, and only his eyes worked. Out of nowhere, he saw the girl come floating, swimming across the air, landing over the crab, she received the full blow of Francis' boot. She curled up, like a worm, and lay there, whilst everyone stared. Francis stood frozen. Shock lent his features a strange look in the night light.

'*Hahaha*,' Matti broke the silence, forcing Francis' foot off the shipwrecked form on the ground. 'Let's go to bed, dumpling. I'm tired.''

The word induced the mechanical trigger in Francis, who let himself be led by his newly wedded wife into one of the tents. The sound of the tent being zipped down reached the rest of them. The others followed, until he was left, staring at the empty space ahead. He could not understand what had happened to the girl or the crab, for both were missing at this point. He heard Arya tell him to follow her and watched in a daze as she moved like a zombie, in clipped movements that both fascinated and filled him with horror. She staggered and wobbled some more before she too vanished from his sight. He sat for a long time, his chin to the sky, feeling the night wind caress his face, knowing that somehow the calm had been lost. He heard the waves from somewhere, a raging sound like thunder, whip up a secret terror in him. The moon had gone to bed, lost in the clouds somewhere, just as he was. He staggered to his feet, a strange urge knocking on his insides. The wind kicked him from behind, planting a solid one, as if his mother were chiding him, for straying. He laughed at his jumbled thoughts. What would he know about a mother's love? He stopped, unwilling to go on, and felt the wind kick him again, a new one that sent him reeling. The wind picked up, cruel and unheeding, it almost packaged him into the tent ahead. He pummelled at the drawn retreat, mad that he could not get in. Just when he knew his lights would dim, the tent opened, and he tumbled inside, colliding with another body. A voice told him it was Arya. He found her in the dark, with his eyes shut, not wanting to open them, guided by a vision of a bed of rocks and two figures planted upon it. He kissed her, picked up on her need for him, a primitive intuition that formed and was shaped between them, a desire he had never grasped before was alive between them, and it was so real that had it required a human shape, it would have been dressed in the best. The awakening stirred in him, so that the numbness melted, and he settled into himself, somewhere deep inside his mind and body, the aftermath of a life spent searching dissipated. He let himself be one with her.

CHAPTER SIXTEEN
THE MISTRESS
ANIA

There were no surprises left. She swept her eyes across the room, raking in the silhouetted figures, their backs to the long windows. The morning light creeping over them, hair freshened with dawn's light, yet it did nothing to turn the image into a work of art.

They were lined up as if waiting for the curtains to drop, a miserable serving of descendants. They ought to be kicked out through the window, one by one, but the likelihood that the pests would crawl into the crevices of the building and cause an infestation in the walls deterred her. She wanted to throw something at them, but held her temper in check. They were useless, not one of them fit to walk in the shoes of their ancestors. She thought of her father, that proud man, who at eighty had sprouted a fertile head and beard, kept a mouth full of teeth, and held a mind so sharp that even at that age, he could have controlled the seasons from there, if he wanted to. She sent up her thanks for the fact that he was packed away, safe from the torment that she had to go through.

It was Beth who moved forward first. She stuck firm to the rules, dipped her chin as was custom before a first address from a family member at important times, wet her lips and said quietly. 'We have news, mother.'

She knew all about the news. Nan had filled her ears with it already. But she feigned surprise, 'Yes? What is it?'

Beth fidgeted with her skirt, keeping her head bowed. She had already summed up this daughter in law of hers a long time ago, within the first month of her arrival at the House. She was a first-rate troublemaker and a master one at that.

'It's about Chris.'

She leaned forward and said quietly, 'If it is about Chris, why is his mother not the one in front of me, or perhaps Chris himself?'

Beth quickly retracted into place, next to her husband, who did not have the grace to meet his mother's gaze. This son of hers was only interested in two things. The first came straight from the kitchen, and the second was a cottage he had built for himself on a small piece of the land belonging to the estate. She had heard the news herself, of her son, lying on his piece of earth, sunning like a lizard or painting, lost in thought as if he were a loose rock. His other passion, she had been told, went into planting potatoes that never found their way to the pot. And the most recent obsession, came in the form of two large dogs, the new occupants of the cottage. Apparently, he had gifted the dogs his home, and got kicked out after. She heard the staff complaining when they thought they might never be heard, about having to tend to the cottage and the dogs, on top of their daily chores. Well, she shrugged, they were being paid for it in any case. But Rod had no interest in anything, beyond his hobbies.

It was Mona, who moved forward now. This one she did not trust either. Quiet, keeping to herself, she had a slippery habit of vanishing and reappearing like an act in a magic show. Her sons had chosen poorly, for both marriages were already doomed. But she knew that between the four, there was no innocent.

It's Chris, mother,' Mona started. 'He went and got married in the quiet.'

She let the words rise into the air and freeze there, suspended like blocks of ice they kept all eyes frozen on her. She watched the useless lot simmer in their distress from under her crown of dignity. She kept her face blank, let her eyes harden so that Mona, finally shaking off the freeze, snaked in beside Matt. He too refused to meet her gaze. It was just like him, a son who spent more time under other people's roofs than his own. He was a mouse, taking his monthly allowance and running. He had many places to go where he was warmly taken in, so that everyone might have a bite of the cheese. She knew all about it. She might have looked the other way too if he stayed long enough under his own roof to take an interest in the business. All that money did not drop from the sky, and both brothers should rightfully have helped with the running of the estate, and the earning of it. But both had made their own habits come first, which she had sadly backed over the years, and now it was too late to change anything.

Sighing inwardly, keeping her shoulders straight, she asked in a firm voice that held a note of disinterest. 'The bride and groom may move forward.'

The straight line heaved, throwing up Chris and Miriam, who on their own, defenceless without the herd immunity, edged forward like slugs, so slowly that she wished she could get up and kick them both from behind.

She did not need time to sum up Miriam's character. She watched the girl looking at her from under a thick fringe that sat on her eyebrows. It made the girl appear demented, the way she stared as if from under a weight. She had changed the colour of her hair too, inking it the darkest black. It was an unfortunate change, lending the girl an awful demeanour. Miriam raised her head fully now, dealt a gaze so fixed it looked like they might engage in a power struggle, one that did not make sense to Ania since the adversaries were not equally matched, so she stared back, much as she would have done with her dogs. Miriam did not blink, looked like a fish with eyes round and wide. Ania felt her own eyes go dry, and quickly changed the game, by saying. 'Welcome to the family, Miriam.'

The smile that spread across Miriam's face was lethargic, and when she finally stepped back, the smile still stuck on her face, the whole room's energy changed, as the line melted, and pairs of feet moved forward, congratulating the young couple. Ania watched them and felt an attack of nausea. She needed to get out and find air that was free of slime. She got up, and the room went quiet. She took her time, moving slowly away, and as soon as her feet touched new ground, she could hear them at it again, and to her ears, the sound was like dragging chalk across a blackboard.

She walked to the kitchens, aware of the staff scuttling across her path, shoulders hunched, feet running ahead of them. She wondered for the hundredth time, how she had managed to invoke control like this. It made her feel high and mighty, but standing tall, she felt alone in this high place of authority. She thought of her husband, gone for more than twenty years, his heart had knocked him hard in the chest, and then turned lifeless like the gold coins he loved so much. Besides his love for wealth, his other passion had been to keep her in place like a mule. She had scrubbed and cleaned and fetched and carried her way through life, her position as Lady of the House was meant to be a literal one, for she was given a list of chores every morning by the Master of the House, chores that he thought unfit to have any paid help perform. But it was her bloodline that spared her, for she was allowed to breed, and that pedigree bloodline is what set her up in such ultimate fineness. She had come in handy, bringing her bloodline. He had come in nicely, bringing great wealth.

The sight of Nan hurrying towards her broke the reverie. She said the first words that came to mind, 'Send fruit and a glass of water. I am going down to the beach.'

Nan had been too long in her service to show any surprise. She simply nodded. 'Right away, Mistress.'

'Good then.'

Ania made her way out of the kitchens, heading towards the stairs that would take her down to the beach. She had no idea what had prompted this adventure, for she had no special love for the enormous bathtub that sat outside her home. If it was up to her, she would pull the plug and drain it, for as she came out onto the shore, the sea was heaving and puffing, as if a massive giant were rolling in its midst, burping, and giggling, the stupid thing made the water bulge. She wondered, if her husband was out there, rolling in the waves. It would do him good, to be tossed about like a cork, shake him up nicely, for the many miseries he had forced upon her in their lives. She told herself not to be bitter about the dead, for she was certain she would join them soon. At sixty, she was no rough eye rockfish, would hardly get past her first century, let alone the idea of a second. But her place had to be put on hold. She could not leave just yet. There were matters that needed sorting out. But as she walked, the sound of the sea came to her, fussing, reminding her again of a fate that was waiting in tow. The voices of the dead. A shiver ran through her body, but she kept her pace steady, feeling like the living amidst the dead. She saw the pile of rocks come up into view. It brought back memories of a day she had squashed into the back of her mind, that like a hole in the wall of time, left a scar when her world changed course. She wanted to block it out, to forget the faces that swam in front of hers, to forget the pain. But it all came back, strangely moulded into a single fragment of memory, yet made up of a hundred snapshots.

She sat on the ground, gracefully. Even as a child her manners had been trimmed, all edges made to fit the mould exactly, so that she moved and spoke with an intuition that was prearranged and curt. Her hands swept through the sand, and it felt as cool as chilled cucumber slices. Still, it was not enough to put off the nausea. It filled up the base of her throat, the illusion of thick and slimy bile lodged itself firmly, threatening to stop her breathing, to plug her hearing. In silent agony, she shut her eyes. Instinct told her she was not alone, just as she felt a touch on the shoulder that was both firm and comforting. It was enough to fetch her out of the nightmare. She could breathe again, but as she opened her eyes, even before she could turn to see whose hand it was that had breached the sacred space and placed itself on her shoulder, as if it had a right to, she caught the sight of a figure on the shoreline, poised on the rock bed straight in front of her, like a sign of new torment. It was a slight figure, and she wondered if her mind had coughed up the image, an illusion made real. after years of suppressed pain. Pain that she had carried, buried so deep, it had nowhere to bleed out, instead anchoring in her chest, close to her heart. In time she learned to bear it, for many winters it simmered, and now wriggling and struggling, it had become stronger, was looking for a way out. She blinked, watching in horror as the figure fell into the waves, like an elastic band, it launched forward, sucked up by the white fringed froth. It disappeared, and she turned to the face over her shoulder.

She could not speak, but turned and looked at the face of the young man whose focus was on her. She pointed towards the water. They both watched as something bobbed in the waves, and then she knew that Ethan was sprinting across the sand. She watched, as one caught up in a movie. Her mind used the fractured time to resurrect the past, so that the images layered themselves out in front of her. Her eldest son James came back to haunt her, that handsome face floating, breaking into a smile, his lips curling and his dark eyes laughing at her. She reached out a hand to touch his face. It faded, sucked into the blank wall of nothing, but then she shifted to a new slot in time, saw his body, as it lay broken on the rocks below, with the waves washing over him, as if he were an offering. She recalled the window, the ominous eye that looked out over those cursed rocks. She saw it all again as she did that night, walking into the room, her favourite son at her side. It was as if their arrival had been predetermined by Fate, for they were in time to see someone standing at the window. She recognised the person poised at the gaping window, the young face, heart shaped, smothered in sagely calm, looked at them, just before turning away, taking the body with it, falling over the ledge like an escaped note from Death's music book. James rushed to the window. She heard him shout a single name, *Carla,* before he dropped out the gaping window too, falling like a perfectly aimed dart.

Ania begged her mind not to take her further into that night. This time it followed a will of its own, and she was back in that room, standing at the window, that framed piece of night sky, looking down into the dark. From somewhere, the wind came rushing, making a fuss, tearing at the curtains. It slapped her across the face so that she became aware of the banging on the door of her heart, as it grew louder in her ears, the thumping grew until she noticed Nan had drifted by her side. Her breeding kicked in, and she calmly asked Nan to follow her. She was aware of the others, all within earshot, and if she called, they would all come running, and then the whole town and every other one in the vicinity would be filled with the terrible news of what had just happened. She could not let that be. She and Nan got to the beach. By now, the wind was howling like a mad thing, a savage thing bred on illness. It raged in its madness, whipping up the sand and throwing it into her face so that it stung, cursing her so that the sound stirred faster inside her, forcing her to walk as if she were in tremendous pain. Stooped, she staggered like an old woman towards the rocks. She saw her son, lying there like a cracked hermit shell under the night sky. Her beautiful boy. Her thoughts grew more disorientated as her body separated from her mind. But there was no girl.

Nan stood in shock, her eyes pinned on the sight, her face drained off colour. Ania shook her back to life and asked her to call the others. Her son had fallen out the window. How Nan managed to get the feat done, when her mind had been bagged with the horror of the night, she might never know, but soon enough she watched as the others tumbled out onto the stretch of sand, crying out as the first drops of rain fell. She stared at her hands, as the rain battered them, coming down faster than an eagle on the swoop, fanned by the wind, the rain attacked them with a fierceness of tiny, pointed tips, the pinches were delivered like sharp tipped knives so that the crowd ran for their lives. She stayed, oddly comforted, until a few hands came and snatched her into the safety of the house. She stood at the window and watched from there, as the storm flashed and ripped into everything, tearing up the trees, threatening to blow out the windows. She thought of her son. If he hadn't been dead before, he certainly was now. It was such a strange thought that it made her laugh. She laughed as if a clown's face stared back at her from the night sky. The sound sent Nan bolting into the kitchens. She came back with a single cup of tea and brought the family doctor with her. A brave man coming out in such weather. He was lucky, he did not need medical services himself. The last thing she remembered, was having a sip of tea, looking at the tip of the needle as the doctor bent forward, his hat tipped at the right angle, his eyes kind but focused. When she woke, none of the trio ever spoke about that night again.

The next morning, they found Carla's body, washed up next to the rocks. She did not know who took care of that, or what happened after. All she knew was that James had been moved sometime during the night. She had not told anybody about Carla. She had no intention of saying anything, and over the years the pattern became set that way. For her part, she moved on, waking the next morning, feeling her memories twisted into a woollen ball; the strands so thickly wound that they stuck to one another as if glued. The woollen ball kept its secrets so rigidly, that she found herself begging her mind for a glimpse and it took her straight to the days when her husband was still by her side, her children fat and happy, jumping over the flower beds like crickets in summer. Matt and Chris were ganging up against their sister, pulling her long plaits, so that she howled like a wolf having its tail yanked at full moon. She saw James then, a boy of ten, with the sun bouncing off his dark hair, running to the screaming Ann, accompanied by the nanny, whose name she could not remember. But her memory knew the face, a long face with beady eyes, both of which grew longer and beadier the closer she got to the child. James reached Ann first, taking her into his arms, hugging and then tickling her until she rolled on the grass with the same energy as if she were rolling down a hill. She landed in the patch of wet garden soil, where her brothers had been playing with the garden hose. Just then, the nanny caught up to her, taking her plank profile to the victim, she landed a solid slap on Ann's face. The nanny found herself on the other side of the gate not long after that. A new nanny arrived shortly afterwards. It was Nan, a young, sophisticated woman, the special sort Ania admired, for her first act of duty was to punch the Cook in the nose for serving soup with crushed almonds to James. James had an allergy, and although he survived the bowl of soup, the Cook did not survive the kitchen. Ania liked Nan, had known from the start she belonged in the House. Nan learned how to keep things in order, but she had also developed a strange side to her personality, an almost hidden talent for eavesdropping. Ania caught her a few times with her ear to a closed door but said nothing about what she had seen. How could she doubt the woman who had been such a loyal addition to the House?

Ania's thoughts went back to another memory – when her children had to be fetched from summer school for the funeral. They returned to a House that was buzzing with the news of the dead. It was as if a secret had been let out, hung to dry under a thirsty sun, but then the storm clouds came out to play and chased the sun away. So, the secret dripped onto the heads of everyone standing underneath, and a modern day myth was born. The gossip told a story of James and Carla, being married in secret; their vows exchanged a year ago, right under the nose of the Mistress, as if she were a clueless flying ant, a queen who had eaten her own wings. She became the branded fool, the wandering idiot whose ignorance was mocked secretly, they settled for the role of jester. She knew it was far easier for them to talk, for talk never bit the mouth from which it came, but it set her ears on flames. Worse still, the family priest had managed to creak his aged limbs into action and scurried into the House on a sunless morning where he paused everywhere, like a squatting duck, for a gulp of air, or for a sip of hot tea. He finally managed to make his way to her, to whisper his condolences, not for her loss, but for his weighted conscience, begging that she know the facts. He was innocent, he said, caught in the whole charade, his words came out in age shocked whispers. He told her that James had taken advantage of the family good standing and forced him to conduct the marital vows, and that both James and Carla extracted a vow of silence from him on the matter. He would have it now that she should know the facts, and the truth, as it came from his innocent heart. She would have liked to rip that lying heart out and jump on it, but decorum stopped her. That and the fact that she was facing a prime example of human nature in its rawness. What else could she have expected. The realisation brought her around, back to herself. Her mind ran freely now as it returned to the present. She cursed herself again for the truth that could never bring her peace.

Her heart reminded her of the time, the day after they lost her James. Left with her two remaining sons, and their wobbly minds, it stuck pins into the place where her heart ought to be. She knew Matt, her second born would never be able to focus further than the tip of his nose, and if he tried, she was sure

Matt would have a cockeyed vision of whatever caught his eye. As for Rod, he could not look at anything beyond his dreams so that in the end, he himself grew into a dream. Her only daughter Ann could barely look out for herself, and she sometimes wished that Ann never made any decisions at all, for they came back worse than barking dogs to taunt her. She could not handle the agony of thinking about the future of her empire. There was no one she could trust. Her favourite son had both plucked out her heart, as it had been, and betrayed the family legacy, all in one go.

Her thoughts grew too big inside her head. It filled her mind until she was sure that if she did not escape, her feet would lift off the ground, and she would float into the sky and pop. And so, on that second night of depravity, she fled from her room without thinking, finding herself on the shore, with the night air chilling her bones, and the moon-faced sky leering at her. The more she thought about it afterwards, that act did not make sense, the fact that her feet took her to a place she did not even like. The sight of regurgitating water made her feel ill, as it did now, threatening in some way as if she would be sucked in and tossed about like a cork. She did not like feeling tiny, inconspicuous in the grander scheme of things. So, she never bothered with the ocean, even though her home was almost arched into it.

But that night, she had kept walking, suffering herself to listen to the water as it threatened her. She had no longing to return indoors and drag her mind through the events of the last days, so she walked beside her foe, trying to tell herself she was somewhere else. With her chin lifted to the sky, the wind nagging at her from behind, the water whispering loudly inside her head like voices in the marketplace, she told herself in this domain she was still queen. But there was a problem. She was angry with her Creator, had plenty of questions, and none of them could be put into words. She could not stop her mind from breeding wicked thoughts, as if she were superior, and yet, she knew her place, went to Church every Sunday. She was not proud of these new hobbies, but for a woman in her situation, there was no other recluse. Blame had to be laid somewhere. Yet, the stars looking down on her that night were passive, wanting to calm the defiance in her soul. The evil bred in her turned a new direction. She hated the gossip, silently willed the nasty breeders to hear a special tune, one that might drive them to the edge of the cliff, a protruding piece of rock, right around the corner of the House, and that from there, they might willingly drop like fish bites into the ocean, where sweet-toothed sharks lurked, waiting for their desserts. Oh, it was a rare thing, but she smiled, happy at last to feel her courage return. She would bow to nobody who was made the same as her, and as she walked defiantly, each step tacked into the sand, her feet collided with something. She stopped dead. Looking down, she saw the wriggling bundle of material, stretching and shifting, a flexible package that emitted a mouse scream. She did a very uncommon thing. She stopped and with a firm hand, moved the soft material aside. A chubby baby lay bare, only a few metres away from the breaking edge of the sea.

Her mind clicked into place again. The flashback brought her back to the moment, and she saw Ethan disappear under the waves, then bob back up, like a dolphin. When the sea rolled him out at last, he was holding the limp body. Long, black hair fell towards the ground in a stream, like a black waterfall. She brought her body into action, meeting him as he deposited the figure onto the sand. As the girl lay there, like a frozen doll, she could not help whispering, 'She looks dead.'

As if her words had penetrated the form, the girl's eyes sprang wide open. Their eyes locked, and she found herself staring into a pantomime face. The face roused fear in her, for she would never dare forget what it was like to be met with something from the other world. With their eyes glued, the body sat bolt upright, like a spring had given up somewhere, with feet in sneakers pointing towards the sky. It sat clothed in layers, as it stared at her as if it would launch. Her fingers reached for Ethan's shoulders, willing to touch something human, and she pulled her gaze away, and saw that he too sat staring at the *thing* he had brought back from the water. They watched together as the form unfolded itself into a straight vertical line, turned like a ruler, and struck out towards the mansion.

Ethan rose to his feet and taking her by the arm, as easily as if he were older, as if he were in-charge, he gently forced her into step with his own, as they shadowed the phenomenon, keeping a respectful distance. The cold fist that had punched her heart and stayed to deliver a second blow, slowly unfolded its icy fingers, melting away. She could feel herself easing up, breathing again, leaning on the strangely comforting presence of this man, one she knew so little of. Yet, the baby she had plucked from the ocean's edge, the young man with the countenance of a king, was here with her now. Perhaps, she thought to herself, therein lay the reason she preferred to keep him in the shadow. The fact that he seemed closer in trait, matching her ways, unlike the behaviour of her own children or theirs, put her on edge. She was not one for an enigma, had no patience for it. Still, deep down she was glad to have snatched him up that night, taken the baby straight to Nan, with instructions to have him raised as part of the House's workforce. Now that her mind had slotted back into place, she pulled her arm away from him, rather roughly, as was her way, to bring back the division that lay between them, so that when they entered the House, everyone would see that nothing lay out of the ordinary, and that she was in control. But he never flinched, kept his stride to match hers, appeared more defiant in his role of bodyguard, both of herself and of the body marching ahead of them, determined. They had left the sea behind.

They wound their way up the staircase, went through the House, reached the corridor that took them down to the main Lion feature, and then on to the sitting lounge. They attracted all the staff. It was inevitable. They got into the family room, where the family were waiting, under the stewardship of Nan. They had certainly been discussing her, more precisely, the trip to the shoreline. Perhaps, they were wondering if her mind had gone off to graze, leaving her body to wander free. Things were riding in her favour though, for she took second place in the drama that was yet to unfold, as all eyes set themselves on the figure standing in front of the piano. *It* stood there, pasting its eyes onto the keyboard. She could feel the tension in the room, spawning in the eyes of the new spectators. That collective fear seemed to leap like a giant frog onto the head of the figure, giving *it* energy, when it suddenly jumped onto the soft cushioned piano stool, becoming still again, like a chunk of stone.

She looked across at Ethan and found that he was looking back at her. She wondered, if he too were thinking the same thing. If she was not taking this in with her own eyes, nobody could have convinced her otherwise. In any case, there was nothing they could do, as the figure raised its hands, about to launch itself into a piano rendition, sending the crowd gasping, praying for protection. But in that stress of tension, the body deflated, became human again, as the girl collapsed on the keyboard. The awful sound vibrated through the walls, with everyone shooting back into life, and Nan could be heard giving out orders to have the girl taken back to the work quarters.

'No, move her to the guest quarters,' Ania said in a clear voice. 'And call for the doctor.'

She wanted to hear what he would say. The poor girl must have been in the grip of some type of fever. Besides if the girl woke up in a trance again, she would need a good jab to jolt her back into her senses. She was glad for one thing though, and that was all attention was now riveted upon the unfortunate girl, who would be the centre of talk and life for the next few weeks. The idea to have her moved into the House, was to keep them busy, steer the talk towards the new House guest so that her life could return to its old trail. But her problems were not really solved. With a new guarded dread, she realised that Ethan, in his drenched clothes, might have already attracted attention to himself, and would be the centre of a new story in which she herself had played a large part. But when she looked towards where Ethan had been standing, he was gone. Quietly, like a gentleman, he had taken himself away from the fuss. She looked across at her sons. Their common sense had evaded them. rallying as they were around the inert figure, calling attention, acting like idiots, they kept looking at her and at the frozen figure, putting the link out between the two of them. She turned about and went straight to her rooms. There was no scrubbing off stupidity, it clung like a stain to the hosts. In the case of her sons, it had tattooed itself upon them, from head to toe.

CHAPTER SEVENTEEN
CORAL

The room was large, intimidating in its antique décor of heavy, hand fashioned oak furniture and a very thick, black carpet. Framed paintings covered two walls, showing imposing forests where the trees stretched up from the floor to just below the corniced ceilings. The robust black iron chandelier dropped from the middle of the dark ceiling, the effect crafted the air, combing the paintings, drawing the dusk from the setting, letting it rest on the bed where she lay. Coral shivered, turning her eyes away, pushing down the feeling that she was being watched. She did not like the room, not even the expensive, ornate furniture that decorated it. She especially disliked the antique wardrobe, towering in front of her, dark and double chinned, with intricate markings, it sat on wooden legs that looked like claws, as if it might fall over, straight onto the bed. And next to it, in equal ugliness, sat two chest drawers, both a metre tall and a metre wide. She knew they were all exquisite pieces, patterned by expert woodsman, most definitely long dead now, and that was part of the reason she forced her way down into the covers.

Her mind calmed down instantly. The past two days had brought her peace, in the form of the doctor's needle. Now, she was wide awake, left to put the strange events that nibbled on her conscience into order. It was all there for her to pick at. Beth having thrown them out for her, like a deck of cards during an afternoon game, sweeping into her room, looking as if she had just come from holiday, bright eyed and eager, she gave her the breakdown of the near drowning and the piano sabotage, poking and prodding at Coral's mind, with questions in that honeyed voice of hers, but it came to nothing. Beth would not give up, and after a while, something in Coral snapped. She told Beth her secret, even though she kept another one hidden. She should have kept her mouth shut about both. But it was too late. The words were out, and as Beth's round eyes bulged greener than usual from shock, her body shot off the bed, and before Coral had time to think about what she had done, Beth was back with the family doctor.

The man with the kind face and brown hat stared in surprise at the thin circle of salt that made a ring around her bed. It had been put there by the cleaning staff. Having taken a vote, the decision was made. Everyone agreed, they stood no chance against such powerful forces, the type that hounded such a meek girl. None of them wanted to sample such effects for themselves, so to side step the contamination, now that she lay in the Mansion, and brought the unseen into their domain, they devised a plan. She knew all about it, having been given a rundown by Karabo, who, with unaffected honesty, told her that recent events had even brought the chills out in her. But she was grateful for the companionship, even though Karabo had only stayed long enough to give her the news. Now, she watched as the doctor stepped over the mark without hesitation, dusted the bedside table that had also been given a frosting, and set his doctor's bag there. He spoke kindly to her, performing his mandatory checks, but this time, he took more blood samples and left, all the while Beth hovered nearby. By the afternoon of that day the results were in. Beth had not kept her promise. She told everyone. The Mansion knew, every window and every corner, every door and every pot plant knew. There were whisperings everywhere, spilling over into the gardens, rising above the tips of the trees, floating away to the staff quarters, where around the campfires that night, it tickled the noses and throats of everyone, as they gasped and choked over the news as if they were hearing it for the first time. They had never thought her capable of such a devious deed, blaming the dead, when she had a huge secret to hide. Putting on such a performance to attract attention and sympathy. The Mistress had been fooled again. And this time, it did not come from one of her own. It was more the pity.

Coral shifted in the bed. She had not seen the Mistress, not since she had been moved into the Mansion. Only Beth had come to check on her, looking more concerned each time, coaxing her to remember, to get better, to shuffle her fears and release the tension. She had been fooled by Beth's green eyes. Now, Beth was back, but Coral had learned how to read the signs, and to be wary of the fake compassion in her eyes, the beautiful reptilian eyes, and the burnt sugar in her smile, put her on alert. But Beth carried on, putting more words into the space between them, until even she had to accept that Coral was shut up tight, sealed better than freshly picked mussels. Beth left in a sulk, and Coral stubbornly held on to her deepest secret. That must stay with her until she took her last breath. Even beyond.

The doctor had not been to see her in two days. She was ready to go back to her mushroom home, as she liked to think of it. She missed hearing the wind rustle through the trees, tall caretakers that would not let anything bad happen. She craved their solitary refuge. It bit into her heart, just before the door flew open, as if it had been kicked solidly from the other side.

Framed there, as if she had paid for the space, stood her mother, her face contorted with anger. Nancy stormed into the room, followed closely by her father, and her Aunt Kesh. A nervous member of the cleaning crew brought up the rear. Coral focused on the woman's face, knowing that she had seen it before, somewhere in the corridors, dusting the frames that held portraits of family members long departed, faces looking out, none of them smiling, all sporting terrified expressions of what this world promised.

'You, how can you disgrace us like this?' Nancy was screeching, her face ablaze. 'Looks like you were born to bring us into the ground.'

Ed stood by, slightly hunched from his burdens, his face closed, unreadable.

'Tell me,' Nancy demanded. 'Did we bring you up so that you can drag our family name through the mud? Tell me what we did to deserve this?'

'Come now,' Kesh crooned from the side, her heavily made-up face in a sweat. 'What can we do? If my girls did this, who knows how I would have reacted,' she paused to mop at her face with a bunch of tissues. 'Especially if it was my Kiara, I know I would have died from a broken heart.' Kesh shook her head, as if she were speaking of someone who was not in the room. 'It's like eating your food from a banana leaf and then eating the leaf too. Who would have guessed? And Coral, this one being so quiet.'

Her words set a bonfire crackling and spitting in Nancy, as she lunged forward, before anyone could predict it, and went straight for Coral's throat. It was all they could do, to pull her off the figure in the bed, and then too Nancy shook with rage.

'Think you are too big for your boots, you nipper,' she

screamed. 'But let me tell you something, I am still your mother. You will answer to me.'

The commotion brought Ethan into the room, with Arya at his side. Nancy had her back to them, lunging forward for a second try, she had built up more force, coming from a deeper need, but Ethan intervened, being the quickest on his feet. He got Nancy away, just as the Mistress walked in. Her presence restored a calm that had the effect of water thrown on fire, and everyone stood as if in anticipation of the smoke.

The Mistress exchanged formal greetings with her new guests, and in the ensuing silence, Nancy found her place next to Ed. When the Mistress spoke again, it was with a tilt of her head, her words firm and polished. 'I gather we have all had a rough day. Supper and rooms have been prepared in anticipation of your arrival.'

It was done. Like magic everyone drifted through the open doorway, followed by the Lady herself. When the door had been closed with a finality, it gave Coral the first sense of security she had ever felt.

CHAPTER EIGHTEEN
THE MISTRESS

She looked at her two grandsons standing in front of her. Francis had inherited his mother's round face and green eyes. She could not explain the rich sunset that coloured his hair. Must be someone on her side. Chris took up after his father, the dark hair and general countenance of moodiness was there, qualities that irritated her. But she needed both boys now, to gear up and learn the ropes. She was not going to be around forever, and the family empire should never get sucked in, all because her grandsons were too lazy to fill up her place.

'There is work to be done,' she said firmly. 'And as I can't see myself getting into this sort of thing personally, I need you both to handle it.'

Francis nodded eagerly, and Chris stared back at her.

'There is news that the scream of a Taitan falcon has been detected in the woods, where we have already acquired plans for residential development. Now, we have half the Earth's conservation groups pitching their tents, crawling up and down the trees, nosing into the ground, searching for any sign to stop work from going ahead. Nobody has a thing to report on, but they will not budge. They are wasting my time, popping up everywhere, the workers are too nervous to start the foundations, and construction should have begun last month already.'

She had no time for protecting the Earth and the volatile

treasures it held. That was a job better left to those who were made for it. She had been born to find ways to make money and hang onto it. That was what she was good at. But she did not want to start a new project with the idea of having to deal with unhappy people or misplaced birds.

'It is good land that is reserved for a forest estate,' she continued, 'and I can't touch a single leaf on any tree, not until *they* are satisfied.'

'But why bother?' Francis was saying. 'We own the land. They don't.'

'Yeah,' Chris gave his two-cent worth, 'who cares? Just torch the land, all problems solved.'

She could not believe what she was hearing.

'You will both go and find a way to resolve this,' she said drily. 'Without laying waste to a single tree or bird.'

They blinked at her rapidly, as if both suffered from the same eye infection. She continued unperturbed, 'And there's the matter of the seaman cottages on the other side of things. They are old, lined up on the shore, and in need of some care. I want a proper inspection done on the thirty of them. The original tenants are already six feet under, the caretaker in charge has only now creaked open his eyes and crawled out of his casket to realise those cottages are neglected. They need fixing up if we are going to clock in rent.''

She grew angry at the blank expressions on the faces staring back at her. For all their years of study, both her grandsons were starting to look very silly. It was unacceptable and unthinkable. The empire they stood to inherit was vast, the ventures both diversified and challenging.

The cousins looked at each other.

'Don't worry,' Francis was saying, 'we will get Ethan to

double up and sort things out.'

'He is paid help after all,' Chris put in. 'let's see, what he comes up with.'

'Yes,' Francis nodded. 'Plus, we promised to take Matti and Miriam into town.'

She would have liked to strangle them both, like a pair of roosters. But she kept her calm and nodded. 'I want feedback by Monday. That will be all.'

They left, too quickly to hide their eagerness at being set free. But no sooner had they gone, than two other sets of shoes entered her office. She had been staring at the thick carpet, her thoughts gone somewhere else, the slight breeze that wafted into the room playing with her face, when these new sets of shoes entered, and she found herself marvelling at the sequin on the one pair. The shoes were bright red, the gold sequin crawled over the red, shining as if each tiny circle had been polished by hand. Next to this shine, the formal shoes of the other pair looked bland. She raised her head to find the owners looking at her.

'Sorry, for disturbing you, but' Nancy said plainly. 'We came here to tell you, we are going.'

'So soon?' Ania inquired, as she got up from behind her desk and approached the couple. The husband stuck out his hand in greeting, but she was not one for handshakes, so she dipped her chin at him, and for some reason, this act worked up his wife so much that Nancy's voice trembled as she spoke, 'We have our pride, and you might think that you are better than us, but let me tell you something, I can take the whole lot of you on with the lift of my thumb.

The woman glared angrily, as she provided evidence that her thumb was in working order. Ania was puzzled.

'Please excuse me, if I have offended you in any way,' she began slowly. 'But you are welcome to stay here for as long as you want.'

'And let you rich people corrupt my daughter some more,' Nancy said, as she elbowed the man into life. 'Why you think that money can buy everything, but not decency! Tell me, I want to know since she won't open her mouth, who's responsible for the baby?'

Yes, the news had reached Ania, she was above everything that happened within the confines of her walls. But she had lost interest in the girl after hearing about the pregnancy. The girl's behaviour still sat uneasily with her. No pregnancy could ratify such a display as the girl put on. Something else lay at the bottom of that pond. It irked her, but she chose not to think about it any further.

'You should speak to your daughter and find out,' she said without interest. 'It is not my business anyway.'

Nancy picked up her pointed chin, pushing out her small chest she could have been a puffer, all swelled up and ready to explode. 'What you think, huh? Tell me? Expelling all your powerful words like a flushed toilet, and you know *nothing?* My daughter came to live under your roof. Letting a young girl behave without manners, and you turn your face to the other side? How you going to look me in the eye, tell me?'

Ania reached her wits end. How could she tell what the girl did in her time? Was she now expected to play babysitter to every name in her household? She did not like the woman's tone, her accusations. It made her feel cheap, an imitation slipping, falling into the abyss that would swallow her whole, take her down into the depths like some sort of creep, bred by the swamp.

'No!' she raised her voice to the high ceiling and to the birds nesting on her rooftop. 'You listen to me now,' and she knew her voice had lost control, her colour bruised her cheeks, she could feel the heat burning them. This was not like her, to behave in this way after years of careful breeding. 'I am not her mother. You are, and maybe you should look at yourself before you lay blame here. You hear me? Now, get out of my rooms and out of my House! You are no longer a guest here and do whatever you please with your daughter. I could care less.'

She knew she had gone over the top, gone too far. She had lost her composure, shown her broken side to a stranger? How could she turn back from this?

'*You!*,' the woman spat. 'Listen to me nicely, what's so wonderful about your doorstep that will bring me back? Let me tell you something, we will go, but you are not better,' she stamped her foot, 'than the dirt under my shoe,' and she held up a foot, showing a piece of gum stuck to the underside, 'see? But I wipe it clean, from your type.'

'Maybe,' Ania could not help herself. 'You should check your shoes again. Clearly, you have not wiped it clean enough.'

She should stop, but she could not help herself. It felt good to be out of the confines of the box, to speak her mind, to be free. She found this nit picking thoroughly enjoyable. She was immensely proud of herself. 'Better be careful,' Ania said, her voice saturated with sarcasm, 'looks like you may be more glued to the spot, than you think.'

The woman swelled. It looked like she might collapse. But just then, in the nick of time, the girl appeared in the room, and it felt as if Ania had been transported to a theatre, front row seat, for the stage performance.

'Oh,' Nancy spat out, turning her anger onto her favourite

victim. 'She managed to wake up and come here. What do you think she looks like?' she asked her husband, and before he could say, she continued. 'Looks like a ghost, no life in her face and very different from before. But that's what happens when children don't listen when big people talk.'

'I want to stay. *Please.*'

The girl was looking at Ania, had totally ignored her mother's words. Ania fell back into herself, the freedom gone. She was once more the controlled voice of reason, of artificial breeding. Yet even, she picked out the look in the girl's eyes. It was haunting, like the look of an animal caught in a hunter's trap.

'You shut up and get your things,' her mother snapped. 'We'll go straight home, and I don't know what we will do, but,' she paused. 'We'll keep it quiet. Nobody else, but Kesh knows, and I will finish her if she opens her mouth.'

'I am not going home.'

Nancy shook her finger in the girl's face, 'You don't tell me what you think. Don't waste our time. Let's go.'

For some unknown reason, Ania intervened. It was not like her, to get herself stuck in the middle of domestic matters, especially those that had no bearings on her life at all. She was doing a lot of things today that were not like her at all.

'You can stay if you so wish.'

'Thank you, Mistress.'

The slap that the girl received across the face rang into the air. It echoed in the room, booming in all their ears, almost sent the girl reeling from the force of it. It looked like Nancy was going to land another thunder cracker, but this time the Father stepped in, waking up from his slumber, he was like a man reborn.

'Stop it!' he almost shouted. 'Leave her alone.'

As he stood there, holding Nancy's wrist in his hand, the woman took a second to register the new turn of events, and then snapping into action, she yelled. 'You taking your daughter's part in this? Think you're an easel, coming out after the rains? Now, you suddenly awake after so many years, you had no mouth, but now you got one, shouting like a madman, telling me what to do?'

The man took a deep breath, and when he spoke again, his voice sounded strange, 'I am going to the car. You better come with me, or you can stay here if you want.'

It was like watching Nancy go into a trance. She took a full minute, then stepped away from her daughter, trailing in her husband's footsteps. The man had left, not looking back once, as he took the drama of the past few minutes away with him, so another full minute relapsed, before Ania recovered herself to finally address the girl in front of her.

'I can never remember your name,' she said almost absentmindedly.

'It's Coral, Mistress.'

'Well,' she made a mental note of it. 'Coral, you may return to the staff quarters and continue with the kitchen, same as before. That will be all for now.'

Ania spent time after that in silence. She did not know why but the feeling that change was around the corner weighed heavily on her. She still did not understand Coral's behaviour, the images were fresh in her mind from that day. She had deliberately not brought it up. Now, she had the added burden of having Nancy's face etched in her mind, seeing the woman's expression when her husband woke up, and performed that turn, full circle. She had played a big part in bringing on the torment of the poor woman. She had picked up a fork, instead of keeping the peace. It was bad behaviour on her part, as hostess, and had given Nancy plenty to chew on through that long drive back, to wherever they were headed. And yet, something warned her that she was not done with them. It made her uncomfortable. She knew she had provoked something terrible by interfering, allowing Coral to stay against their wishes. Now, it would be her turn, somewhere in the future, to face her own drama.

CHAPTER NINETEEN
MONA

Her conscience? It had flown away. But something bothered her, scratching on her insides, making her feel like an injured insect. She walked into the Mansion, her lips fresh from the warmth pressed into it by another man. Philip. The time they spent together, those loose hours like newly spun thread, was enough to make a carpet that would connect two cities. She ought to be ashamed. But there was another matter, a deeper one, that caused her anguish. She had carried the weight for too long, and now, she wanted to shake her shoulders free off everything, and walk away, a straighter and remade version. She did not care, if it was Philip's cottage that she walked into. She did not love him. That space was only reserved for one man, and Matt never looked at her in that way. If she confessed, at least she would not have to live with the guilt. This girl, Coral, a simple serving girl, had shown her the path. If she could carry the weight of her shame, there was no reason Mona could not do better. The news about that girl had filled every crack in the House, spreading into the towns and even, if she could guess, over the seas and into the neighbouring countries. She envied this girl, wondered how she dared flaunt her state with such abandon. It made her desperate to seek her own freedom.

'Mona!' Matt suddenly came into view, his tall frame dressed for his favourite game. 'Where have you been?'

Something about his casual, unaffected stance made her snap. She knew he was being true to himself. The difference came from her.

'I want to talk with you,' she heard herself say, 'and with everyone else. Anyone at this point.'

If luck had been eavesdropping, it certainly jumped out from behind the pillars now, for she had the fortune of seeing the big three passing by. They stopped in their tracks.

'I want to talk,' Mona said again, looking at Matt, who had the grace to blush uncomfortably, 'Now.'

Matt did not say anything. He took off his blue checked cap, looked inside it, and set it back on his head. His behaviour was like a drink of vinegar, and the sour taste was only getting more concentrated as she watched him shrug, before turning his head away.

'Do you even care?' her voice picked up. 'What is wrong with you?'

At this point, the Mistress, who stopped in her tracks took charge, and like a hostess, she gathered the group and ushered them into the large drawing room. The portraits were there, arranged in heavy wooden frames, old faces made bigger, chicken eyes looking out.

Mona kept her attention on the Mistress, and once she got the first few words out, the rest followed easily. The two short sentences eloped, one put an end to her affection for Matt, and the other shut the door to her marriage. When she was done, she felt worse. She should have kept her mouth shut.

'You are drunk,' Beth rushed at her, shaking her by the shoulders. 'Go lie down. You will feel better soon and realise you have been talking nonsense.'

'No,' Mona said, stepping back. 'It's done, you hear? I

cannot live like this.'

'So, you had an affair with some Philip. People have affairs all the time. You and Matt can sort things out.'

'It's not an affair,' Mona told Beth quickly. 'It's more than that.'

A silence followed, as the words fought for balance. The Mistress spoke next, quietly, 'How long?'

'Years.'

And then she asked the impossible, in a matter-of-fact tone, the single word that said as much as a diary, as if it was the most natural thing to ask, 'Chris?'

'He is Matt's.'

'Then,' the Mistress replied in the same tone. 'You are free to settle things with Matt as you both see fit.'

The truth was out. Her big secret had filled the ears of everyone there, and she should have felt the release. But she felt worse, as if she had stepped out of her body, gone up to the ceiling and spread herself out like a bat.

Meanwhile, Beth was gasping like a fish. She put her hands to her lips and stumbled so that Rod brought her a chair. Beth collapsed into it. Rod himself did not have the courage to look at her. Perhaps, he was worried. Mona thought, a smile of irony playing on her face that she would spill the beans on him too. Meanwhile, the Mistress and everyone else fixed their eyes onto Matt, waiting for him to take charge. He said nothing, only looked at his wristwatch, and then took off his cap again. Mona had seen redwoods with more life. The seconds ticked into minutes; the only movement came with the blinking of their eyes.

'I am late for the game,' Matt finally spoke. 'Should have been there already. But it's a tournament, will run over the whole week.'

The Mistress nodded. It was as if they had scheduled tea for next Sunday. He left the room, without a glance at Mona. She stared at them. The tears washed her face, her heart stomped and bounced, and she feared it would burst through her chest and follow Matt out. She should have known. She should have kept the truth. It would have been her sweet revenge on them both. But it was over now. She needed to go pack. But first, oddly enough that it came to her at this place in time, she pulled Beth aside, waiting for the room to clear.

'Did you give that ring back?' Mona asked quietly.

'What ring?' Beth frowned, gritting her teeth. 'You fool. How could you do this to us?'

'The ring?' Mona pressed her again. 'Where is it? The one mother showed us.'

'Oh,' Beth shrugged carelessly. 'I was trying to get a better look at the thing, under the sun, and it fell. Somewhere on the grounds.'

Mona shook her head, then walked away.

'You are the loser,' Beth muttered quietly, under her breath. 'Yet, you are shaking your head at me. I will never be as reckless. Not me. Never me.'

CHAPTER TWENTY
BETH

Her sister was an imbecile. There was no other way to look at it. Beth felt the anger rushing into her head. The swell was like blowing air into a balloon, the way it filled up and stayed bloated. Well, her head might have sailed away into the sky, if it could have detached from her body, with the thoughts that were going on in there.

She watched as the last of Mona's luggage entered the mini-bus taxi. Her stupid sister had taken one night only, to contemplate her fate. That theatrical display, the great revelation that was meant to put her soul to rest was a joke. Why, she had bigger skeletons dangling in her own closet, giants in fact, reason enough to call her a witch and put her on the stake, but the world could go upside down and spin like that, and not even then, would she open her mouth and blab. Did she work so hard to crawl out of the dirt, just to slither back in? Her sister needed therapy.

She had found out only this morning, that Mona's decision was made. It was to leave the Mansion and go straight to one Philip and his thatched roof. They were going to live off his dreams, for that is all he had, from what she had heard. It was enough to put her off breakfast. How could she do it?

Beth thought of the rumours that were doing the rounds, and it stank. But her concerns were not for Mona, it was for her own self. Mona's grand exit left a place that would soon need filling. It made her uneasy. She would not play the flute to any upstart, especially one that was not related to her by blood. Mona had stayed clear off her path. Mona knew her place, substandard as it might have been, she never tried to upstage the pattern of things. Beth felt a pang, that lasted only a few seconds, for the empty space Mona's departure would leave. She was too much of an old war horse. She knew all the tricks to survive, and she was not afraid to use them. Matt could bring in the competition. That new woman would never last, not unless she played puppy to the hem of Beth's skirt, learning to follow the lead, never to take first place. Beth knew how to hold her position and keep it. Still, the idea made her skin sting, awakening old wounds. It was Mona's fault for putting her into this position.

As it was, Mona had refused any help, but the staff, high on the latest gossip, and under the command of Nan, rushed down the stairs, fetching and loading Mona's possessions, thrilled to be a part of History in the making, until the carriers had exhausted themselves, and the room lay nearly bare. With Matt gone, and the Mistress nowhere to be seen, Mona seemed to be taking her time. Beth wondered if her sister was stalling. Perhaps, she had changed her mind and did not want to leave at all. She hurried from the window, down the winding staircase, determined to challenge destiny, but then her attention drifted, to the family office and to the door that had been left open, only slightly. Her feet took her there, natural instincts telling her it would be worth the effort, her ears were already primed and ready. The room was mostly used by the Mistress, and it was reserved for issues that concerned the family.

She stood and looked through the slice of open door, enough to see three profiles.

'It's not fair,' she heard Chris whine. 'It's not my fault. My mother is the liar.'

'I agree, it's not your fault,' the Mistress could be heard saying, 'you should not let these recent developments define the person you are.'

'So, nothing changes?'

'Nothing needs to change for now.'

There was a short period of silence.

'Is there any news on the wooded areas, and the sea cottages?'

Francis was quick to reply, as he thumbed across at Ethan, 'We asked him to sort things out. He should know.'

Beth winced. That no good son of hers was messing things up. He should be one step ahead, leading the way, seeing that he was the next heir.

'Well?' the Mistress sounded irritated. 'Is there any news?'

Ethan's voice came back at her, and something in his voice matched that of the old lady. It drew Beth's attention.

'The sea cottages can easily be fixed up,' Ethan reported. 'I have the new plans that need taking a look at,' he moved forward and for a space of time, was out of her visual orbit. 'Each cottage will have the finest conveniences, all with the appeal of the original architecture.'

'Well, there is no need to waste any more time. You can give them a go ahead on that,' the Mistress said clearly.

Ethan nodded, before continuing.

'We are up against a mountain with the other matter. There is no way we can say whether the Taitan falcon is roaming the woodlands or not. Not for now, at least. I've been there, and the area is too large and too dense. As it is, nobody would believe us no matter what we say, seeing as our intention makes it that way. All they anticipate is construction and destruction.'

'Yes?'

'I've been thinking, what's wrong with a sylvan surrounding? Maybe we don't need to focus on changing anything, rather let's use this to our advantage. I put a team up, not in your ordinary scheme of things, they are more a tribe of ex-suburban folk, currently forest dwellers, and the idea is for each one to spread the word, urging others to go off the grid, put people who are fed up with cities and pollution or each other into tents, and have them live in the forest, with the forest.'

'What?' Francis jumped in. 'It's the worst idea I've heard. And the cost of setting this up? Do you think your grandfather will foot the bill? Where will the water supply come from, and are they just going to use the bush for the rest of their needs? They will end up contaminating the same forest you are trying to save.'

'I agree,' Chris chimed in quietly. 'Just get the construction companies out and let them do what they have to do.'

'Can we work out the details on this?' the Mistress asked, her attention piqued.

'Yes,' Ethan remarked, ignoring Francis and Chris for the time being. 'I was hoping, we could meet with the team to discuss the ideas they have. As it is, there is a huge demand for this sort of thing, and once we portion the land off, selling won't be a problem. But the draw card seems to be a call for assurance. The buyers are not just buying land, they want the necessary knowledge and basic plans put into place so that the hard work's done, and all they do is show up, then follow the guidelines.'

'They want to pay for that?' Chris asked, bewildered.

'Yes, in their minds, they have made the jump, and that is enough.'

Beth waited.

'We cannot afford a public scandal,' the Mistress contemplated loudly. 'And this estate business is not worth the risk, but we are already drowning in it, so if this will sway public favour and make me a good profit, it is a starting point.'

'It's a good idea?' Francis asked, puzzled. 'But who is going to head this thing, in the *wilderness*?'

Beth shook her head. Francis was playing right into Ethan's hands. She had to do something.

Beth pulled the door shut, so silently that she was sure nobody noticed. She landed a good thud on it, as if she had just got there, and was promptly told to enter.

'Oh, I am sorry,' she heard herself say as clearly as if she meant it, dipping her chin in greeting to the Mistress. It was a pity her son lacked such tolerance for protocol. He was without the finer tunings of a future heir, she knew that. She would fix it soon.

'I had no idea there was a meeting.'

'Well,' the Mistress said starchily. 'You were not intended to be part of the meeting.'

Beth chose to ignore that.

'I wanted to see you, Mother. It's about our new estate. Matti came to me about it,' she nodded towards Francis. 'She is a conservationist and a gentle soul. After listening to her, I decided that it's only proper the family show our faces, especially the future heir,' she stopped herself from smiling. 'People need to see Francis, to get used to him being in charge. This issue with the birds is getting out of hand, but it is a perfect opportunity to get things started for him.'

'But we were just discussing that,' Francis chipped in.

'And when did Matti see you about this? I never knew she was soft about birds.'

'No,' Chris laughed from his side, 'She is not. I saw her the other day, throwing stones into the trees. Man, her aim was good. She dropped a few of those birds out of those trees, and she was having a good time, a great time actually.'

Beth wanted to box both their ears, her dim son, and his half-wit cousin. But she had to turn the conversation around, for now, she had both the Mistress and Ethan staring at her, both looking confused.

'Ah,' she laughed the words off, putting a hand to her chin, and then opening her fingers as if she were letting loose a couple of butterflies. 'Matti is pregnant, so women in that state do strange things sometimes.'

'Pregnant?' Francis and Chris both chorused.

'Yes,' Beth smiled like a saint. 'Just this morning. She told me in confidence, but news like this should not be kept quiet.'

The Mistress had stood up, and she was now in front of Beth.

'Are you certain?' she asked, her eyes boring into Beth's soul.

'*Mmmhmmm*,' Beth nodded her head and it felt as if someone else were holding it and shaking it so fast that everything was starting to spin. She pulled herself together and said, 'I know, it means the future is secured. And yes, she is pregnant, but lying down now. So, I think we can give her some space, and then when she gets up, we can see her.'

She could not believe the new power she wielded. She was advising the Mistress as if their roles were swapped.

'Yes, that would be best.'

'As for the matter of the estate?' Beth put out the reminder. 'What should we do?'

She had the situation by the horns now. A small lie of course, told in honour of protecting those that were hers, was nothing. She had in fact told two. Matti had not spoken to her in days, and when they met, she could hardly stand her daughter in law.

'What would you have me do, Francis?' the Mistress asked him, and this was his chance to take charge.

'I want to take Matti to Italy,' he pronounced. 'For two months. She always wanted to go there, and now that she is pregnant, we can celebrate.'

'But what about the estate?' Beth reminded him, her eyes shooting daggers. He missed the warning, charged instead by the dreams in his head. 'We will have sweet tomatoes and pasta, and visit Pompeii.'

Beth was livid.

'Who will manage the estate then?' the Mistress asked.

'Why, him of course.' Francis said, pointing at Ethan. 'It's not like he has anything more important to do.'

'And,' Chris pointed out, 'I've seen the place. It's a jungle, not a forest. Where would we live?'

'I'll go,' Ethan said. 'If it is required of me.'

'Yes,' Francis snorted. 'It is required of you. You have a funny way of speaking.'

The matter was settled, and there was nothing more Beth could do. There was one daunting task that waited for her. She needed to see her daughter in law. As much as she disliked the prospect of forming an alliance with the woman, Matti had become a key player without knowing it. If there was anything she could be grateful for, it was that Matti had already displayed a selfish, conniving side to her, that went far beyond her years. In fact, if she could be honest with herself, Matti was the perfect partner for the job.

CHAPTER TWENTY-ONE
MATTI

For a month now, she had gone about displaying the necessary pregnancy side effects with so much joy that nobody would have guessed otherwise. She was nauseous when it suited her, had wholesome cravings day and night, demanded a Lily of the valley for herself, and when the plant arrived, fresh from the woodland somewhere she would never go, she sent it back, the sweet smell and the flowers shaped like bells gone belly up sent her mind straight to Church. The association put her conscience on the scale, and the idea that she might have to take penance made her uneasy. She sent the rare plant away, deciding to focus on other ways to irritate her mother-in-law. She knew Beth was obliged to her, the stunt needed to be pulled off, for both their sakes. But Beth had more riding on the gamble. It was not something to be taken lightly, the fact that a woman like Beth might stay indebted to anyone. But she was indebted to her. It filled up her ego pots, so that everyone sat like coloured eggs in an Easter basket, and she could jump on the whole lot for fun, and watch them crack, if she wanted to, and nobody would do anything about it. She had so much power that everyone was paying dearly for it, but in the end, she was the one making off with the jackpot.

Francis had just finished making their bookings for the trip to Italy. They had wanted to leave earlier, but the Mistress stopped them. She surprised everyone, with her concerns for

Matti and the baby. Matti was only allowed to fly after she had reached three months into her pregnancy. Well, she made the announcement last week that she had reached the end of her trial period.

She was on her way now to meet the others in the garden for a quick lunch, and then it was off to the airport. She was flushed at the idea of going away. She had never been to another country before. Her cheeks were red, and she had taken to wearing loose fitting clothes recently. She had put on weight, but it was not her fault. Everybody indulged her.

'You're looking exceptionally well this morning, Mrs Francis,' Miss Nan told her as she met her in the hallway. 'Is there anything I can help you with?'

Matti would have liked to tell her to get out of her way, if she was so intent on helping, but she got a hold of herself and smiled so that her puffy cheeks collided with her eyes. 'No thank you.'

Miss Nan dipped her head and was gone. Matti continued, letting herself out of the house and into the gardens. They were magnificent, spread out and maintained perfectly. But as she went further, she entered a new stretch where the trees were taller, and the pathways, mostly swept clear of fallen leaves, were scarce, disappearing into the trees, the few that kept to their lane, avoiding any crisscrossing, lent themselves into a small clearing. The water fountain that sat in the middle of the clearing gushed. A table and chairs for eight people had been set up. Everyone got up as she neared.

Francis came running. He kissed her on the cheek. He never came too close to her any more, always afraid, and uncertain of his behaviour now that she was pregnant. She preferred it that way. It made it easier to keep her secret.

As he drew away, she made a mental note of the others. Ethan and Arya were there. She liked Arya, and Arya liked Ethan. She had made it her mission to connect the two, starting from the day she got married. But as for the sister, that Coral, it turned out she could not stand her. They had been best friends, too long ago... She watched her now, standing there, acting as if she were sorting out the things on the table, looking the same as she always did. She hated her, more than ever.

There was another one, Miriam, almost breaking out into a sprint, as if a timer had been set. They were building up fast, like a blocked drain, these types that she did not like. She hated the way Miriam acted, so desperately trying to fit in, that it made her stand out in the same manner that the quills stood out on a porcupine. If anybody asked her, she would say, Chris could have done better for himself.

Brushing past Miriam, Matti locked her target into view. She reached the table, pursed her lips before launching the attack. 'So, how many months are you?'

Coral stopped arranging the table and looked up. 'It's three months today.'

'Oh,' Matti laughed. 'Just like my wedding anniversary, three months to the date. How funny to think you made out with one of our guests. So, tell me, who is the mysterious Father?'

Coral looked away. There was an awkward silence, as the others tried to think of something to say. The slight breeze that had rocked up offered a topic for conversation, and Ethan seized it quickly. 'I think the weather's turning. How about we get started on this picnic, huh?'

'Yeah,' Arya piped up, digging into one of the baskets that were lined up next to the table. 'Look at what I brought you from home.'

She held up a packet of ripe mangoes, and then tipped them onto the table where they rolled about, plump, and freshly sweet smelling, in their yellow jackets. Then she brought out another packet, and like a magician, produced two more fruit.

'Papaya,' Arya announced, smiling broadly, her red lips matching her sleeveless red top, her light skin glowing under the clouds that peeped out. 'It's from our own tree at home.'

'*Oooooh*, I love papaya,' Matti sounded excited, reaching for the green one.

'No!'

It was Coral. She was so agitated that she knocked the green fruit straight out of Matti's hand. It dashed to the ground, where it lay like a fallen green stone.

Matti looked from the fruit to Coral before shoving her away, so that the girl almost ended up on the floor. It happened so quick, before anyone could realise anything.

'I feel sick,' Matti moaned, straight after dishing out the push. 'I can't eat anything any more.'

She put a hand to her mouth, while Francis rushed to her side. 'My love,' he stroked her back. 'What must I do?'

'It's her fault,' Matti whimpered. 'Now, I don't feel so good.'

Francis turned towards Coral and shouted. 'What is your problem?'

Coral visibly shrank into herself, and she opened her mouth as if she wanted to say something, then thought better of it and kept it shut.

By now, Miriam and Chris were hovering near Matti who held her tummy and wailed. 'She doesn't know her place. If something happens to this baby, it's *her* fault.'

It looked as if Francis was going to jump out of his clothes, as he turned again to Coral, anger in his eyes, but before he could say anything, the sky spat a sudden shot of thunder, and a jagged blitz tore it up, letting loose a heavy downpour. Matti shrieked, and dashed out of the clearing, with Francis following hot on her trail. Chris and Miriam ran after them.

Meanwhile, Arya picked up from where Matti had left off, and she lashed out at her sister, blinking in the pouring rain, as the cheap eyeliner that gave her eyes the Egyptian curve, melted into rivulets, running down her cheeks. 'You had to ruin the moment! You pushed that fruit out of her hands, just because it came from *our* garden. Because Mum and Dad don't ever want to see your shameful face again. You are pathetic, you hear?'

By now, Ethan had removed his jacket, and was holding it above Arya's head, but she pushed it aside. 'Let me tell you something else,' Arya's voice turned spiteful. 'Veru had to promise her mum-in-law that you won't be at her wedding, and as for me,' Arya laughed. 'After today, I want you out of my life. Matti is more of a sister to me than you ever will be.'

She walked away, and Ethan turned to follow, but he stopped long enough to ask her. 'Why? What made you do that?'

'I heard them say,' Coral mumbled, as if she were talking to herself. 'Back at home, that green papaya is bad for pregnant women.'

Whatever Ethan thought he had no time to put it into words, as Arya's voice carried over to them, and he turned and went to her.

CHAPTER TWENTY-TWO
CORAL

They left her there, with the picnic table. She watched as the rain dug into the loaves of bread, until nothing was left but a mushy mess. Some of the glasses were knocked over, rolling on their sides, tickled by an invisible hand. In their serving dish, the strawberries simmered in sky broth, the water bringing out a fresh redness that she had not noticed before. The cutlery came alive, quivering under the onslaught of short rain jabs, until the wind came and rolled them up into the tablecloth where they lay still. Oh, she was going mad.

There were locusts in her heart. The way her heart thudded as if it were launched from long legs, a hop in the air, then a landing, only to start the whole process in quicker spurts again, a shred of quiet, before the jumping and hopping resumed. It was getting difficult to control her thoughts under the pouring rain, but nothing in her stirred to make a dash for it.

Into the chaos, the wind churned the air again, striking her in the back, knocking her to the ground on all fours. It was a new thing, dropping from position, to survey the short, wet grass and smell the fresh earth. Relief crawled through her spine, settling in her fingertips. She felt alive, with her head hanging towards the ground, as if her neck had walked off and left her crawling out of the cave. The weight lifted off her shoulders, as her fingers dug into the grass, bringing up clods of earth and roots. Her fingernails were short, as if clipped and made ready for the job at hand. She carried on clawing, the garden shovel could not have done a better job, the hole in the ground grew, her brain stirred, her eyes lifted, and she thought she saw a garden gnome peeking at her, from under the picnic table. The small, hunchbacked figure in the long, pointed hat seemed absorbed in her labour, so that she too became more determined. With the unnamed goal in sight, her own shoulders lifted, water pouring on her head, her hands working as if her fingers would run off if they stopped, she felt something solid laid bare in the scavenged soil. She plucked it out, held it up, to show the watching gnome, but it was gone, vanished as if it never was. She looked at her treasure, took it and slipped it onto her finger as if it belonged to her. And then, she lay down on the ground, exhausted, closed her eyes and slept, for how long she did not know, until a voice brought her back, and the touch of human hands picked her up.

'My goodness!' Miss Nan called out from under her umbrella, as the two staff members who had accompanied her in their raincoats, lifted the unfortunate girl back onto her feet. 'What are you doing child?'

She was up, supported on both sides by the two pairs of hands to keep her in place. Miss Nan's voice rose above the racket of the wind and the rain, giving orders that they return to the Mansion with immediate haste, and that she would send others to clean up after the storm had passed. Coral blanked out somewhere on that trip back, had no idea how she ended tucked up in the grand bed again, the same guest room that played host for a second time.

When sleep lifted, her eyes slowly opened, weighed down as if with gold nuggets. Adjusting her sight, she saw Matti sitting on her bed, and tried to push herself up, when from the other end of the room, Beth's voice carried over. 'Rather stay down. You look dreadful.'

Her body obeyed, slipping back into bed, where it lay, comfortable, flat. Her body was tired, her mind still hazy.

'So, you're finally up,' Matti said ironically. 'Strange, how you manage to always end up the victim, isn't it?'

Matti was dressed in her pyjamas, her hair coiled into a knot at the back of her head, her feet in slippers. She wore no makeup, her face looked pale in its nakedness.

'I. I don't know what happened.'

'Yeah, poor little mouse you,' Matti said through clenched teeth. 'Imagine, if Ethan had not told Miss Nan that you were left outside in the storm? We would be kicking you into an early grave now.'

'Well,' Beth said quietly, coming into full view with her hand on Matti's shoulder. 'You have caused chaos. The Mistress cancelled Matti's tickets, calling her condition too delicate. And Ethan told everyone why you pushed the papaya out of Matti's grasp. It seems we are stuck with you.'

'Not really,' Matti said slowly. 'I could have her sent back. To her house.'

'No,' Coral pleaded weakly. 'Not that.'

Matti stood up, the smile that shaped her face went up into her puffy cheeks, and it hung there, frozen, rather eerily, as if it were stuck. She looked like a child again, one that had been bullied at school, before turning the tables around on everyone else and becoming the master bully herself. It was written into her features, especially hidden in her eyes, but it gave itself away, when she spat out her words, her nose wrinkled every now and then in tune with her eyes, which at that precise point, would scrunch itself and force her head to the side, so that she developed the habit of looking at her victim from an angle. It was an unnerving sight, and Coral was sure it was something special, reserved for the unfortunates, like herself.

'You remember the forest queen?' Matti was talking. 'The one I gave you when you turned your back on me? I remember that day as if it happened yesterday, the day you showed me that promises are negotiable, that they just go away, like this,' and she snapped her fingers. 'That you can make your own rules if you feel like it,' and here she wriggled her fingers, stretching her arms above her head, she carried on with the spidery movement until at chin level, she dropped her hands to her sides, and stared stony faced at the figure in the bed. 'You showed me that you don't have to care how someone else feels.'

Her voice was getting dangerously grim, and Beth put herself in between the two of them, but Matti pushed her aside, 'You will never be a Forest Queen,' Matti laughed. 'Why, you won't even be the caterpillar, because they have a headpiece, which makes them special. You will always be the dead thing, like that butterfly in the frame. I hope you still have it,' Matti laughed. 'Because when I'm done with you, that's all you will be left with.'

'Matti, I never meant anything bad by it,' Coral said quietly. 'I was afraid. Too scared to leave.'

Matti shrugged, 'Oh, you remember that book I told you about,' she stared at Coral, waiting to see if she remembered, then carried on, 'It's funny what money can do. It's brought the same bunch of people, with their bright red pens, straight to my door, begging me to publish. I told them exactly what I will say to you now, that once you hurt me,' here she paused to place a hand on her chest. 'This heart never forgets.'

Matti turned to Beth, and said coldly, 'I want her taken

from the kitchens, put her with the cleaning staff. I want to see her planned task sheet, and I want to see it by the morning. She starts pronto at five.'

Beth looked from Matti's vanishing back to the pale figure in the bed. Sighing deeply, and shaking her head, she went from the room, and closed the door behind her.

CHAPTER TWENTY-THREE
ETHAN

The venture in the forest had paid off. For three months, he had tried his best to save that natural piece of charm, and succeeded, benefitting both the enterprise and the natural wilderness. The hard work and isolation worked a change in him. If he were of the spiritual sort, he might have read into the situation. Looked at the change as if it were a send from above, a message bobbing in the ocean, bottled in glass, washing up at his feet, only he would never shatter the glass to get to the message. He preferred to go by his own resolve. Things worked better that way.

  He was back from his travels, had earned the new title from the Mistress, though he had learned to think of her as Ania now, seeing that he had become her chief official advisor and overseer, the authentic whisperer in the ear to the woman everybody knew almost nothing about. In that cloudiness, without doubt, lay the anchor of her power. Yet, he had seen a side of her that brought the woman to ground, made her a wholesome being, one that was capable of deep emotion and even, fear. He would make nothing of that day on the beach though. Going by his own standards, he had kept his mouth and his mind shut from the events of those hours. He turned his focus back to the present, glad for the new crowned success that was his, having earned it as truly as the fishermen braving the North wind. The tide turned for him, his head was out of the deep, he had no reason to feel as if he were swimming against the predatory wave. No, the way he saw it, that wave had been tamed, rolling him out onto an island, where he got to plant his feet in sand, his eyes feasting over water that lay still. The dream was sublime, the feeling very real, and for this rip in time, he knew what it felt like, to hold the coconut in his hand, sipping the sweetness, no worries about it landing on his head. Yet, this new fortune came with a bittersweet slant. Something chattered, making noises that filtered into his brain, setting up a jabbering and a chirping, just enough to make him uneasy.

It all went back to that night on the beach, and to what happened inside that tent. His memory fed him a teaspoon of the event, only enough to let him know that whatever he felt that night, in those moments, he had never been able to feel again. But then, there had never been a repeat of the night. He had made sure of that. It was too soon, too consuming. He preferred to leave things for after the wedding. He needed to put himself into order, and this uneasiness that ransacked his thoughts, he likened it to anyone with acrophobia, stuck in a situation where the mountain got to settle the score between life and death. In his case, love would decide his fate. But as things stood, he was not sure if he wanted to trade solitariness for love. That was where his insecurity lay, he was almost certain of it. He would need to move past it. He had the ring in his pocket. It was time.

He watched as Arya came up the pathway to join him. He was standing on the patch of ground where the tent had been. He gazed at her, as she made her way towards him, her face exquisitely profiled by the setting sun, the deep red dress draped expertly about her tiny waist, riding up well above her knees, showing off perfectly shaped legs. She wore sparkly high heels again, and he smiled at that. He expected not many would go for that option, not when the trip was one to the beach. He felt less of an idiot now, standing there, holding a large bouquet of red roses that matched her dress, all bunched up under his nose, so that he felt like a hypocrite. He was not one for it, he preferred the stems to be left exactly where nature put them. But Arya loved flowers, especially roses. He had asked the florist for a very large arrangement and been told forty-six roses went into the arrangement. He had no idea why the number in its precision set him on edge, like counting the heads at a funeral. It left him with the same bitter distaste. But for now, the flowers filled up his arms, and fitted the bill of a romantic notion. He had something else in his pocket that reminded him of that strange night. He could not wait to give it back to her. He wanted to watch her expression, had already figured out her reaction, and it made every sacrifice in his life worth the pain.

'*Heyyyy*,' she called out, in her usual voice, as she approached him, bright red lips smiling, lightly blushed skin cool under the aging day. She dropped into his arms, squishing the roses, and drawing him to her. He relaxed, feeling the warmth of her arms as they reached for him, the excitement flowing from her countenance into his.

He kissed the top of her head, above the sweet smelling flowers, it coated his being, the floral pungency gave him the lead. He gave her the flowers. She took the bunch, and it filled out her arms, went up past her heart shaped face so that they laughed together, and he took it back from her and set it on the ground. Very slowly, he straightened up, reaching into his pocket, he brought out the small box, plain and black, that contained the first hidden surprise of the evening. She took it from him, quickly, and he noticed that her burgundy manicured nails, shaped into pointed tips, had sparkle in it, little bits of silver that shone like studs as she carefully popped open the lid. Her face froze, something was wrong as she stared at what lay inside. It was not the reaction he was expecting.

'You left that behind in the tent,' he said, as if reminding her. 'Must have dropped off the chain. This sneaky charmer,' he indicated the pendant. 'Found its way into my hair, just as you found your way into my heart.'

He thought she would find the pun in that. But she was still staring at the silver pendant, that had been fashioned into a plump, tiny mouse with oversized ears and a long nose. He did not tell her that he had done some research on the small creature's real-life family and been intrigued by what he learned. He waited for Arya to tell him, so that they could compare notes. But she was quiet.

'I looked it up,' he offered as consolation. 'It's an elephant shrew?'

It was a strange looking thing.

'Yes, yes.'

He watched her reaction closely. He was sure he saw her flinch, her eyebrows creased for a very tiny second and her lips draw into a pout. But it must have been his imagination, for in the next second she had thrown her arms about his neck and buried her face in the base of his throat. She felt so warm, and smelt so good, that he kissed her.

'We can tell our kids someday,' he said, drawing back. 'That our fate rested in a pendant.'

She nodded quickly, 'Ya, that's what my grandfather said when he gave us the pendants. The other two,' she paused, referring to her sisters. 'They had different animal pendants. He said we had different fates, but that mine was special. He said that I might be shy, and small, like the elephant shrew, but in life I would meet my other half, and that would change everything. Looks like he was right.'

Ethan covered up his surprise. That description did not fit Arya.

'Where you shy as a child?' he asked her.

'Very,' she remarked, batting her eyelids, looking away 'I didn't want you to know.'

He gathered her into his arms, his mouth on the tip of her ear so that they both looked out towards the rolling waves. 'You are the most important person in my life. There's so much ground we need to cover. But we will do that, soon. For the first time, I have someone who belongs to me. There is nothing I would not do for you, so long as I know I have your heart, in all its purity.'

He turned her around to face him. 'And you have mine.'

He waited for her to go on, but she only nodded. She said nothing more, the change in her demeanour worried him. She looked troubled, but that was not exactly it. She appeared vexed, and he was at a loss. He sensed what needed to be done, to lift her mood, so he went down on bended knee, watching her eyes light up, hearing her gasp and then shout out, as if he had gotten up and were running off with the ring. But he held his place, lifted up the gold wrapped box, as an offering, his conscience struck by the gravity of the situation. Arya's grandfather, in his wisdom, had correctly predicted her fate, by gifting her the elephant shrew. As things stood, they would be married, in a short space of time, and Ethan knew he would stop at nothing to bring the world to Arya's feet. Her life as his queen would be extraordinary, and for the best part, he knew that in his lifetime, once he took a wife, his soul would be partnered up forever. It was a strange thing, handing over his life to another. He did not know if the quality he possessed was a curse, or an endowment. Either way, he shared the same fate as the elephant shrew. The idea brought a smile to his lips. Whether Arya was the one, he could not be certain. But the smile lingered as he recognised the truth, that Arya was a good woman, clean of heart. She, much like him, would never go out of way to harm another. She had given him a place to belong to, in a world where he knew no attachment. Other than the respect he harboured for Ania, he had kept his world a sieve, so nothing remained to hold on to. It was different now. He was not made like everyone else – he knew that. It was a stubborn and stupid conviction, to vow to take a wife for a lifetime, but it was his to make. People talked, and he knew that feelings changed, sometimes people forgot who they were. And that was their right, earned in a place where the rules were set by somebody else. It took guts to define who you were, no matter what that decision meant. It took him a lifetime to find his footing. He was nobody to judge, but he had earned the right to his own biscuit cutter, and he knew what shape that biscuit would take. Once the vows were exchanged, he would spend his life making Arya happy, if she would have him.

In the meantime, Arya snatched the box out from his hands. She threw the lid open, and as her eyes found the ring, balanced perfectly on a neat cushion of burgundy, she gasped. The fat gold band had an enormous diamond sitting on top. Arya had never seen anything like it before, and it showed on her face. Her hand went over her mouth, she bobbed her head up and down with excitement, pushing the box out to him. He smiled, took out the ring and placed it on her finger. It was a perfect fit, and Arya held it up in front of her nose so that she could get a better look.

'It's gorgeous,' she squealed, her voice rising, her hand stretched out, sunlight bouncing off the ring, 'Oh, it's too beautiful. It's heavy too, must be the quality,' she winked at Ethan mischievously. 'It's eight hundred times bigger than Veru's. And shinier. I can't wait for her to see it.

Ethan smiled. He would have to get himself a suite, a burgundy one if it made Arya happy. The idea made him nervous, but then he imagined the giant bows of burgundy that would deck the fancy hall, with the wedding guests all made to wear burgundy hats, pressed into single file down a burgundy carpet, only to be faced with a bride dressed from head to foot in the same colouring. It brought him back to the moment, felt the smile light up his face again, but in his heart, something was amiss. He dismissed it, seeing as they were now engaged. He would have to set a date soon.

CHAPTER TWENTY-FOUR
ANIA

She was almost there. The large tents were pitched on the fringe of the shoreline, taking her mind back to a time when she was a little girl, waiting for the circus to come to town. She went, and found out that she hated it, watching the other kids, wearing their silly faces, smiles too big, sticky hands clutching fluffy clouds of candy floss. Nothing seemed real, and when she got home that afternoon, she welcomed the poison of the real world.

The tents were upon her now, big white outlandish things, made of material, with clear spaces for windows, so that the mice inside could take a good look out from their internment. It was ridiculous, the whole affair, and the large number of people milling about spilled inside and out from the white sacks, as if they had forsaken their manners, and been left to graze like cows. She heard their laughter, their voices mingling around the tables. There were mountains of fresh bread everywhere, that being Matti's favourite. People were busy with the loaves. The act was so ripe, the air carried the sweat of yeast and butter to her, and as she got by close enough, she saw the knives cutting into the freshness, hands holding the bread in place, squashing the baked goodness into a pulp. For the first time in her life, she preferred listening to the sea, rolling out the overfull troughs, like a water stash on a greedy farmers land.

'Mistress!' Moira hurried over to her. 'I have been waiting to see you. Waiting just for you.'

Ania nodded, her suffering had begun. She was not one for social drama. She preferred to be left alone. The woman in front of her was no ordinary character, and she could not stifle her surprise at the way Moira extended herself, stretching like a chewed piece of gum, leaning into another person's orbit. Thankfully she missed the mark and ended up kissing the air in greeting. Still, the woman kept her close stance, reaching just below Ania's chin, the head of hair so thick and high, so decorous and artificial they must have charged for three instead of one at the salon. Ania took a few steps back, with as much tact as she dared, while Moira flexed the muscles in her face, turning it into a frown, waiting for Ania to say something.

Her husband broke the uncomfortable greeting when he shouted at his wife, 'Moira, get away. You know she likes her space. How many times must I tell you the same thing?'

His words brought Mona running, flanked by the new addition, Philip. The four of them stared at her. She dipped her chin at them, before walking away, as fast as her dignity would allow her, straight into the centre of the next group.

When the half a dozen heads were done bobbing in greeting, the ruler of the pack fixed her with a straight face. 'The weather is very nice today. Lovely weather for a function.'

Ania picked up on the hint of peace and nodded quickly at Nancy.

'*Ohhhhhhh*,' Kesh was gushing from the other side, the bun coiled on the top of her head looking dangerously wobbly, the flowers and studs that were poked into it showing their weight. Her face was coloured in shades of pink and red, the charcoal lined eyes and glossy red lips were hypnotizing 'Now, our Arya is going to be married too. Look!'

She pulled Arya's hand up, showing off the magnificent

ring that dazzled there, but it was the dress that the young woman wore that grabbed attention. The bedding of two rooms must have gone into that dress, which paid tribute to a hot air balloon turned upside down. The final effect made her look like a stuffed pigeon. Meanwhile, Kesh was still speaking, 'her mother always said she was made to be a princess.'

Ania kept her thoughts under the lid, although personally, she would have been the last person to put Arya and Ethan together.

'*And,*' Kesh was not done, 'Veru's wedding is next month. I think my brother,' she nudged Eddie in the side, 'has beat us all. Both his daughters set up for life.'

Veru blushed, and Dinesh moved closer to her so that they looked almost intertwined.

'One thing though,' it was Nancy who cut in bitterly. 'I must find out, how is that other daughter of mine doing?' She doesn't know she still has parents. Not even one letter, or word from her.'

Ania frowned. 'She is somewhere, hereabouts.'

'*Hmuf*,' Nancy looked even more displeased, 'trying to avoid me, that's what she is doing. After everything her father and I did for her, that ungrateful dog.'

Ania remained speechless.

'You see Ed?' Nancy barked at her husband. 'Every family has that one rotten egg. And you always take her part. See, where that got you.'

'Enough,' Ed said quietly, looking very uncomfortable in a suite he had clearly outgrown. 'We are not here to fight.'

'No,' Nancy returned smugly. 'You here to show the whole world how wonderful your daughter is. Can't even come greet us. Big shot, that's what she thinks she is.'

Nancy finished her tirade, worked up and flushed, it was the worst possible time for Coral to appear, but that is what happened. She pitched up suddenly, should have stayed far away, but it was too late. The girl looked exhausted, the dark patches under her eyes were deep, giving them a sunken look. It was like staring at pirate's treasure that nobody wanted. Her face however had taken on a rounder profile, but then she must be at least six months into her pregnancy. She greeted each stone figure in turn, wiping her brow every now and then, rogue perspiration slipping off her face, landing in wet splotches on her dress, like make believe holes, the shapeless material hung on her from neck to toe. It was nothing more than an ugly piece of grey cloth. Ania did not like it. She had not seen the girl in a while. Did they not pay the girl enough. She made a mental note of checking up on things herself.

'What's this?' Nancy was scolding. 'Looks like *they* can throw such a big function, but very thrifty with the money,' she rubbed the three fingers of one hand together and gave Ania the terrible eye. 'The only thing missing for her is a cup,' her voice was getting louder, and drawing attention from inquisitive ears. 'Why, I can put in the first coin myself. Shameful!'

Everyone was spared any further agony, with Ethan's arrival. He must have overheard the drift of the conversation, for he stepped into the midst of the group, planting a kiss on Arya's forehead, while balancing a stack of parcels.

An extra note of cheer fed his voice, his countenance remained one of nobility, the way he claimed his spot and made everyone else sniff with respect. His complexion looked richer, his physique broader, his hair more lustrous, the air about him exemplified adventure and excitement. He had always stood out, but now, he ran the race in his own league. She would have been proud to call him her grandson. If only...

'What are you holding?' Nancy turned her attention to the gift-wrapped packages.

Ethan's smile grew, handing out the gifts, finishing off with the last one for Coral. She hesitated, before taking it.

'Open them,' he instructed, as if it were the season for Christmas, and caught in that spell, they did exactly that. He had brought them an item of clothing each.

'Thank you,' Ania remarked in a tight voice. She held the scarf in her hands, a ruby piece of cotton, the first gift anybody had dared give her, starting from the day she lost her husband, and became the Head of a vast empire. That was another piece of the puzzle knocked out of place today. Nobody thought about gifts, not when it was supposed to go to her. She was above everything, no bread -and- butter pudding for her, not unless it came with a side serving of goblins gold. She knew the talk. She learned most recently of the two islands she was supposed to have bought, one to use as a spare they said, seeing as the ocean levels were rising, so it made sense that if one got gobbled up by the sea, the other would come in handy. Talk was rich, the truth was sometimes not far behind, but the effect of isolation it created was a different matter. Of late, the latter prospect bothered her. She had started seeing large circles of light on the walls of her bedroom at night, as if something evil had attached itself to her, separated her. The dancing orbs moved as if they were in a trance, her eyes told her she was not dreaming. She believed what her eyes told her, they had not let her down all her life. So, she figured it must be her mind. That was a different part of the story. The mind was like a lemon tree. If the thorns did not stick it to you, then a nice bite of the sour fruit would. Either way, you took your chances. Her mind was running out of chances, but if she was going down, it would not be without a good fight. So, she lay in bed at night, staring at the dancing orbs when they appeared, thinking to herself how perfectly underestimated beautiful round circles were, until she dozed off and woke the next morning to find she had yet another day with her mind intact.

She brought herself back to the present, the scarf in her hand. She did not have a scarf, not one like this, and it warmed her heart, even though her face remained rigid in its setting.

'I got these from the ladies who live close to the forest. They earn their living by making everything by hand,' Ethan was saying proudly. 'They are amazing, the talent natural, unmarked and never feigned.'

'So, each piece is original?' Arya asked, looking at the folded piece of material she had unwrapped. Her eyes flitted to what her sisters were holding. Veru had something similar in purple, but it was Coral's gift that brought the malevolence out in her.

'What colour is that?' Arya asked, in a voice that sounded strangled.

'Oh, that will be a shade of green,' Ethan laughed, not having picked up on the tense abrasion, intent as he was on watching everyone open their gifts.

'A shade of green?' 'Arya asked, in a voice of venom. 'I've never seen one like it before. What, did they get silkworms from Mars to make it, since hers is glowing and mine isn't.'

Everybody turned to look at the material that Coral was holding. It was soft and silky, a light green, as if the colour had been borrowed from the leaves of the weeping willow. When she unwittingly shifted the cloth in her hands, a shimmer ran across, as if the sun had picked out its favourites in the shallows, and the silvery dash of fish sparkled in the clear water.

'Ooooooh,' Kesh sang, oblivious to the predatory expression taking over Arya's features, 'now that is something special. I never seen anything like it before.'

Her words released the spite in Arya, 'You bought me a brown dress. I don't like it,' Arya said sourly. 'Everything you give me, is either burgundy or red. So, what's this?'

She had not bothered to be discreet, and the group heard everything as clearly as if she were the storyteller, their eyes and ears automatically tuned in. It was getting very uncomfortable.

'Well,' Nancy made her voice higher on purpose, to shift the tide. 'I love my scarf. Kesh does too. And how interesting your father's shirt looks. Must be pure cotton too,' she said approvingly. 'But I must tell you about the scarves, we get very cold weather only now and then in Durban. Still, it's very nice, right Arya?'

'Why did you get me brown?' Arya chewed the words slowly, her voice trimmed with irritation, 'when look at what you gave *her*?'

'You can have mine,' Coral was saying. 'Please, I will trade with you.'

'Veru has purple,' Arya continued, unswerving in her anger, 'Fine. I get that. She's not as fair as me, so purple is a flattering choice for her,' Arya was losing herself, and Veru was shooting darts at her now that she was being attacked. 'And I don't want your handouts,' Arya snapped at Coral, then turning back to Ethan she said, 'How could you put me last?'

Ethan held her gaze, and his words.

Arya pushed back her hair on both sides, looping it behind

her ears, and held up the dress next to her face. 'See? This is not my colour. How can you be so inconsiderate?'

'I would never put anyone above you,' Ethan said slowly, looking to Nancy for assistance, but she was too busy staring at Arya, a frown on her face, so Ethan took up the battle, sticking his foot out, hoping he would not fall over it, and he said, 'I got you a dress that signifies everything I experienced over the past three months. The earth, the trees, my resolution to make you my wife, everything is tied up to that forest and the choice I made to go there. I wanted to get you something that reminds me of that, and it came up in the form of this dress. I never knew you hated brown. That is my fault for not checking first.'

Arya softened up instantly. She was about to say something when Coral handed her the green dress. She shot out her hand, sending it into the air, where it slowly floated to the sand. 'Can't you see we are in the middle of a conversation?' she barked at her sister. 'How inconsiderate. I love my dress. It was handpicked for me by my fiancé. What makes you think I want yours?'

Arya bundled her hair into a knot at the base of her neck, and was about to throw herself into Ethan's arms, when Nancy's voice stopped her.

'What's that on your neck?' Nancy sounded confused, pointing at the elephant shrew. 'That's not yours. What happened to yours?' she demanded from her daughter, her voice becoming anxious. 'Your grandfather will be spinning in his grave if he saw the things I am seeing. In my time, we respected our elders. When they gave us something, it came because of hard work. We looked after it. He told me loud and clearly before he went away for good, each pendant belongs to each grandchild. No exchanging, no throwing away, no giving to anyone else except to your own children. The thing is,' here she paused to breathe. 'Be decent, if you don't want to wear it, then keep it in the drawer. And he told me in a straight fashion, he had a very loud voice, like thunder, and he was big, like a giant, and his brain worked fast, went faster than the ticking clock, not even your father and his whole side stood a decent chance, that's how smart my father was,' she sighed and gave Ed a look of regret, before turning her attention to Arya once more. 'I gave him my word. Now, that man has been dead for years, you want him to come haunt me, for breaking my promise. You think I got nothing better to do than run from ghosts, and what if he brings those relatives back with him, the ones we were happy to lose, did you ever stop to think about us? No, you only thinking about yourself. Give that pendant back to Coral, I know it's hers.'

Arya did not flinch. She looked at Coral, 'You threw yours away. You told me you liked the fox. That was mine. And you took it, without asking.'

Nancy filled up her lungs too quickly, with the giant gasp she took, Kesh moved in behind, ready on call, in case she passed out. But the lady was built for bigger quests, 'How can you do such a thing?' Nancy barked at Coral. 'Right under my roof. No wonder I been dreaming all these years, bad dreams, and it's because of you. You brought bad luck into the house, to me. Let me get my hands on you, think you're a big shot, I'll turn you into a small shot, when I'm finished with you. Got the nerve to do such a thing, this has broken our house.'

She was kept in place by Kesh, who held her arm and shook her head, pointing towards Ethan. His face had lost all colour. His demeanour had changed so quickly that the group was now fixated on him, forgetting about Nancy and her honour.

Arya put her hand on Ethan's face, saying slowly, 'Everything I've said is true, my love. But I was too embarrassed to tell you the truth, so I made up the part about my grandfather's words. He did not tell us why he chose them, he died before he could. She threw her gift away. She could not shut up about how unhappy she was, complaining forever, and being spiteful. She tried to steal our pendants, Veru's and mine, and throw it over the neighbour's wall. Lucky for us, the dog started barking, they had one on that side, and everyone came running. That's when Veru and I saw her holding the chains in her hand. We didn't say anything,' Arya paused, catching Veru's look, and emboldened by what she saw there, continued, 'Just because everybody loved us, saying how beautiful and fair we were, and Coral wasn't, she hated us. They said how come she was looking more like a duck than a swan. I think that pushed her too far, she became a jealous thing. She used to poke her fingers in my face, telling me that I got a fox, and she got a rodent, it's all my fault for being so cute, and that someone told her, mice have teeth that don't stop growing, and she had no idea why grandfather would leave her something like that,' Arya drew breath, 'It must be that she was a mouse, insignificant, going to cause a plague of misfortune wherever she went. She was going to use her teeth to make holes everywhere, and she bit my hand, like she was biting a chicken bone,' Arya's voice rose, 'and I closed my eyes. Everybody was still sleeping. The next day I gave her my fox, my darling fox with the bushy tail and the orange eyes.'

She paused. Ethan was looking at her intently. 'It hurt me, thinking of how hard my grandfather worked to buy us the gifts, so I went to the bins outside the kitchen window, and looked inside all of them, with my bare hands,' she paused, to hold up her palms, soft and fully fleshed, they looked the mirror of health. 'Dug into the peels and through the leftover curries and found the pendant in the trash. It was mine, and I put things together for myself, and figured it was always meant to be with me. Can you blame me, my love?'

By now, Kesh was livid, 'You nasty, vindictive one,' Kesh fumed, staring at Coral, 'looking so innocent. This will go from one house to another, people will talk, they will say our family is no good. How will our girls get good marriages. Never mind, I will tell them Coral went and got bitten by a dog, picked up rabies. Yes, that's it. We will say they gave her treatment. At least our family name will be safe. Nance,' Kesh almost begged the woman. 'We must arrange a big cleansing ceremony. This is too much,' she took out a face cloth and mopped her face. 'I don't know what to say any more, shameful, the whole thing makes me sick.'

Everyone turned their attention to Coral now, waiting for a reaction of some kind. Coral said nothing.

Nancy flapped her hands like a distraught bird, 'throws it back in our faces. So bad, rotten to the core, that she is causing problems everywhere. How must I face everyone, in our old age when we supposed to be happy, this child is bringing misery. I don't know what I did to deserve this. The world must be coming to an end, my heart is good, and I suffer, but yet, I saw aunty Vani the other day, looking half dead, totally useless, but even that one, got all her children cooking and cleaning, pressing her feet, making her two cups of tea a day. And me – I make my own and his,' she thumbed towards her husband. 'And I never complain. This ungrateful daughter of mine will be my downfall, can't put one decent foot in front of the other without falling, got the nerve to do so many things in the quiet. Wait and see what happens when I get a hold of her now.'

'You right,' Kesh was saying, stoking the fire with a big iron spoon. 'Put your foot down. If one of my girls did this, threw my gift back in my face, I would pull her hair. And you are handling it so well, not even doing that. These children of today, they must be put in their place. Think they grown too big for their boots. And what about us? Washing, cooking, cleaning, mopping, ironing, drying clothes. What, we must expect nothing else. Husbands on one side, and spoilt brats for children on the other. Who is going to speak up for us?'

Nancy, fired up by her sister in law's sympathy, took one large step, only to have the men in the group step forward and create a human barrier between her and the daughter she was going to sort out. The Mistress looked as if she might grab the opportunity and flee the scene, to find more neutral ground, but she was bound by etiquette to stay.

Ethan brought the attention back to the crux of the matter. He fixed Coral with a definite stare, and when he spoke his voice shook slightly, 'Is what Arya told us the truth?'

CHAPTER TWENTY-FIVE
MISS NAN – PART ONE

It was uncomfortable, standing there, watching the drama unfold. By now, the Mistress had lapsed into some kind of shock, an elegant type, that turned her into a chunk of stone. She said nothing, stood and stared, as if she had made a duplicate of herself, and long abandoned the body. Miss Nan had only just arrived, to get the gist of what was happening. Somewhere deep inside, she knew this day was not going to end, until something broke. She felt it, a premonition of sorts, wished it away but the feeling stuck to her, making a home in her gut, so that she felt the wave of nausea strike her, and quickly put a hand to her mouth. It subsided, the feeling went and made itself a new home, close to her heart, so that she felt the anguish of heartbreak, without even knowing why. It was ridiculous. It must be the company she was keeping, she decided, intending to slip away, but the sight of Ethan's face stopped her. She felt guilty, knowing the secret she kept put her in the lead role, a pawn of deceit, the secret she kept so unthinkable, that if she let it out, the tables would crash. No, they would burn. She was no fool. There were already plenty of cracks, the secret she kept was riddled with it, and if anybody had played detective, by now they would have it all figured out. She knew that, had prayed that it would happen, set her free from the burden of it.

She watched Ethan closely now. A new strain had set itself

into his features, showing trouble that brewed beneath. How she wished she might go to him, a mother figure, yes, without the accruing rights, for she did not deserve that, but with enough love in her heart. Deep inside the blankness that was her soul, Ethan was the animation, the colour and the charm that kept her heartbeat on course. She was not young any more, a middle-aged woman with an alacrity for running a household, a crow, they said, an endangered, invasive species with an apathetic interest in other people, an interest that kept its nose and feet everywhere. She heard the rumours, was happy that her behaviour and life made such headlines around supper tables, and frankly, never cared about minds that worked like cheap fish tank filters, all that muck getting clogged everywhere. No wonder there was no space left over for clear thought. She shuddered.

But now, she returned to the cause of her concern. Ethan was looking at Arya, his forehead mapped in a frown, while his fiancé had her face turned to the ground. They made a good couple, but she knew Arya would fall short of the position that might be hers one day. In any event, the girl's mother Nancy, the woman was a brainteaser, an enigma at its best description. With both hands on her hips, her head moved from one to the other, like a locust with reading glasses, she was almost hopping on the spot in her agitation. Her husband put a hand on her back, seemingly to keep her from flying off the spot, but it did not look like it helped much. Kesh, the aunt, stood on the other side of the couple, hovering over the situation, like a mad flea. The pregnant girl, pale and looking worse for the wear, stood with pursed lips, breaking the silence, her words fetched the desired release. 'Everything Arya said is true.'

Her words released the spell for everyone else, but Miss

Nan, she sensed trouble, picked it up with her nose, a special gift she had received, for sifting through gibberish. It should be an excellent gift, but it failed her at times. Her thoughts went to Matti. Her nose must have been off duty with that one. It started with the letter from Matti's aunt, all innocent like, leading her to take pity on the poor girl. She went out of her way to push Matti into better circles, prepared to jump on Coral if she had to, or anyone who got in the way, of her pet project. Matti reached the top with no problem, and then she was left to watch as the girl flaunted a heart of charcoal. There was no better way to say it. She returned to the moment, and to Arya spluttering, 'You see, she always gets me in trouble. I feel so bad now, as if I stole the pendant.'

Arya began sobbing loudly. The emotional discharge, which should have brought sympathy had the opposite effect. The impact was most severe on Ethan. Miss Nan watched him, and because she knew him so well, she could see that under the look of shock that still etched itself into his features, there was a new strain of anxiety, and in his eyes, she saw the reflection of his thoughts. It looked like he needed to get away, but the cries that filled the air put a stop to any escape. The drama needed grounding, and Nancy took charge, gathering Arya to her, she forgot her place and her manners, barking as she did, 'What kind of boyfriend are you? Waiting for the world to come to an end, before you do something. Standing there and staring, like an outsider. What, cat got your tongue and holding it ransom?'

Oh, she would have liked to take that woman and feed her to the rats, or better, throw her into a medieval well, a deep one, and leave her there, giving her time to use every alphabet, its derivative and possible futures, exhaust them ten times ten over, before she let her out. That would be the mark of redemption, not just for mankind at large, but for that husband of hers, who should have put his mouth into better use, and shut her up when he had the chance. It was too late now, of course. Miss Nan liked to think of herself as a neutral person, but when it came to issues of common decency, that was a different matter. She did not approve of the manner in which the woman treated Coral, it put her nerves on edge, jumbled up her constraints, so that she feared she might overstep the mark and take matters into her own hands.

For now, her thoughts were mostly for Ethan, and if there were any boundary bashings scheduled, then she would take up his fight first. Sadly, she could not. It was his place to hold, not hers. His potential mother- in- law's words shook him into orbit, he took Arya into his arms almost mechanically, and however he managed to placate his personal demons for the while, he kept it closed under a tight smile. It was a new thing for him, she could see, being bossed around. Usually, it was him doing the bossing, but in this case, the stakes were too high, and to get the girl and keep her, he would have to make sacrifices.

He was extraordinary, she thought, not just in appearance, but the presence he exuded came from another world. She knew she had deprived him. But she had protected him the best way she knew. This secret that she carried for him; she would take it to her grave.

Nancy intruded on her reflections, bringing her back to the present, and from her shadowed space, she watched as Nancy nodded in approval, directing her words to Coral. 'Nice thing you did. It suits your sister better. Look how it shines, shines. What's the sake of you keeping the pendant when you can't even look after yourself properly. See, how damaged your hair is.' Nancy shook her head in disbelief. 'Simple thing, like taking care of yourself, and you can't even do that. Lucky you gave that family heirloom to your sister. At least she will take care of it.'

Coral's reaction was to quickly recoil her hair into a knot at the nape of her neck. Some of the strands had become undone.

Then Kesh did a very unpredicted thing. Something seemed to have shifted in her. She did something quite extraordinary. She volunteered to help Coral into the new dress, to make her more presentable, going by her mother's standards, of course. Nancy seemed pleased. But then, Arya dropped another shocker. She admitted, rather proudly, that the dress Coral was currently wearing had been her choice.

'Oh,' Nancy piped up. 'Why you didn't say so in the first place. I see the beauty coming from it now. Very nice dress. It would have looked better on you, anyone can tell, not so shapeless and plain, like a sack, but what can we do?'

Kesh seemed to possess a new strength, going against her sister- in- law, she shook her head, insisted that it was no problem to help Coral into the new dress, took the girl by the elbow, even looking surprised at her own actions, and marched off. Miss Nan looked across at the Mistress, wanting to see what she thought of the new turn in events. The grand Lady, still suffering under shock, looked trapped, caged like a chicken, going from beast to bird, oh, the world was turning upside down.

'At least she will look decent in the photos,' she heard Nancy say, as Kesh and Coral vanished from view, the last words filtering in. 'Let her go and dress up. I must go change now too, wasted time for nothing. Children these days, can't think for themselves.'

CHAPTER TWENTY-SIX
MISS NAN – PART TWO

While the shoreline filled up, Nancy stood patting her hair, a small figure dressed in a glittering Indian outfit, a gold sequenced stunner. She wore costume jewellery that sat at the base of her throat, and from her ears, chunks of fake gold and glass diamonds glittered. On her forehead sat a beautiful red, tear shaped sticker, glass studded. To everyone's horror, she plucked it off and stuck it on the Mistress's forehead, landing it in the middle of her eyebrows. 'It will stay,' she declared, patting it firmly into place, unaware she was trespassing. 'I don't need to ask you, we going to be family. Family shares with one another. I got another one, see,' she opened her small purse, produced a card from which she took out a fancier one, and placed it precisely on her forehead. 'This one is proper. Yours is not as good, but never mind, I bought so many, all useless like that one I gave you. They don't make things like they used to, nowadays, they make it like their grannies are working there. And look, it's nearly falling off already. Just a little bit of sweat, and it falls. You better not sweat. At least keep it on, for now. Let me tell you, I can see the difference already. Makes you look nice and pretty.'

Everyone stood shocked, even the grand Lady herself seemed to be at a loss. It was clear she had never faced an obstacle in this form before. They were all spared in a way by the arrival of Francis and Matti, who looked as if they were arguing. They had a little girl with them, one she had not seen before.

'I want to play the piano now, Grand Mum,' Matti was saying. 'And *he* wants me to wait until they finish planting the trees.'

'It is a tree planting ceremony,' Francis reminded her. 'And we are going to plant a special one for our baby. Can't you wait, it will only take a few minutes?'

'And what must I tell Lucy's mother?' Matti asked angrily. 'Her bedtime will be up before I can start playing.'

By now, Chris and Miriam, were there too. Miriam had changed the colour of her hair again, this time into a brilliant shock of purple. She had chosen a deeper shade for her lipstick. She combined the look with a bright orange dress.

'Who is the little girl?' Chris asked right away.

'The daughter of a friend of Matti's,' Francis said. 'Matti is playing a piece today about a mother and child.'

'Oh, cute,' Miriam said loudly, as she bent towards the child, looking at the five-year-old as if she were a lab sample. 'I never get a chance to spend time with kids.'

The girl shrank visibly, into herself, putting her thumb into her mouth, stretching her eyes at the face in front of her. Matti started laughing. 'Lucy is afraid of all things purple and orange.'

Miriam dismissed the joke, always too keen to be on Matti's good side. She changed the subject and asked, 'What time are we going to start?'

'Why start anyway?' Chris asked flatly. 'What is the good of planting more trees. We will need more people to look after them. It's a waste of money and time.'

'He's right,' Matti replied drily, 'and besides, why can't we get the gardeners to do it? It's too hot. I had far more fun planning this function.'

'You should listen to your wife,' Miriam chirped up. 'Think about the baby.'

Francis looked distressed, sending a look for help towards his grandmother. She had recovered herself enough to settle back into her role, a quiet picture of dignity, her poise remarkably elegant, her thoughts watertight, fluid grace of body and mind that belonged to another era. She fixed Matti with an eye of good breeding, and when she spoke, it was not so that the other might have an opinion. 'Matti, we have guests here to witness the ceremony. Let's get started, and then you may do as you please.'

The pronunciation of order finished the argument, just as Beth and Rod arrived. Beth had chosen a dress that hugged her figure, missing half the purple satin at the back, the other half in front had a plunging neckline, the day being saved by a lavish green bow, tacked on so that it fetched Beth just the right level of modesty.

Next to her, Rod was dressed for a day at the beach, his toes with unclipped nails sticking out of his sandals. He seemed totally unaware of the picture he presented, moving around with surprising agility, he covered much ground, bellowing at the top of his voice, pumping people's hands, as if testing a new system for extraction. He was in the highest of spirits and it was extraordinary.

'Yes,' Beth cooed, turning her head away from him, as he took his place at her side once again. 'I think we should start. The walk back to the gardens is going to hurt,' she pointed at her stilettos. 'Whose idea was it anyway to meet here?'

'Mine!' Matti beamed. 'That old piano looks good here.'

'Okay then,' Beth changed tactic, sending an imploring look towards her mother- in- law, 'Can't she play us a piece. She has been practising so hard, and I see she has brought props along.'

Beth pinched Lucy's cheek playfully, and the child giggled.

'Oh, and she is so friendly,' Beth giggled. 'Children are a great judge of character. They just know the bad ones. They stay away, as if they can smell the big, bad wolf from a distance.'

Everybody took great care to look away from Miriam, who being tactless, pressed the issue further, 'It's not always the case,' she said brightly. 'Who puts their faith in a child, anyways?'

'I do,' Beth replied coldly. 'Only a fool thinks otherwise.'

An awkward silence followed, and it was left up to Rod to bring the conversation around. 'I'll bet the food's getting cold, while we doddle over unimportant things,' he sounded concerned. 'I missed breakfast this morning, and I don't like my food cold, so any piano playing can wait till after.'

Whatever Matti thought never made it past her lips with the appearance of Matt and Mona. After they had performed the usual greetings, the estranged couple stood next to each other, looking miserable.

'What are you doing here?' Chris growled at Mona. 'You are not part of this family.'

He had clearly not forgiven her. He edged closer towards Matt, fired up and ready for a verbal combat. He looked to his father for back up, but Matt was clearly unaffected by Mona's presence. Chris started to sulk, then approached the topic from a different angle, giving Matt some advice, making sure it was loud enough for everyone to hear, he almost shouted out, 'You should not have to deal with her, Father. It's unnecessary baggage for the day.'

Mona bit on her bottom lip, and it looked as if she might cry.

But matters were about to get worse. Moira and Pat joined the group.

'What's the big deal?' Moira was saying, attacking the group at large. 'My grandson can have two Fathers. Who can be so lucky?'

'Or so unfortunate,' Chris muttered, his head hanging, rubbing his one ear irritably, as if a mosquito had visited there, 'so, where's your new other half/' he asked Mona, sarcasm biting into the words, 'I saw him here. What, is he gone into hiding, too scared to face us?'

'I asked him to leave,' Mona said quietly, 'we are just friends.'

'See,' Moira said proudly, dressed as she was in a knee length office suite, balancing on heels that she was clearly not accustomed to, wobbling this way and that, before wagging a finger. 'You think the worst of your mother. It's not natural, you can't ignore her forever. Look at it this way, in a way, you can get double the gifts at Christmas. Now, that's not a bad thing, not a bad thing at all.'

'Shut up, Moira' Pat growled from her side, his face sweating, his body heated up under the layers of formal dinner clothes, his shoes scrubbed and polished clean, so pointed that the tips stuck out like two noses on the hunt.

It was Matt's turn to intervene, and since he rarely spoke about anything except his hobby, his words, given up in the usual non-committal tone, made more of an impact than they should. 'Chris is my son. That is a fact. If his mother and the new guy want a part of his life, I don't mind.'

'You see,' Moira said to her husband, pausing to tighten the man's tie, although if it went any tighter, the knot looked like it might strangle him, 'not even you could put together such an offer of peace. Matt, he is to be admired, admired for his charm. Look at us, he told everyone off, put them in their place. He said we are still his parents, everything we have we keep. Everything stays, more will come too. How about that? I bet nobody believes us, I don't blame them. We are lucky, very lucky.'

Miss Nan wanted to laugh. It was a strange thing. The woman, Moira, should have brought her piggy bank with, because itchy, rich fingers had a habit of dropping gold nuggets from time to time, and she was in the right company for that to happen. On a similar note, Matt's big heart and good manners were putting more tears into Moira and Pat's dry eyes, pumping fresh blood into lethargic hearts, quicker than the slicing of an onion or being chased by your neighbour's dog. They took turns, telling everyone how Matt was a true hound of the bloodline, for he had rescued them, helped them earn the respect of their fellow beings, those that mattered. It was not an easy thing done, but they had baked and gobbled their own fortune cookie. It was a matter to be proud of, and the more they thought about it, the more they realised there must be something special about them that everybody had missed, for why would Matt insist on keeping them in his company. Miss Nan knew why. If he had done things any different, the fools would have turned the family name inside out, given it the stink and the look of uncleaned tripe. She was not one to play with her words. Matt had handled the situation well, even giving Mona a very generous settlement, making it known that he would be the first one to offer his best wishes, should she marry her lover. Looking at them, Miss Nan wondered if Matt had ever really loved Mona. She knew their marriage had not been a happy one. She wished more for them, felt saddened. It was obvious Matt's mind had gone off elsewhere. Mona, for her part, could not keep her eyes off him, moving closer towards him, so that their hands almost touched. She might have had more luck if she just went ahead and kissed him fully on the mouth, for at least then, she would have had the satisfaction of having that last kiss. As it was, he pulled out his phone, checked his calendar, advised anyone who was listening that a new tournament had come about, that he would be gone for the next three months, but that he wished everyone well during his absence.

Rod jumped in at the same time, saying that he had plans to visit an art exhibition and that he too would be gone for a month. He asked Beth if she might be interested in going with him.

'Oh no, darling,' Beth shook her head. 'There is a baby on the way. You know I will be needed here.'

'I can take care of things, Mother,' Francis reminded her. 'You can go if you like.'

'And abandon my *daughter* in her time of need?' Beth cooed. 'Never, my darling. This baby is too important for that.'

Rod pulled Beth closer to him. She went still. Rod seemed oblivious to this reaction, raising his voice even higher, more than he needed to, he practically shouted. 'My wife may have many skills, but childrearing is not one of them,' and he winked at the Mistress, as she gracefully looked away. Rod's laughter dropped onto the listeners, stale wine filling up cracked glasses, When Francis arrived, wifey dearest nearly rolled him out into a phyllo pastry, the first night he slept in her bed. He brought out such a howl that Miss Nan came running, called for Mother, and that's how he got rescued, and set up in the nursery, permanently.'

A thunderous look settled over Beth's face as everyone, except the Mistress, enjoyed the joke.

'Yes, I remember,' Mona shook into life. 'Francis was toddling about, baby fat cheeks and the cutest waddle,' she stopped to laugh softly. 'Beth managed to find one of those diapers. I remember she said it worked better than any drainage pipe,' she looked at her parents and shook her head, 'She rolled him up, nice and tight, then Francis,' Mona playfully patted Francis on the shoulder. 'You went straight for the pool. Dropped in, and it was the only time I saw your grandfather move that fast, a scary thing to witness, and he yanked you out of the water, holding you up like a pint of beer, but then the diaper dropped, landing on the paving, and stayed there, looking like an inflated car seat.'

Now, everyone was laughing, even the Mistress had tiny butterfly wings fluttering at the corners of her lips. The only one selling hate, was the one in the green bow. Beth managed to hide some of her face behind that bow, but not before Miss Nan had seen the look on her face. She did not like what she saw. It raised the fear in her.

'Oh, come now, my sweetie,' Beth removed her arm from Rod's with some effort. 'You forget that we all have our moments. Remember the prom night. I had Rod on one arm, and your date on the other,' Beth laughed, but she was the only one enjoying herself. 'Why, you were so happy for me, watching me go around with two very handsome, young men, to help balance the weight of that crown,' Beth paused, patting her hair where the crown would have sat, and when she brought her hands down, the only thing missing was a cigarette in the one, as the other gripped the side of her hip, striking a poise that everybody finished off in their heads, 'Mona was always the independent sort. Made of something durable, I can never understand that type.'

Something moved across Mona's face. Whether it was years of neglect, trapped under her sister's shoes, or the look that Matt gave her, drenched in sympathy, the same kind he would give to an injured animal, either way, it popped a cork somewhere in Mona. She took a step forward, spat words out that squashed Beth's joy, and sent every pair of eyes reeling towards the ground in embarrassment. 'You might understand more if you paid attention to your husband,' Mona spat out. 'I've learned first-hand, he is also of that type.'

The glass dropped from Rod's hand. His mouth released itself, his eyes blinked open and shut, he had turned into a fish. At last, his brain processed the turn of events. He stopped looking at everyone else, took matters into his own hands, going down a path nobody saw coming, and instead of denying the sledge-hammered words, he gave them a body and a face.

Yes, it was one night,' he turned to Beth. 'But you were never around. And Mona was ready to jump out the window. I saved your sister, in a way.'

It should have stopped there. Things were getting out of hand.

'*And*' Mona beeped excitedly, clearly far from done, her face stretching with insane delight, as if she were pumped up with something combustible, and the more she fixed her eyes on Beth, watching the misery unfold there, on the other's features, the more eager she looked to feed the volatile situation. It was as if she had gone mad, lost track of her senses, 'By the way, Francis is not Rod's son.'

The collective gasp that filled the air had no time to rise. They watched as Beth flew at Mona, pulling at her hair, wanting to scratch her face, but Mona was not in the mood for intimidation. She pushed Beth off her, as easily as if the woman had been a broom. More aggravated than before, bent on causing more pain, she pointed a finger at Francis and said, 'He is John's son.'

Into the hushed silence, a gloom had fallen. The implications of what Mona had said were too great, the pain deep reaching. Francis had his hand over his mouth, Matti stood next to him, so perfectly still, she might have turned into an ice sculpture. But it was Rod who took matters into his hands, as he fixed Beth with an eyeful of pain, 'When?'

'Before we were married,' Beth said quietly, picking herself off the floor, she made sure to keep a distance between her sister and herself, 'I was already pregnant when I met you.'

Rod did not say anything. It was Miriam who put into words what everyone was thinking. 'My father? Is Francis my brother now?'

When nobody replied, Miriam said brightly, 'It's okay. My mum is a very forgiving person. She won't mind. As she would say, there's always space for more in the family.'

Nobody else shared her enthusiasm. It was too early, too out of place for such a quick change in matters. But for Rod, he had already worked things out in his mind. He went to Francis, whose hand was still over his mouth, and gently prying it free, he held the hand in the palm of his own, and in a voice that nobody had heard before, a gentle whisper, so that they strained their ears, not wanting to be left out, he said firmly, 'You are my son. Nothing changes that.'

He grabbed the boy, hugging him tightly. The moment stretched, lasting forever, and all the while, Beth, stood alone, her face masking her thoughts, but her eyes never lifted off the ground. All her secrets were out. Beth had lost everything.

Miss Nan, like everyone else, had trouble digesting the turn of events. But she felt no pity for Beth. Frogs never became princesses. That was how it went. Just as well. Beth's reaction, however, affected her in a way she did not like. The woman was just standing there, staring into the ground, as if somehow the ground might crack, offer her a cave, into whose depths the troublemaker would go, searching for more hearts to break. Oh, how could she sympathize with the woman, but in her own conscience, something whimpered. She was, in her own role, a woman contaminated by lies. How could she judge? The turn in events forced something back, made Miss Nan's eyes go bigger, as it brought back matters, she did not want to think about. The diary in her head released itself, the lock unlatched at last, barring pages that contained terrible secrets. She had kept them hidden, closed inside the nightmares that haunted her. If they had dug the Kimberley Diamond mine any deeper, they would never have reached her level of despair, or guilt. Those secrets she carried, a double set, overlapping into a single horror, that in the dark, when she lay in her bed, came to visit. It was no better than a young strangler fig tree. She heard those trees put roots so deep that they took over the host. The tree in her head put roots into her, and for years, she had fought the battle, the better part of her brain stayed adamant, refusing to budge. But now...

Her memories took her back, to that night, years into the counting, and the things she had seen, watching inside her head as it all happened again. She saw that witch, for there was no better way to say it. Beth, climbing out of the bathtub, the great swirls of fragrant steam blinded the mirrors, but not Miss Nan's sight, as she watched Beth slip into a white gown, then thinking herself truly cloaked by powers from the grave, the woman went and simply stared into a single misted glass. She uttered her confession, words so wild they had the power to stalk a person to death, and Miss Nan, she got attached to the sinister presence, frozen, standing there, holding an armful of bath sheets, the only witness to the words that filled the air like old cabbage stew. Beth had told the mirror, how she was already with child. A certain John's charitable act. That she, as new Bride of the Mansion, had deceived her husband, found herself a helping hand in a time of need. Miss Nan had an immediate sense of indigestion, took the tainted laundry with her, and made her way blindly along the corridor. Her feet took her straight into new trouble.

The room belonged to James, the eldest born of the Manion, and the nicest of the brothers. But he was not in his room when she entered. Carla was there. Miss Nan knew with a certainty that comes from good instincts, the only reason her body had taken her into that room, was to tell James the dreadful truth. She could not keep it to herself. The burden of it would have aged her, she was not bred to be a tortoise, carrying around that extra weight for the rest of her life. She was prepared to give all of that over to James, leaving the decision in his hands. But she was faced with Carla's back instead. Carla stood at the open window, looking out of it with her head turned to the sky. The sound of waves rushing to their doom filled the room, the moon was no chandelier, the eerie dim lighting was worse than the glow from the dinner candles. She did not like it, and beneath the towels that she still carried, her fingers clenched themselves into fists, so eager were they to switch on the lights. But it was not her domain, she had no say here. Still, as she watched the figure at the window, she knew first hand, that James and Carla were running around behind the Mistress's back, in the quiet, thinking their love made them invisible. People saw and talked, but for some reason the news had not reached the Lady's watchdogs, who at that time, were too busy chasing the neighbourhood cats, to worry about keeping their chief informed. The Mistress would pay an unthinkable price for their negligence. She liked to think of the Mistress by name, only in her head of course. She would never dare address her as such to the face. Certain things were just not done. In any case, affairs went from bad to nostalgic when Ania and Carla met, the two women, face to face, bright and early one morning. James introduced Carla as his friend. It was a mistake. Ania pricked her ears, kept her chin up, did an odd thing, and everyone watching agreed, that she rolled her pupils chameleon style, the one pupil fixed on James, the other one on the unlucky Carla. Not long after, she uttered the most infamous words of the day, and those words must have stuck the fork into poor Carla's chest. 'Yes, you will do for a friend,' the grand Lady said. 'But I do not see any other prospect ahead. My advice is do not attempt to cross the line. The Bride of this House and Family will not be common, there will be no other like her. If you ignore my words, nothing good will ever come from it.'

Word of that orientation spread faster than the time it took to scramble the morning eggs. It did nothing for Carla's reputation, putting her into the same spot as a hunted fox. She made a choice, and fast. It was to latch onto James, tighter than before. The pair grew more inspired to write their own tale of unrequited love and did it so well that Carla soon fell pregnant. There were rumours that the pair set up house in one of the unused rooms in the Mansion. The place was a maze, going deep into the architecture of the building. It had been sketched and built in the old school days, with hands that created dens everywhere, both inside the walls and underground. In a place like that, where brooms and mops would not go, people were convinced, the two had chosen to make a nest. Miss Nan herself, at first amazed at the skill of the story tellers, had to eat her bad thoughts up, for she was soon to become a part of that small circle. Carla came to her, confessed everything, taking her to the small room where an empty cradle sat. James had it secretly made by expert craftsmen who created the crib in a country far away, too far for anybody to walk to, and so it arrived by ship and sat there, waiting, a monument of change. Carla went into labour after that. The baby boy was rightfully brought into this world by the family doctor, whom Miss Nan fetched to Carla's door. It was not easy, but it was done. The good doctor pledged his support quickly, promising to keep the secret. He was more afraid for himself and what would happen if the Mistress ever found out. So, the plot primed itself for success. In any case, Miss Nan paused in her reflection, the thought only occurring to her now, that the child must have been watched over by an angel, one that put in overtime, for if Carla had not confessed to herself, it would have been the end to everything.

Unfortunately, it was Carla who went ahead and made a fateful mistake. She left the child unattended, in his cradle, just three months later, as if she had been summoned. Threading her way upstairs, appearing smack in the room that belonged to James, the unfortunate woman could never have guessed that once she entered the cursed room, she would never pass through that door again, at least not in the form she had taken since her first breath. Miss Nan gulped down a sigh, put her mind to the sieve again, letting the memories fall like flour, flashbacks that needed a good shaking and sifting. For she had reached the end too, wanted nothing more than to set the memories free. She saw Carla again, and in her mind the woman looked as if the brightest stars were shifting, leaving a space for her, as she stood at that doomed window, one so ill-fated to die young. What Miss Nan had seen that night, was a fairy like creature, an orb of translucent radiance, a supernatural ballerina, drifting in slow motion, tilting over in a way that human bones were not made to work, slipping over the ledge, gone from sight, more likely pulled away by that two- faced smiling moon. Miss Nan had never trusted that amateur ball of light, with good reason too. But while she had been standing there, her brain in shock, James ran in. He looked out of the window, saw the death act. What followed was more like a crawling of sorts, for he appeared to crawl, up and over the ledge of the window. Since he was no spider, he dropped out. His lips must have been pressed tight, so that in the following tortuous seconds, no sound shifted the air, and the sound of the sea had become too redundant to count. She imagined him cutting through the air swiftly, where the jagged rocks, still salivating after the last spearing, their towers and peaks dripping and waiting, took his life. She awoke, ran to the window, fear in her heart, her brain still. She got there to find the Mistress joining her. She must have walked in with James and witnessed the scene herself.

  The two women stood quietly at the window, watching with dread, as the waves picked up, the tide rolling in, smash after smash, keeping what lay on the bed of rock out of their sight, as if a timer had been set so that when one gulp of water covered the rock bed, the next was rolling in to cover the treachery. A strange thing happened next. A gust of air, as if it had been boiled in a pot with the lid on, suddenly rolled in, popping the lid, the steam escaped, heralded by the wind that was born from inside the room. The duo, herself and the Mistress, conjuring with each other in silence, felt the force on their backs, as the wind, sounding strangely as if it were made up of piano notes, unknown and haunting, left the room, as if it were sucked out, gone in a single breath. The only remaining sound, was of tiny Christmas bells, shuddering and tinkling, huddled by the moaning wind that roamed outside, over the sea. It was enough to drive a sane person mad. The piano notes returned, a rustling of leaves in Autumn, chilled prematurely by Winter, the music hit differently this time, a sourness that descended into the pit of the stomach, like the juice of fat yellow lemons, burning, uncomfortable. The ambience was round and dark, as if the musical fruit wanted their history told, of a citrus burst for the nose and a sting into the eyes. Now that the music notes had settled in their tummies, it moved them in circles, until it too rushed out of their mouths and out the window. Everything went quiet.

The Mistress turned to her. She saw the flickering orange, like a flame brewing, in the depths of those charcoal eyes. She imagined it was the same glow, the diminutive volcanic streaks, that slowly bit into the coal, just before the first flame broke through. Well, she had seen that ignition, once after, in the eyes of somebody else, and it was a rare sight.

'You understand?' Ania said under her breath, making as if nothing had happened, indicating with just the slightest tilt of her well-bred neck. 'We must keep the Family name, at any cost?'

Miss Nan took a while, she had not yet recovered from the double tragedy that lay unexplored, somewhere below the window they were both looking out of. But she snake rolled her eyes as if she were poisoned in her soul. It did not sit well with her, but Ania's will was the same as hers, and as she obeyed, she saw at the corner of her eye, two heads, two spies, peeping above floor level, hiding behind the heavy closet. In the next instant, they took off, running for their lives, as if each had a personal poltergeist chasing after. She understood what was expected of her.

CHAPTER TWENTY-SEVEN
THE MISTRESS
ANIA

The afternoon was an evil one, changing the course of life. Francis had lost his right in the line of succession. No matter how deep she searched, something inside her had woken. She tried switching her mind to other things, wondering why Kesh and the girl had not come back yet. In some remote part of her, a niggling worry raised itself, a maggot, soft bodied, the spawn of a house fly, edging itself on an adventure, coming out of hiding, from deep inside a forgotten supper. She shook herself free of the thought. It was disgusting. Yet, the feeling stayed, a premonition of a kind, as if the approaching night was not done with them, that something worse was about to happen.

'It's getting dark,' Nancy interrupted her thoughts, and she was thankful for once to be brought back, as the woman checked her watch. 'It's only seven, lucky not twelve. Still, that music sounds just like a ghost is playing it.'

'We must go to the tent,' Miss Nan interrupted with new urgency, and Ania, like one waking from a nightmare, realised they were stuck in one already. She missed her soft bed, the familiarity of the duvets and blankets, a crumpet of bliss, going strong over many years. That vaulted room, where she lay rolled up, snug as a sausage roll, had given her the luxury of a quiet shelter over the years. One that she took for granted. The pinch of the demented wind stole into her thoughts, as it tugged at her hat, crawling up her back, stabbing the point of her nose, so that it felt as if she had put an ice cream cone to her mouth, and let the tip of her nose taste the swirl of ice cream at the top. She forgot about her bed, thought instead how cruel the wind might be, going after a woman of her age. It carried on growling, intent on setting a course of madness, lifting the sand into their faces, stinging them like wasps out for revenge. The wind set itself up a few extra notches, sending some of the fancy wooden tables and chairs into the air. As the flying furniture shot straight up, a few smashed into the ground, and where others had not been hurled upwards, it was their turn to come alive, shivering and shaking, they hobbled in a wobbly march. She watched hopelessly, had no idea what to do. Mistress of a fancy Mansion, and where was her power now. It occurred to her, for the first time, in the grander scheme of things, the bank notes she had gone and stashed everywhere, they were never going to get up and come find her. The way she saw things now, the road had come to an end. It would be a far better deal to suck in her breath, stick out her chin, and face the barrage, head on, and those stashed bank notes, well, they could fry like hot chips. She felt such a fool, a coward. The wind moaned, reminding her that she was not getting off that easy – she deserved more – much worse. She managed a tight smile, it came of its own accord, she saw a few of the faces that had pained her in the past, stuffed into trash bins, the wind taking the garbage out to a place where the sea met the sky, far enough to never come back again, and close enough for the mind to see. She was getting ahead of herself, and the frigid wind, coming with its ancient fury, made that clear, with one blustery move, it nearly knocked her sideways into an undug grave. She moved closer to the others in the group, seeking herd immunity, something she had abhorred all her life. It was a hard life, made heavier by the art of etiquette, but she was no stranger to her flaws. She knew that her personage, put together from a need to survive, did not set her above the rest. It just enabled her to function better than the lot, to lead them to believe that she was a brand above the others. Ever since the loss of her husband, she had gained control of her mind. She told herself to make double sure destiny never shot itself twice, that she was safe in her own making. But all that control came at a cost.

The idea fetched Carla to mind, that girl whom James had brought home. She remembered the girl's untamed beauty, her abnormal behaviour, for one so low in status. Why, how could she ever forget that first greeting, when their eyes met, and the girl jumped into her head, so that it almost dropped in servitude, almost bowed to the newcomer. It was too much, so she took the Human way out, used her power and her scorn to humiliate the girl. She told herself she was doing it for James, that it was for his protection. All she had managed to do was leave behind a fat scar covering what might have been. Now, in this moment of the present, she found herself wishing for a second chance to put things right. That, when she had first spun her wicked ball of twine, it should have been picked up by the wind, and the threads scattered somewhere far away, so that the girl and her beloved son stayed safe. But now she knew, as if slapped by a thing of leftovers, a scarecrow, that in trying to keep the two apart, she had called the crows, home to roost. Why had she not seen that most people, the ones who were the first to pass judgement, had plenty rotting fish in their own kitchen storage. She had betrayed herself, and her own. The truth was a sad thing. She had known all about the culprits, even before they landed in front of her eyes. Her spies had brought her the news, of the lovers, jumping wilder than locusts, roaming everywhere. It irked her, the fact that she was left out, the last one to be told. But in the end, when the deed was done, she knew a mistake had been made. She saw it that day, in Carla's eyes, watched that girl's gaze flick, between James and herself, filled with arrogance and a dogged will, a calculating resolution forming in a stubborn, young mind. She knew that the girl was planning to stick it back to the grand old lady, the Indian Mynah. It was not a strange thing to have come to her mind, since she had read up on the species, had a great respect for those birds, especially the ones with the yellow rings around their eyes. They must have stories to tell, but in their wisdom and low-cost appearance, hardly anybody gave a snuff about their being. Well, she did, because she had always considered herself modelled on their type, a ruthless protector of her family. Bringing herself back into the present, she was in time to see the new trouble they were in.

The group she had joined, standing and staring as they were, caught the wind, as it brought a buddy, the ocean, to join in. Waves came crashing towards them, leaping fingers of spray, like eyebrows riding high on a bald head. As the freak energy subsided, the white fringed edges, like a bride's veil, swept over everything that had been knocked off the tables, taking some of it back, leaving a wet sopping mess of the others behind. The water only brushed the tips of their shoes, but still, it was enough.

'Come, we must hurry,' Ania broke the reverie, and the group rushed into the packed tent, to be drenched in the music and confusion that was now the beating heart of the place. All the sides of the tent, curtain drops that had been let down, squirmed like the arms of a restless squid, the wind punched and billowed, wanting free passage. The petrified crowd squashed itself into a human bait ball. Having lost their senses, the clump blinked, a circle of eyes that moved between the flapping tent and the piano player. When that frightened crowd spotted the Mistress of the Mansion and the ladies with her, they shrank further into themselves, so that she may go first down the path of terror and uncertainty. The space between the piano and the crowd was large, stretching like the gap left by two front missing teeth, and she crossed that quickly, realising only later she had done it alone. Both Miss Nan and Nancy had lost their will to advance and were now part of the bait ball. The lights had gone out, the inside of the tent remained cast in a strange light, an eerie shade of daylight, and through the large squares, the see through parts in the cotton canvas functioned as windows.

    A figure sat hunched at the piano, with a head full of hair that covered the shoulders and most of the face, fingers spinning out the notes frantically, working like a spider's legs. The music escalated into a carousel of madness, the notes twirling the brain around as if it were a piece of cheese, the demented pitch searing sensitive ears. Ania stood and stared, as the face lifted, slowly. She recognised Kesh's artwork. The thick layer of foundation was floury, the cheekbones polished with blush took on a bruised patchiness, the eyes had been given a thick bold lashing of black, so that when the tears started, they left a trail. All that was missing was a rogue moon hanging over the girl's head, with a ghost at hand to complete the effect. The entire thing was preposterous, the performance all too dramatic. She had to put an end to the novice acting. The nonsense had no hold over her. Ania took that determined step forward. But movement behind halted her. It was Ethan. He came in, striding angrily, his hair dripping, the little girl at his side barely keeping up with his footsteps. He stopped by the tight circle, raising his voice he yelled, as the maddening music continued in the background.

'What is wrong with you?' he pointed at Francis. 'I found her wandering on the shore. She was your responsibility.'

The child stepped towards Matti, and the ball drew her in.

No sooner had he uttered the words, than the music settled on him too. He left the girl with the safety of the crowd, marched forward to give Ania the complement of two. His raised eyebrows showed his confusion.

Fuelled by Ethan's presence, her confidence rose. She moved as if sword in hand, her mission was to take down the possessed doll, release the frightened crowd, restore order to the norm. When she reached the girl, she raised her hand, and slapped the face. It seemed to work. The fingers stopped.

The masquerade should have ended, but Ania saw something that grabbed her attention, the sight put her heart into misfire. Ania pointed at the ring on the girl's finger.

'What are you doing with that ring?' She hissed, shock and fear written on her face. '*Stop* pretending, we've had enough of this. Just tell me, where did you find that ring?'

She heard her voice quiver, felt the tightening in her chest. She had not seen the ring since that day – the day the body had washed up ashore. Carla's body. It was all there in the memory bank. She saw Miss Nan and herself head straight for the shoreline the night before, followed by most of the house folk. They saw James, in the ounce of a second's luck, lying on his bed of rock. The sea had not claimed him. He was already dead, unmoving. They could not approach him, the waves made sure of that, in a tide of violence, dashing and submerging his resting place, as if the sea wanted him pure, unsullied by the touch of Human hands, in that space after his death. The rain brought the balloons for the party, the extra that was needed to send everyone running for cover. She stayed. She waited, to hold James in her arms. But between the wind and the rain, both behaving worse than school bullies, she stood no chance. For the first and only time in her life, she passed out, right there on the shoreline, collapsed into a heap, that she needed to be hauled into the House, a fire set up in her room, and the family doctor called for. They would not let her out into the darkness, and she was sure that as her eyes struggled to keep focus, the faces of Miss Nan and the good doctor magnified in front of it. She felt a sting, and then nothing. When she woke, it was to a sunny morning, the birds were chirping in their misfit gangs, everything seemed back to normal. The visions of the night slowly returned, and as she pushed herself up into a sitting position, Miss Nan came to her, straight out of the armchair, from where she had been keeping a close eye on her. Miss Nan told her that James had been seen to, safely brought indoors at some point during the night. As for Carla, her body had washed up early the morning. She had personally seen to it that the two pairs of watching eyes, the star witnesses to the tragedy, the peeping faces in the room with that doomed window, were given new spectacles, that with it came a promise of secrecy and a stack of notes, enough to ensure the owners of those eyes did not have to work another day for the rest of their lives. As for that night, she had put the news out that James had fallen through the open window, an accident, one that could have happened to anybody. Carla's misfortune was put down to an unrelated drowning, and that was the story they stuck to. Carla had no family, so nobody came forward to claim her body. They took care of that too, giving her a separate burial of course, a quiet one. That same day, as she sat watching from her window, Miss Nan came in again, pressing the ring into her hand, she told her with a great big sigh, that the ring was the only thing of significance they had managed to find on the poor unfortunate woman.

James had a matching one, he went buried with it. She knew, she had been there for James. Now, the cursed item, rather the second of the twin, had come back to taunt her, the black ring mocked her, hugging the engraving of the lovers to its insides, knowing that she knew. It became a sign of her suffering and everything she had lost. That day, the one when her feet took her down to the shoreline, she had done something. Tossed that dreadful ring, the sign of bad luck, taken straight off the finger of that strange girl, somewhere between the gardens and the ocean. She could not remember. She had not been in a state of mind to recognise anything. And, after the omen was gone, a new sign emerged. The wriggling bundle on the shore, as it turned out, was a baby. It looked as if the sky had kicked it out. She had not questioned, simply picked up the baby, wiped her mind clean off the ring, went straight into her House, armed with the determination to start a new chapter.

Seeing the ring again filled her with rage. It was not something she a right to, this display of common emotion, but it consumed her, so that her hands moved of their own accord, reaching for the girl's throat, she had no clue what she was doing, but it felt right. Her ears collected the gasp of horror from the crowd, brought the sound to her, but it was too late. The intent to extract a horrible revenge for her loss, for a son who had been everything to her, filled her body, her mind. She could not make Carla suffer for the pain in her heart, the object of her hatred being safely tucked up on the other side of life, but the bearer of that dreaded ring in this world would be a nice substitute.

She was not thinking straight. She knew that, but she did not care. The same heart rot that destroyed so many trees on the estate, in that one year of devastation, following the death of her son, she had pushed out of her mind, thinking nothing of it, well, that torment returned, taking advantage of her weakness, bringing with it a loss that overwhelmed her aching body, reminding her of the pain she had suffered in that moment, when her eldest and dearest left. She was not ashamed to think it. That rot made a home inside her, over the years, the rot turned her insides into dust. There was nothing left. She was going somewhere else today, and she would not go alone.

A terrible gale flew inside the tent, stirring up the sand so that the guests stood like chickens in a dust bath, with the sand filling the air, the wind tackling them, they had become figurines, with wide eyes, as they watched their host in action. Ethan was the first to break free from the bewitching. He tried to pull the Mistress off the girl, when the girl abruptly stood up with the strength of an ox, in a sudden show of paranormal gusto, sending the Mistress flying off her, to land almost on top of Ethan. He was quick to react and found himself catching the Mistress with a quiet dignity that could have been rehearsed backstage. Making sure the Mistress stood firmly on her own ground, he turned to see the girl.

The sight put him on edge. She was standing now, raising her hands into the air, wriggling her fingers as if the air had hatched worms. She brought them down with a crash so that they pounded the keys. The powerful vibration resonated, with her leaning forward, a thing with its head almost at a right angle to the neck. He was certain there was no beating heart there, no more. It had been replaced with something else. There was no hope for rescue, and somewhere behind the eyeliner that dripped thin ribbons of black down her face, past the badly behaved lipstick that crept beyond the contours of her lips, smudging itself, as if she had deliberately run circles over her mouth with both hands, lay something inexplicable. The face looking back at them, and the only reason any sane person would keep the idea that it was still a face, came down to the fact that it remained attached to the rest of the body. The only moving part of that body came in the form of a pair of eyes, and even those rolled about from side to side, wary of the crowd like a frightened animal.

A full minute stole past, and nobody moved. The girl called the shots. She lifted a hand very slowly, the movement riding on punctuated seconds, as if the gesture were feeding life into her, in agonising doses. One finger unfolded, pointing towards the figure in the crowd. All eyes turned as one, every heart thumping so hard. The pointing finger led straight to Miss Nan.

CHAPTER TWENTY-EIGHT
CORAL – PART ONE

Her mind took her back, to the year she had turned fourteen. She had gone to the dentist. It was an odd time for any recollection, but she saw herself lying on the chair, looking at the man in the white coat with misgiving. An old assistant limped quietly by his side, and together, they looked worse off than a pair of starved hyenas, inside white jackets, having just missed their lunch. Fear moved within her, whilst she quietly nursed her paranoia of being there. Then she was told about the extractions, two of them, and the idea of playing dead grew more attractive until common sense intervened. She sent her mind off, to a better place, to the sea, where the salty air filled up her nostrils, and she could taste the ball of salt sitting at the back of her throat. She felt the pinch of a needle, could not be certain if there were more, since her mind fled and hid somewhere under that chair, but her mouth had gone numb, the pouches of her cheeks became nuggets of rubber, the sensation to clamp down and test bite drove her insane, it was her tongue that worried her most. It lay limp and heavy in her mouth, and she was sure she was never going to talk again.

When it was over, her mouth still felt dead, but she was irritated to discover that everything else was in working order. She had been too dramatic, and life was meant to go on as normal. She left the rooms, but instead of going to the bus stop, made a brave decision to go to the village park. She had never done something so impulsive before. It made her feel good.

The park looked deserted when she got there. It was arranged in a circle, with a small lake in the middle, but everyone knew that if you left that circle behind, and climbed the softly rolling hills that lay beyond, you would end up in the true heart of the park, where the trees fought for space, and the pathways were covered with soft petals. She had never gone that far out herself, but word got around. Now, she pressed on, eager to see the lucky bean trees which, according to everything she had read about, concerning the park, should not be that far away. As she passed the Wild Date palms, with the Tree ferns sucking the shade in, she was sure she saw movement out of the corner of her eye. It was a still day, so hushed that nothing had a right to move. She carried on.

From somewhere, a giggle broke the silence. She guessed there were couples hiding in the trees and shrubs, stashed far away from prying eyes and ears. Something she had not counted on. It made her sad. She wondered what it must be like to have a boyfriend. She never had one.

The trees she had been looking for came up. Picking up her pace, noting that she was now leaving the central space of the park and going into the denser, quieter region, she moved on, anxious to get to the lucky bean trees. She did not have far to go when the coral trees appeared. She saw the lucky bean long pockets, as she liked to think of them, all dark and clustered and ready to explode. They had chased away the flaming flowers, but there were a few flecks left on the branches.

Getting down on her knees, sifting through the dried grass, she found a red seed, with a black eye. She put it in her pocket, checked her wristwatch, and gasped. They would be waiting for her. She was late.

She got to the bus stop to find the bus over packed, the conductor cranky. The girl in front of her got in, but the conductor put up his hand, stopping her even before she got onto the first step. She tried her luck, using her numbed mouth, she attempted to give him a wide smile, having heard that a bit of female charm worked wonders, but she must have scared the guy, and got the doors shut in her face instead. When the next bus rolled in, she got into her seat, her heart thumping. She was in a lot of trouble.

Nancy waited for her at the gates. She was furious.

'Since when we take so long at the dentist? Nancy shouted. 'You want me to get into trouble with your father. I told you to go straight there and come straight home. Where did you go after that?'

Coral held her breath.

'What, you making up excuses in that useless head of yours?' Nancy snapped. 'You better tell me now. What, you got a boyfriend already?

Oh, how she wished that were true, but the boys were smarter than they gave themselves credit for, looking the other way, barely noticing she was there. It was a wretched design in the scheme of things – she had a feeling she was doomed to be alone.

Arya walked in just then, 'What were you doing at the park?' she asked, her eyebrows drawing together in confusion. 'Mia saw you there.'

'The park?' Nancy asked, puffing up, her eyes growing wider as each second put the puzzle pieces together. 'Which boy you went there to meet?'

'I didn't meet anyone,' Coral shook her head sadly. She brought out the lucky bean, holding it up. 'I went there to get this.'

'You're an idiot,' Arya smirked. 'You always get us into trouble for nothing.'

'A seed?' Nancy shouted now. 'You think I was born yesterday?'

Nancy took the seed and threw it into the air, 'Quiet like a cat, but carrying on behind my back. From now on, no such thing as roaming. You go straight to school and come straight home. Arya will walk with you. And tell your useless friends to stay away. Bad influence, that's what they are.'

'She has *one* friend,' Arya muttered. 'I have a dozen. Why must I babysit her?'

Nancy considered this for a small second, 'Right then, let Veru bring her home.'

Arya smiled, 'Thanks ma. I will tell Veru.'

'And as for you,' Nancy hooked Coral with a severe eye. 'You go wash your hands and come help me with the roti. Aunty Kesh is coming for supper, and on top of that, I got seven dozen to make. Your grandmother always said, better make more, never run short. Such an embarrassment, to make just enough, when you can have leftovers for the neighbours too. From now on, you will help me in the kitchen every day. Think you can have your own ways. I'll put an end to that so quick your head will spin. Young people these days,' she muttered to herself, 'Think they know everything.'

That day marked a turning point in her life. She learned that she could suffer in silence, that she could take a punch in the one eye and rely on the other to help her through. But she had never counted on the fact that there was a limit to everything. Her mind came back to the present. It seemed she had been kicked out of her own body. Her resolve finally broken, gone up in smoke. In the tent, with everyone watching, something had grabbed hold of her, and kicked her out. She watched her body move, standing outside of it, wondering how it was able to move on its own accord, as if it belonged to something else.

It was a funny thing to realise that her body and mind had each gone its own way. If she crossed the road on this one, took a nice long look at it from a different slant, it was the same as getting out of a coat, then taking a step back and surveying that hangered coat. Her body took the place of the coat right now, she was standing watching it, a mechanical thing, except the coat would have been easier to look at. She was not able to think of her body as her own, watching *it,* as it moved its hands and head. It twisted its neck around to look at her, eyes so weird, each pupil went its own way, spinning like the wheels on a bicycle, only at a slower pace, and it worked her up, to see this version of herself. Her range of view was limited, seeing that the position she found herself in, was preposterous and about as unimaginable as flying rabbits. But if her body had thrown her out, and she was forced to look at it, the image confronting her did nothing for her dignity. It was better that a roaming bear find it and put an end to the madness. In the meantime, her mind opened, bringing her bits and pieces of memory, and she started to piece them together, from her inevitable position. The impending situation was turning into a hostile negotiation, a joke really, for now she must play detective, if she wanted any chance to regain what was hers, she had to play the game.

It was not easy to catch her mind and hold it still, but she was the one asking the questions, drawing the confession from some part of her mind that had turned rebellious. It kept secrets, refusing to let her in. But she was firm, and fought with herself, until the events played out before her, as clearly as if she had the television on. Memory served up a particular day when she was back at the kitchen, in the Mansion, holding onto a tea tray, ready to go into the dining hall. As she left the kitchen behind, she was not aware of any presence other than her own. But then, she remembered how she had been violently jerked from behind, the intention was to lift her feet off the ground, for her to be yanked upwards, at an angle, the force was powerful, yet gut instinct told her somehow, no harm was meant to come her way. The tray however met with a different conclusion, as it crashed, the pieces of porcelain cracked, their white insides bright like snow. She saw the damage, heard the smack of the tray as it hit the ground, but her body slipped away from her, the something terrible was taking her out of the Mansion, drawing her by the elbow, marching her across the sand and onto the rocks, her footsteps were fast paced and rapid, the measurement between each movement was too small to make sense. And then her sight went away, the sea hung from where the sky should be, and her eyes shut themselves out of fright.

When she opened them again, her eyesight was restored, but better that it had not. She was in the water, thrashing about, drowning, yet her heart still beat, it thumped and bumped, telling her she was alive. She never learned how to swim. There was no time to think further than that. The flashback ended. She knew the rest, waking up in that unfriendly room in the Mansion, being hounded by Beth. Her mind refused to give up anything else that might help fit the pieces together, that rogue part, the chunk of her brain, the traitor hushed itself, and she was back to the present, looking at what should be her body, and the pointing finger. That finger was directed at Miss Nan.

The poor woman had turned to jelly, quivering in her spot, she looked as if she would melt from the terror. That dignified woman's heart could stop at any point now, the thought brought more pain. She had caused this agony by turning into something ugly and unwanted. All her secret pining and whining about her depraved longings and inadequacies made her vulnerable. Perhaps, she had created an alter ego, put all that pain into a part of her that thought it ran the show. Still, nothing explained how she got to be outside of her body, that physical arrangement of blood and bone and something else was sitting there, a demented thing, it had no place in the ordinary timetable of life. Whatever she had done, she was sure she might be dead now. How else was she staring at her own body. She must have turned into a ghost. She needed to tell everyone, to warn them. She tried, using her voice to call attention to her. There was no other way. But nobody heard. They could not see her. The realization did something to her. All her life, she had been fine, playing second tune to whoever held the fiddle. But now, she was sure if she got handed a bright red juicy apple, and if she was able to take a sizeable bite from it, then she would chomp on it and smash that sweet apple into the face of the first person she saw. She was tired of being nice, of staying the underdog, always checking her steps, laying herself down as a mat, for everyone to wipe their shoes on. The time had come to flick the light switch, press it so it went the other way, taking her conscience with it. Now that she was dead, who cared if she grew malevolent. If anything, it counted for experience and that was something she was short of. This feeling, an abandonment of herself, was different, in a dangerous way.

 Her eyes went to her body. She sighed, and after a while, she realised she wanted it back, and with that recognition, the bad ideas left, taking their bad vibes with them. She saw her body moving its feet, the terror in the watching crowd forcing them to cling to each other like barnacles, doing a better job than the sea creatures themselves, so that as they stuck together, it was difficult to separate friend from enemy. She felt sorry for the lot, they appeared so vulnerable. She wondered why she had ever thought less of herself. *They* were no better than her, not when it mattered. In that mood of discovery, like a bird scratching for crumbs, her family clicked into sight, the four of them, with Arya in the middle, huddling together like a blob of sticky toffee, so tight that a passing mosquito would have been robbed of a good bite if it had Arya in sight. The realisation hit home, painful, compounded by what she already knew. There was no place for her in that herd. Watching them connected like that broke her heart. She did not belong anywhere. If she never got her body back, she would exist as nothing more than vapour, but even vapour showed itself to the naked eye. Her fate was worse, and she made the deduction that she did not care.

Suddenly, like a match struck when darkness grows, a new fear took hold of her. The baby. She had to make things right for the baby. She must fight her way back, somehow. There was nothing else. She noticed her body had paused, feet still, the barricade of two people in its way. They shared the same spirit, it was easy to tell, from their stubborn pride and tenacity. The Mistress and Ethan moved her, their courage fed hope to a renounced mind. From her viewpoint, she saw Ethan locking gaze with her body, a misfit, towering above it, his arms folded, his chin lifted into the air as if he were headmaster and it a truanting kid. His stance comforted her invisible self, it pushed the panic down. She could not shout out to him, suffocating without a voice. Why had she never made use of her voice before. She had always held more than she needed. She had always had herself. Now, she had half of that self, but things were going to change. The walls of the house she built, the one in her head, the gloomy, dark one, suddenly showed windows punched into them, with latches for safeguarding. She allowed herself to feed on the glimmer of hope.

Her body was moving again, it went at a lopsided angle. The crowd groaned. It was more than the combined lot could bear. She caught a glimmer of terror reflected in Ethan's gaze too, but he stood his ground. The body, with hands that moved to pulsating seconds, inched its way towards him. The jiggly hands latched onto his shoulders, quivering there, as if they would move up to his face, as if whatever compass it was using had malfunctioned for the moment, providing a resting place. The head on the body clicked a notch, the eyes rolled feverishly around, until finally they found each other. The eyes stopped spinning, focusing on his face in a rare space of time. By now, the Mistress had enough. Her body and mind would not hold on any longer. She teetered on the spot, and a few feet stepped outside the circle of heads, long enough to quickly drag her back into its fold, from where they all watched. Ethan was left to fend for himself, but that look of terror was not there anymore. Compassion filled his eyes, as he held the unblinking stare of the creature. She did not know for how long they looked at each other, only that she was starting to feel something, as if her physical body were once again attached to her. The nausea hammered her body into a darkness from which she awoke, to nothing else but an intense sorrow, burrowed somewhere, so heavy that the tears flowed down her cheeks. She was back in her body, but it felt as if her heart might break, that it was a borrowed piece of glass, that if she did not die now, she might spend the rest of her life wishing she had. It was too painful, the kind of pain that burns from the inside, robs the breath, tortures the memory, kills the soul. Yet, it was not her memories that she saw. It was the recollection that belonged to somebody else. The attachment of someone else's memories, that brought back a life lived in furnishings that were not familiar to her, but the final relinquishing of a hold, the turning of a back, forever in its finality, to foot worn floors, furniture that had become closer than family, to say goodbye to the kitchen where the old mugs sat in chipped rows, and the kettle that had boiled its way into silence. The sadness filled up every inch of her body so that she knew somehow, the end of a chapter was near. The accessory, the holder of those memories that had kitted itself to her finally detached itself. It left. Just as quickly as it had entered, it was gone and she was back to herself, fully now, her mind and body put together in relation to each other, attached and whole. She still felt the sadness, but it had weakened itself out.

She pulled herself up into a sitting position. It was as if she were looking at everything through a sight reborn, that the people around her were as fresh as newly hatched eggs. But the hour of bewitching went swiftly past, peace broken again as Nancy made her way towards her, the shade of her face appeared monstrous.

'A big disgrace,' Nancy was saying. 'Dragging our family name through the mud, like a mad thing. What your father and I did to deserve this I don't know.'

She was in front of her now, her eyes big and round, her mouth twitching at the corners from anger. 'Get up, we are leaving, now, now.'

She was too tired to move. Her body was drained, her mind light so that even with her mother giving the commands, she could not summon her body to obey. She looked up at her mother, willing her to change. She needed her to understand, to love her.

'Why you staring at me like that for?' Nancy snapped. 'As if you seeing a spook or something? That will be funny, coming from you. Tell me something, I want to know, why you can't be like your sisters, look at them, both got rings on their fingers. I don't' understand, but I'm telling you, it's your father's fault. From the time you were born, with that name he gave you, it started all the bad luck. I knew something was going to go wrong. And I was right, performing like this in front of all this people. You brought disgrace to our family. Tell me, who's going to marry you now?'

Nancy shook her head, 'I don't know why we have so much trouble. You are going to put us in the gutters,' she paused to draw breath. 'Now get up. Let's go.'

Coral gave up the fight. She would obey and bring her body to do what was required of it. She stood up, like a rickety old thing, and managed to take a wobbly step forward, and just then, Miss Nan spoke up.

There were words coming out of her mouth, falling over each other, roughly jumbled in fast flowing sentences, short words like bricks going up into a wall, plastered into place, bites of substance that held space, nuggets of truth, fitting into each other, to reveal a truth that when built up, resembled a logic that brought home a story from the ashes. She left nothing out. Miss Nan had placed the baby on the shore that fateful night, no sooner had she heard the Mistress was going out for a walk. She had been left no other choice, the dignified lady pleaded, but to keep the child in the family and hide the truth. There was no other way around it.

Everyone listened. When the poor woman was done, the wind had stopped, ushering a silence into what was left of the tent and its people. Their ears, pricked to attention, listened to the power of a truth that had forged its way into the present, an alien force that refused to lie down, born of a hunger, to bring word from the grave. It echoed more significantly than the taps brought back to life after a drought.

The Mistress was the first to move. She seemed to glide, as if she were brought out of a movie, an ice queen, covering distance on a frozen floor, with all the ambience fed by a strong ancestry. She faced Ethan, put a hand on his shoulder, tilting her chin up at him, she gave him the same recognition as if a family crown had been placed on his head. He was their future, the grandson and heir that finished the circle. It was all said and done in that silent gesture of dignity, of glorified power that comes once in a lifetime.

'I wish I had given your mother the chance that I now give you,' Ania spoke loudly, firmly, 'I was afraid of the unknown, and she presented that to me. I should have approached things differently. Please forgive me. An old woman, who will in due course, pay her own debts.'

For his part, Ethan embraced the woman, his strength and dignity leading the way for a new generation. It was a moment to seize, and it burned itself into the memories of the onlooking crowd, that finally detached, an entanglement that broke, restoring old resentments. Everything was back to normal, so that the everyday tidings could go on.

When the two turned back to the crowd, it was Nancy who broke the spell. She was already shouting out to Arya, calling her forward, ecstatic in her motherly tones of victory.

'I told you,' she yelled at Kesh. 'I always said Arya was going up. Now look, if she goes any higher, she'll fall off the hill. We must cook and feed the village when we go back home, to give our thanks.'

Kesh was nodding her head, slowly, still recovering from the drama. She pushed Arya forward, 'Go girl. Go take your place next to him.'

Arya blushed, and all eyes fixed themselves to her, she moved like a queen, her head up, her shoulders straight, her beautiful figure and face cutting an impressive sight.

When she took her place next to Ethan, the pair were so well fitted to each other, both in looks and height, that everyone felt inclined to dip their heads in acknowledgement of the great union. They were blessed by a new couple, by the continuation of a great bloodline, and nothing in their eyes could convince them otherwise. Ethan held the future, and in his hands, their future rested, a collective whole. Nobody was more fitting to the role than him. And the woman, whomever he chose to take, well, that woman would be their queen. What could go wrong with a pair that were blessed with such beauty and promise sent from above.

CHAPTER TWENTY-NINE
CORAL – PART TWO

She was allowed to stay, until the wedding was over. It was due to happen in a day. A compromise had been reached. She was left on kitchen duty. She was happy to be there. It was the thought of returning home with her family that troubled her.

She had no idea what would happen once the baby was born. She did not want to subject her child to the hardship of growing up in a place, following the pattern of her old life. She knew deep down, the icy mindsets and rigid preconceptions that most people kept, were never going to change overnight. She did not blame them. It was their right to choose for themselves, to form their own footpath, take those along with them, who wanted to keep things the same. She did not want that. Not for her child. Not for herself. But choice did not form a pact with the life waiting for her, compromise had offered her a grim alternative, and she knew in her heart, happiness could never be hers, not when it came at the expense of another. Arya and Ethan were made to be together. Their wedding would soon put everything to rest. She wanted to tell them about the baby, that at least, her child might have a chance at a life that was different. But she knew her sister well enough to keep her mouth shut. She was in the end, the odd one out. She had formed a ladder, used poison ivy, worse, had taken advantage of a sleeping man, done her sister in. But in truth, that night, on the beach, when the storm pierced the heavy clouds, she could not stop herself from loving a man who was not hers. It was she who carried a love for him, an unrequited love, a curse that stalked her, all times of the day and night, lighting up her insides whenever she saw him. The feeling had grown worse, with time. She felt as if she were wearing her feelings like a flamingo, the pink colouring getting more radiant with every heartbeat, and like that elegant bird, twisting her neck, scooping up every second of his presence as if lost in a feeding frenzy, hooked onto the echo of his voice, unable to tear herself away from him. Oh, why was she made to suffer this way. The tears should have dried out by now, been enough to germinate an impressive weeping willow. But not a single tear fell. That would not suit her. She had to take it a whole yard further, spare her eyes from the degradation of a simple right to do what they were meant for, rather let her heart weep in silence, a heavy mourning that had no sound, no physical witness, but a deep hollowness, an entrapment, that carried on, like a stray dog seeking love in silence. That way, the torment was real, a consuming punishment, a befitting way to suffer.

Retribution in her case arrived swiftly, in the form of a confirmation. She was to return home, day after the wedding. She was going back, to a place where the sun rose every morning to the chatter of life, that came in borrowed chimes from the walls of the neighbouring house. And where the sun set to the clatter of dishes washed and stacked away, the breathing of a hard life showed in the worn soles of the shoes left on the other side of the front door. She wished better for her child, but fate had decided.

Her thoughts were interrupted by the door to her thatched home swinging open. It was more likely kicked open from the other side. The intruder stepped into the small space, leaving the door ajar.

Coral got up from the small kitchen counter where she had been sitting.

'Don't come any closer,' Arya snarled, her face contorted with anger, the beautiful features marred by a nasty scowl. 'Stay there. The way I feel now, I might kill you.'

Coral sat down.

'Tell me,' Arya scrunched her eyes, her face plastered in afternoon makeup, the beauty hiding something awful, her fingers pointing, the painted ends waving, 'Is that Ethan's child?'

Coral tried to make her lips move, to dislodge the cruelty, of deceiving herself and her child, but in that bit of space, Arya beat her to it. Arya pounced on the time delay, embracing the deceit, scooping her talents together, she combined her keen senses and spotted the expression that flashed across Coral's face, studying it with the speed of a predator. Arya's eyes were getting rounder, growing wider and larger, like twin mirrored pieces of glass, unnaturally primed, like the eyes of the owl, yellow and primeval, 'I knew it. You crept into the tent, that night, and took advantage of my sleeping fiancé, didn't you?'

'Yes,' Coral admitted, although she should have said that Ethan found his way into her tent, but she did not want to divulge the truth, hanging her head in shame, then brought it up quickly, 'But he doesn't know it was me. He thinks it was you.'

'*Ohhhhhhhhhh,*' Arya barked. It was a howl, one that should have brought any wild dogs in the vicinity, to her side. It brought Veru. Delirious with worry, mad with thought for her sister's welfare, Veru appeared, her sister's caretaker, the look in her eyes glowed with a hunger for revenge, a direct retaliation to the words she had heard, from her hiding spot, somewhere nearby. It was a fellow beast Arya had cried out to, and her new recruitment moved with the same grace as the leader, taking the spot next to her sister, having chosen the one sister over the other.

'So, it's okay, because *he* doesn't know?'

What could she say, faced by the two, it sent her mind off to the wild, and she started thinking of wild dog ears, ravenous eyes, and primitive instincts, a blood thirsty pact to protect their own, a circle that kept them in, and her out. Her sisters wanted revenge, and when it mattered the most, her instincts went dead. She was tired, did not have the energy to make a stand. She had been standing alone for too long. It had taken its toll. All she wanted was a nice soft cushion for her tired body to sink into, the pressure on her back made her give thanks for the support of a spine, the baby kicked as if had a football to land, the foot got stuck in the side of her belly, would not relax, protruding from under the light dress she wore, like a stone on a grassy path, when the lights are out, and a goblin rises, in the form of a sharp toothed piece of rock, showing its flat eared, shark shaped head. And then, the lonely wanderer hits the rock, gets a red toe, maybe more. She told herself to wake up, get back out of her dreams. Her ankles were far too swollen, fat with pain. Luckily, the baby was settled now, taking whatever part of it that was sticking out, back into itself. But her troubles had a long tongue, and a round nose, for that type of trouble rarely subsided, once it got started and heated up, it simmered somewhere inside, forcing her body to hoist itself up onto feet that were already strained.

'You horrible thing, you piece of deceit, stinking rotten garbage, you think it's okay, because he thinks it was me?'

'But it's not like that…'

'Then tell me,' Arya spat through gritted teeth. 'Like what was it? Huh? You seduced my fiancé, left evidence, so I would know, and expect me to feel sorry for you?'

Veru gasped, as if hearing it for the first time. But Coral knew the display lacked authenticity. Still, the words made her feel worse, the throbbing pain uplifted its status to a stabbing, so that she put a hand to her swollen stomach. Her sister was not wrong. She could have stopped things from going as far as they did. She had not known, back then, that Ethan and her sister were going to find each other. She would never have let things progress to any point, had she guessed. She could have slapped the sense into Ethan and asked him to leave. She found out, too late, painfully, that Ethan thought he was with Arya. She was the guilty party. For that, she owed her sister the silent respect to keep that night's events to herself.

'Yes, I seduced him. He thought it was you.'

Arya was not expecting that. She put her hands to her temples, shook her head, and at this point watching her, Coral wondered if it ran the risk of falling off. Her mouth hung open once she was done with the shaking, her hands went to her hair, and there they ran a busy preoccupation. Arya ruffled up her hair, until with the static it stood on its own, before she finally took out her frustration on her face, running her palms downwards over the made-up features, stressing the eye make and lipstick, but this time they held their own under the pressure, did not smudge at all. Irritated, probably sensing so herself, she bit down hard on her bottom lip, until it started to bleed. The tantrum had run its course.

'I'm going to kill you,' Arya screeched, rushing forward so quickly, as if she were airborne, kicked from behind by a horse, both would have had the same result anyway. 'You will never take what's mine.'

She had no time to escape. Arya's hands wrapped around her throat, closing so tightly that her own hands went up automatically to pry them away. But Arya was stronger, her grasp fuelled by hate, nails, manicured into perfect daggers pierced into her skin, drawing bubbles of blood, scratching, ripping, so that her hands fell away, and she quietly resigned herself to the fate that she deserved.

But things were not going to end so easily for her. The tiny Nancy appeared, with extraordinary brute strength, managed to do the impossible. She pulled the two of them apart, as easily as if she were pulling at a chicken bone, a wishbone to be precise, like those times when she placed both hands on either side, to see which hand, her right or left, would fetch her more luck, the bigger piece when the bone had been broken, of course bringing the luck. Usually that act was meant to be taken up by two different people, but in Nancy's case, she wanted all the luck for herself. Now, her girls like the two broken pieces of the chicken wishbone, looked over her head at each other. They were not equal pieces of the broken bone. Ed and Kesh arrived, taking their places with the lucky side, beside Arya.

'You stupid thing,' Kesh scolded Arya, then remembering her share in the rewards, quickly changed her voice, puckered up her painted red lips, and cooed. 'My sweetie, imagine if Ethan caught you, looking and behaving like this,' she quickly patted Arya's hair down, wiped the blood away gingerly from her lips with a face cloth that she always carried. 'You must press your foot on the accelerator, honey, don't tramp the brakes, or that wedding band will never come. You're so close, I can see that wedding tomorrow, imagine our status after that. Brings tears to my eyes,' and her mind thought of her son and daughters, how mothers like herself, yearning for status, would be lining up outside her front door, 'You just think about Aunty Bomi,' and here she paused, to give her brother a wink. 'That sour fig, sister of ours, but useless gossiper, with all the things coming out of her mouth about our family. Now, she will come, and see with her own two eyes how we have risen,' Kesh had to stop, to give herself breath, the excitement was building up in her chest, not good for the heart. 'She will go pumping the grand news, herself, from street to street. Let's hope she bites her tongue if she dares to lie,' and now Kesh picked up Arya's hands, remarking with shock, 'look at how you chipped your nails. But we will fix it, don't worry my dove.'

Arya pulled her hands away, as Kesh continued, glancing at Nancy, 'See what good comes when my brother marries a decent woman. The children bring us fame.'

She had caught Nancy's attention, who returned Kesh's look with a proud dip of her chin. Inwardly, Kesh recoiled, but it was time to side with the greener side. She gave Nancy a slight nod. It went further than what their old relationship had the decency to demand.

'Yes,' Kesh continued, unaware she was trespassing on dangerous water. 'Our honey is going to give us what we rightfully deserve. This sweetie, she is landing a prince of a man,' she paused, secretly wishing the fortune had come for one of her daughters, thinking Nancy's girls were not brought up right, fighting as they were like chickens over a rooster. Her girls had more grace and tact, brought up like their mother. In truth, she had never liked her sister- in- law, always thinking her brother had married beneath his standing. But that was not important now. 'Your mother was always right,' she nodded at Arya. 'You were meant for something better than the rest of us.'

'Oh, just shut up,' Arya yelled. 'Stop with your honey this and sweetie nonsense. Do I look like a bird or your pet dog. Just stop it.'

Kesh found the grace to look away.

'As for her,' Arya shouted, pointing a finger at Coral. 'She doesn't know her place.'

'Why,' her father asked. 'What has she done?'

'Nothing much,' Veru put in. 'Except steal Arya's boyfriend, get pregnant, and now she plays the victim. I write her off, from this second, she is nobody to me.'

Veru folded her arms, took her chin into the air, and looked away.

Ed suffered an attack of shock, delivered swiftly to his forehead, and he held it with one hand, whilst he looked upwards, his head bent in an awkward stance, blinking in the daze that was new to him, his feet rooted to the floor.

'I told you,' Nancy wailed, being the quicker one to react, 'Gone too big for her boots. The single chance we got she must come show her true colours. One thing is going to happen today, either your father has a heart attack or Kesh,' she turned to her sister-in-law. 'You leave now. Take this one back home.'

Kesh shook her head so fast it went from side to side quicker than a devil wind, 'No. I want to dress up for the wedding. Everybody will be there. And I got an outfit already. She will behave,' she nodded her head towards Coral. 'Or we'll just lock her up and leave her here, wait until the wedding is finished. Why should we have to miss the wedding? Because of her? And she is spoilt with that rotten attitude, stealing her sister's boyfriend? I'm telling you, she has no chance, look at Arya. Now, she got the looks to fit the moves.'

Ed spoke at last, softly, 'She is our child as well.'

'Child?' Nancy scoffed, puffing out a generous breath through her nostrils. 'She is spoiling our name, and you feel sorry for her? That's why they always say, never let a man rule the house. He knows nothing. Now, shut up and let's do what Kesh says. For once, your sister knows what she is talking about.'

Kesh looked confused. Just for a single second, she was at a loss, her enemy from before, now her buddy in strife. She took it like a cheerleader, picking her head up, she looked down on Coral.

'I will do as you say,' Coral mouthed numbly. 'I won't do anything to cause trouble.'

The pains had subsided, somewhere in the hassle. She just wanted to be left alone. It suited her perfectly, even if they locked her in.

'Listen to her mouth,' Kesh said angrily. 'Talking like she is above us. What do you think, can we trust her?' she turned to Nancy. 'You know, if any of my girls made trouble like this, I would have taken these hands,' she held up both her palms for all to see, 'And wrung her neck like a farm chicken. You are too nice, sister-in-law. That will be your downfall.'

It was Nancy's turn to look confused now. It seemed like Kesh was paying her a compliment, twisted in the reprimand for not holding her ground. That, she equated to an insult. How dare the woman question her authority. It was time to show Kesh who was boss.

'No,' Nancy shook her head; 'We won't lock her up. What will the people say, when everyone finds out, that I locked up my own daughter? They won't see the pain I'm feeling. Or the pain she put on her sister. No, they will talk about me like I am a witch. I say we trust she won't open her mouth, or else.'

Nancy looked at Coral, using up her motherly rights, picking up her shoulders, she seemed to rise into the thatched ceiling. 'If you do anything to hurt Arya, we'll make as if you never existed, you understand? *I* will never forgive you. You will become nothing to this family, and you, our daughter,' here Nancy titled her head towards Ed. 'Will be dead to us.'

Ed bowed his head, under the weight of the words. But nothing came out of his mouth.

For some reason, the old question of love and obedience entered Coral's mind again, coming from a time, that seemed to be eclipsed into another era. She had once chosen obedience. Nothing had changed.

'I promise. I won't let the family down.'

CHAPTER THIRTY
ETHAN

It was his wedding day, but deep down he felt different. He tried to net his thoughts, bring them together and make sense of them. No good came of that. It was misty, this instinct, that barrelled its way up his gut, gathering into a dense fog it clouded his senses, made him feel as if he were the candy floss at a carnival, rising high, ripe for the taking, sinking into nothing after the bite. Something was wrong. He knew it. It had to do with the woman he was about to call his wife. And what did the other girl, her name never made sense to him, for what was she to him, but she was there like the fog that roams the plains, on a cold morning. *Coral.* He had nightmares, excursions of something lying next to him, as if it owned that space. When he opened his eyes in that dream, *the girl* was lying next to him. He would reach out and hear her mouth his name, in a voice, as foreign as if the sea had spoken to him. But in that spare moment, like a movie ended on cue, he awoke, to find the nightmare finished, yet the feeling lay curled inside him, sinking into his gut, merging into his blood, so that his body reacted as if this were normal. He did not sweat, did not feel upset. It was as if it were the most normal thing in the world to dream of this girl, to share an uncommon connection with her, and then to wake up from it, and expect to move on in life as if the nightmare and its object lay peacefully sleeping inside him. That the enigma would vanish. It was foolish.

It was not fair, especially to the woman he was going to name his bride. But he could not escape the feeling, that gnawing, it munched on his insides, eating away at him, a silent night worker, raising havoc in the quiet. He got up from the bed, convinced that a good shower would set him right.

The good shower only made him feel worse. Standing in front of the mirror, dressed as the groom, his image looked back at him, shouting words of abuse. He had done wrong. But what was it that lit his soul on fire? His body and heart, about to be given to his bride, the woman he shared his being with, that night in a tent on the fringe of the robust ocean – under a moon that gave them a blessing, that woman was set to become the centre of his world. He did not give a green bodied fly's behind about what others thought, and he knew many had their opinion, but for him when he said those vows, his fate and that of the woman wearing his ring, they would become one. She would have him, his undying support, no matter what, until the day the last breath wafted out of his body. Perhaps, it had something to do with the missing denominator in his life, his childhood spent craving for someone he could call his own, being left loveless, not connected, with anyone, in the same way a child craved love. In his adult years, he learned to make his own way, to breathe inside a bubble, the breathlessness made a silent will with his inner spirit, a sacred place, where no human contact might ever shatter his carefully built haven. But then, it was shattered, his peaceful life shifted, one that had its origin at the fingertips of his newly found heart, Arya. The pact was unbreakable. And yet, he had no idea what love was. He could not fathom if it was meant to be a feeling, or a branch that reached out, drawing him into the tree itself, becoming a part of something whole, a network of roots and leaves, a sense of belonging in an existing framework, where one was dependant on the other. All he knew was his word was his own, and he had given it to Arya. Better a bullet rip through his heart, than he turn his back on the vows made to a decent woman.

The rap on the door brought him around. He pulled it open, to find a smiling Francis on the other side, in a blue suit with a burgundy tie. His best man, his family. Seeing him in the ensemble, it made for a colourful escapade, and Ethan smiled. He felt a moment's peace, and in that smile, he wondered about his own appearance, but he should not have wasted the effort. Francis was having a rough time keeping his face straight.

'Colour suits you,' Francis said sternly. 'You could have gone the extra mile and got your hair done too, bro.'

They laughed, sharing the special moment, just as Francis reached into his pocket, producing a bright red rose, he planted it into Ethan's pocket. 'A gift from the wife,' he rolled his eyes, 'apparently, it will provide the extra touch.'

'And it does just that,' Ethan laughed, as the mirror reflected a burgundy figure, from shoulders to shoes, the only mark of difference being the red rose and his dark hair, and that he had left untouched.

'Hey man,' Francis beckoned him from the doorway. 'I know Matti is going to kill me. We must go, I promised to bring you, perfect and in one piece, to deliver you on time, straight into the arms of her bestie. Time's up.'

Ethan joined him, as they made their way through the corridors.

'You remember those words we sang, when we were in school,' Francis said out of the blue. 'When we were so young. Something about girls being a hundred per cent made up of everything nice. Just a heads up, brother to brother, you never lived to tell a story, not until you have a wife.'

He wondered why Francis would offer him this bit of advice, just as he was about to be married. He got his answer soon enough.

'Still, it's worth it,' Francis continued, 'if you are marrying the right one. Your soul mate, the one who melts into your heart, as if you knew this person, from someplace before, and when the eyes meet, it's like you are home. It's funny, I know she has faults, but for me, Matti is in my heart. it's like she lives there.'

It was an uncommon admission of delicacy, and between the two men, a show of emotional attachment, a glue that brought their relationship to a new level of understanding, of bonding. Ethan put the man at ease, his hand on the shoulder of the man he considered his brother. It brought him back to the comfortable space. Francis landed a soft punch on his shoulder, and he returned it, but unknowingly, Francis had just sent his mind off, like a rollercoaster, doing the highs and the lows, the thrill bouncing his heart, but there was no steadying force, no awakening of the spirit, that he might want to jump off that coaster, to call the name of his other, to save her, to save himself.

It was too late.

'I am ready,' Ethan heard his voice play the keynote. 'Brother,' Ethan looked at the man who had become so much more to him, 'let's do this.'

'Let's,' Francis replied, as they left the twisting corridors behind, to trace their steps down to the beach, back to the place of that night, where a love watched over by the stars and christened by the sound of the sea, had merged, a natural thing, an unexpected act that had changed his life forever. But it was not a random coincidence, he told himself reassuringly, and with each step that took him closer, the haunting wrestle of his mind with his heart settled. He knew he could never walk away from his commitment. His future, he told himself firmly, belonged to Arya. Whatever doubt had played with his mind, he was not strong enough to question it. He would stay true to her, pick her up in her worst failings, be a good husband to her, the kind that kept the tears away. He would do that, for her. The curse of his loneliness ended with him. He would see to it that she never felt that pain. His feelings did not matter. Not when Fate gave him the chance to start over.

CHAPTER THIRTY-ONE
THE BEGINNING OF THE END

She was ready, the lucky one who had landed a shark -everyone agreed it was the biggest catch of the time, and all hers to keep. She had caught it, branded it, earned the reward, a big, fat ring sparkling on her finger. People were busy, whispers went around that the ring must be worth more than ten times the value of what most people's houses cost, and when Ethan put the wedding band on today, she was sure she could buy herself half a town, with change left over. The idea brought her chin up, a slight chuckle escaped her lips. Not bad for someone who had no former training in much, but she had played the game and won. She had done the hard work, now things were going her way. She planned to make the best of it.

With her head held high, the sun bounced off her forced curls, the spray had made then stiff, causing them to stick together like a couple of guppies, newly hatched and bullied by the tide, all going in the same direction, but with time, Matti's hairdresser had assured her, the curls should, like dough when it is put into the oven, rise up into bouncy rolls. The tin of silver dust they had emptied over her head must be holding its glow now, the shine painting her like a princess, in her short, burgundy dress, the expensive material trimmed low at the back, cut carefully at the front, hugging her thighs so tightly, as if the material might rip. But there was a reason for that special cut. Her steps were small and measured, to bring attention to the high heels that had been specially designed for her, Ethan had them made according to her specifications, and flown in for this day. There was not much covering the sandals, just a strap here and there, but the heels, those were longer than pencils, and thinner than the lead that filled the insides of them. The balancing act was impressive. She was proud of herself, not knowing anyone else who had the nerve or confidence to stand in her shoes. She smiled proudly as the marital arch came into view, covered in the colour of her heart, an arch so magnificently stacked with burgundy flowers, put together by her fiancé, it pulled at her heart, made her want to cry. She held on tightly to Matti, whose arm was linked into her own.

Matti. It was hilarious how the tables had turned. Now that the truth was out, Ethan stood to inherit almost everything, as head of the family, and only child to the deceased eldest brother, James. Everyone knew James had been the firm favourite of the Mistress, soon to be former Lady of the Mansion. Yes. That position would go to her, just as soon as the missing band got onto her finger. She needed to put on some weight, she told herself slyly, to balance out the gravity of her new power. She was going to be married to a man who never did anything halfway. She did not have far to go to see that for herself. Looking towards the front row, she saw them all lined up for her, everyone on their feet. Ethan had embraced everyone, welcomed them into his family circle. Now that her family and his were to be joined, he had given his permission to Kesh and her parents to invite anyone they fancied. It was a dangerous thing to do, she chuckled to herself. The crowd was large, and she did not recognise half the faces turned towards her. It made her feel significant, almost superior in a way. And to think, she would soon be Ania's equal. Yes, she preferred to think of her by name. Things were different now. But Ania had surprised them all, being one of the last of her kind, dignified and rarified in her old ways, had bent the rules, cried real tears of joy for a full thirty seconds when she found out her precious grandson was there, to save the family, and the day. She had kissed his forehead, breaking every rule that she had so painfully laid down over the years. The news had spread. But it was clear that she loved Ethan. It showed on her face, a very strange thing to happen to such a resolute woman. And then there was Miss Nan. The change in her was remarkable. If Arya did not know better, she would have sworn that Miss Nan had secretly adopted Ethan. With both grand ladies tucked into his shadow, Ethan was already more settled than anybody she knew. This only meant that the woman he married, well, here Arya bent her head briefly, finding the emotion overpowering, could enjoy a level of power, unknown to anyone else. She pulled tighter on Matti's arm, looking sidewards at her maid of honour. Matti, true to her loyalty, looked ordinary and insignificant, dressed in the palest blue dress, a long thing that started from below her neck, going all the way down to her toes so that not even her shoes were visible. She was glad that Matti understood her, that she never did anything to upset her, and she knew her place. Matti was not one to take away her limelight. Personally, she did not care much about Matti, although she felt bad for her, since Matti had miscarried recently, and with the pregnancy gone, she had become rather dull and boring. She was still useful to her though, having replaced both her idiotic sisters. Veru and Coral had proved themselves unnecessary. They were expendable, as time proved, and deep down, she resented both horribly, so let everyone talk, it did not matter to her.

She caught the admiring glance of Beth, standing next to Rod. Surprisingly, they had put things together, with Rod having more of a say now, than he ever did before. They were still an odd couple, her dressed for the catwalk, and him looking like an escaped breed, the jungle in his veins, wild hair and the growing beard kept him faithful to himself. But the two of them had dealt with enough skeletons, and had managed to dodge the falling bones, so that, instead of becoming pinned underneath, they were moving on, together. She liked Beth anyway, despite everything, knew they would get on like the way your eyes adjust to a new pair of sunglasses. But she knew Beth could not help it. Soon enough there would be a new scandal. Beth was a troublemaker. Arya preferred it that way. It gave Beth character, spunk. Something her unfortunate sister lacked – the bland Mona, with the permanent sour expression that never seemed to change. Not that she could blame her, but everyone knew that her lover had eloped, found himself a new set of lips to attach to. Now she stood demurely, between her ex-husband and Chris. Arya did not feel any sympathy for her. She had played and lost the game, was too stupid to go for a next round. And then there was Miriam. Even though she had turned out to be Francis' sister, Miriam had a strange habit of never knowing her limits, of running after people who did not want her there. Now that Matti had become part of her family, she had lost interest in any chance of a friendship, turning her talents rather on getting Arya to notice her. The silly girl was annoying. Growing bored, Arya shifted her eyes back to Mona, and saw that Mona was staring at Matt, who was staring at his phone. He seemed to be enjoying his new lease on life. It was clear that there was nothing left to salvage between them, except maybe for the small fact that Mona still loved him. Arya smiled to herself again. It was in her power to push for a reunion. She might do it, just as an exercise to show her influence. To go a step further, if it suited her, she just might reconnect the relations between the two sisters. It was obvious that Beth was still annoyed, more so that her husband had been seduced by a plainer version of herself. Arya turned her head away from the row, thinking how quickly Matt and Rod had accepted Ethan. Nobody rejoiced that day, not as much as the brothers did, for now they could pass on the burden of keeping the empire intact, to somebody else. Each was happy to return to his own way of finding joy in life, and the situation seemed to have worked itself out perfectly. Even Francis and Chris were relieved, knowing that Ethan could have kicked them out, but rather chose to keep them close. They respected him, it was clear to everyone, and they loved him. As for Ella, she put her broken heart together very quickly, after finding out that Ethan, her newly found cousin, had made all the correct decisions from the start. She stood next to her mother Ann, and from that position, as advocate for Ethan, beamed with pride and a different kind of love for him. Relief showed in her features, and she smiled at Arya, with all the love of a new sister. Well, she was on her way to becoming a permanent part of that family, and as Ethan's wife, life was going to be better than great. She could hardly wait.

Taking her gaze off the family, she moved forward, looking at the rows that contained her relatives. Her appearance, as she had anticipated, being modern and unexpected, was sending shock waves straight through their wide eyes. She secretly enjoyed it. She would never forget the look on Aunty Bomi's face, as her heels took her teetering past the older woman, on the specially designed carpet, that covered the ocean sand, soft and thick, it had been placed there to take the stabs of her heels, leaving a soft dent, only to recover itself and look immaculate in the next blink of an eye. That was Ethan's idea as well. Oh, she was growing to love him more by the passing second. Turning her thoughts back to her father's sister, she wondered if she had pushed her aunt Bomi too far, what with the dress, and the fact that she was on the arm of another woman. The old lady had clearly not expected such a drastic change. Well, Arya thought to herself, her aunt had only the next hour to suffer through, mostly to keep her breath flowing. After that, well, she couldn't say.

By now, the duo reached the priest. Mattie took her place next to Arya, both turned to the man dressed in clothes of the church, both gave a nod in greeting, both received a nod that would not have scared off a fly. Not sure what to do, she turned her face to the watching crowd, thinking it was a strange thing to stick to your own values, to go up against convention. It was a new thing, for most watching, especially her family, to see that she stood at the altar, waiting for her groom. The way she saw things, there was no need for the element of surprise, she wanted no horse taking her to the marital arch, unless it was a unicorn. This was her idea, and Ethan had let her have things her way. She had toyed with the option of having her father walk her down the aisle, if he could manage three steps without falling over his shoes, but she foresaw the comic tragedy unfolding. She saw herself hopping about, trying hard not to spear him with one of her heels. The drama needed to stop somewhere.

Her eyes dropped in on Veru, taking in the sight of her permanent sulk, as she sat wedged, between her fiancé and his mother. Veru was dressed in a plain purple sari, with very little accessories to match. She had not even bothered with her hair. It lay about her shoulders, shouting out for a hot iron, looking as if she had just woken up. And to complete the picture, she had the luck of having her future mother put a cupped hand over her one ear, every few minutes, to deliver the latest lot of garbage into it. Arya should have felt some compassion for her, but she had none to spare for her sister. Veru deserved it. That was Veru's luck. As for matters between the two of them, things were not good. Veru could not forgive Arya for replacing her with Matti. Arya told her conscience for the hundredth time, it was not Veru's day, it was hers. She could do as she liked.

The whole mess started with the idea of having half a dozen little girls, all dressed up as fairies, leading the way. The more she thought about the display of childish innocence, the more that idea grew into something that brought tears to her eyes, for all the wrong reasons. She preferred walking down the aisle with the focus on her, no fake fairies struggling to keep the line, too full of breakfast, too round to move properly, covered in dresses that made them look like wobbling mushrooms. She could not bear the idea of having the crowd crowing and quacking for the wrong reasons, while she, their flower queen, took second place. That was not for her. Neither did she have the time or patience for a bunch of noisy, fussy bridesmaids, all secretly lusting after her groom, their eyes growing bigger when they saw him, their smiles so practised and stretched, it almost reached their ears, making them look stupid. She had seen it during practise, and sent all of them packing, faster than the chicory flower head had a chance to lose its petals. She liked to think about it in that way, made her feel smart, especially since she had found out that it might be a true story – the chicory flower lost all its petals in a day, blooming at sunrise and bald by the time the sun reached its peak. Well, that was how long the bridesmaids lasted, so it must be accurate. As for Veru, she ought to be lying flat on the ground, begging for mercy. The worm. Arya had caught her making eyes at Ethan, blushing, smiling as if she had stepped into the bride's spot. She was as bad as the other sister of hers, both spitting cobras. One was here, to see first-hand, what she had missed out on. The other one was safely tucked away in the forest behind a locked door. That was also Arya's doing. The only people she wanted at her wedding were those who arrived to serve her, not steal what was already hers.

She was happy to think of them no more. Holding the bunch of flowers that Ethan had given her, closer to her heart, she knew she was the luckiest bride. Ethan had seen to her every wish. The flowers were made of satin, just what she had once wished for, mimicking large roses, they had individual bows attached to each. The burgundy flowers set the trend for the decor. Everything was done in her favourite colour, even the guests were given no choice, being handed, at reception, the specially designed brooches and tie pin, each large, fancy piece of artistry had stones set into it that paid homage to her. She listened as the imported band reached a new crescendo, and knew instinctively, her groom had arrived. She locked him into her gaze, saw the smile on his face, but it was no ordinary smile, it played on his lips, danced off the corners of them, lighting up those unique eyes. She was so lucky to have him. But from somewhere inside her mind, a cry, like that of a newborn, stung the insides of her eyes, so that, when the first tears came, and he had reached her side, it looked as if she were weeping tears of love. They were far from that. They were tears of guilt. He brushed them gently aside, holding her close, not caring about the world around them. He kissed her forehead. There were sounds coming from the crowd, everybody sighed in wonder at this display of tenderness, and saw for themselves how much he loved her. He looked into her eyes, and a flame lit itself there for a second. She had never seen that before, and it stirred something inside her. She was no fool, but it reminded her of a lighthouse, a warning to ships at sea. She was one of those ships. Before she could check her words, keep them locked, they jumped board, landed flat in the space between the two of them.

'We have never been together, not in that way. It was Coral's tent, the one you went into.'

It was as if the pause played on, infinitely. She heard him draw breath, saw the clouds gather in those dark eyes, where a flame had just played. She knew how to read them so well, recognised the struggle, the definition of her words putting distance between them. This man, the one for whom she would have let a candle burn down into the palm of her hand, just to keep the flame alive for as long as she could, for whom she could change, keep herself on a straight line, kick out the bad habits, just to be in his arms, she had let him go, let him slip away, by her own stupidity. What business was it of hers, if Coral kept her mouth shut, why couldn't she have done the same. Those seconds haunted her, switched the mood, because every occupied chair on that piece of shoreline, came attached with a set of ears. They heard too. The truth climbed the air, set free, the smell of the ocean came riding in. She had never taken time to breath that in. She did now, deeply and with regret.

But Ethan, he hooked her with those eyes. Whatever claim her words had on him, they were gone, digested. His gaze restored the calm, set her right back on course. She would never forget that moment, no matter where life took her.

'Thank you,' he said, in the voice, that belonged only to them. 'For the truth.'

'There's something else,' Arya looked at her feet. She could not bear it, but the truth had to come out, all of it. 'The elephant shrew. I lied about that too. I made up the whole story about Coral throwing away her pendant. You found it in the tent because she was wearing it. She always wore it.'

She felt so ashamed of everything, the pranks, the lies. She could have just told him the truth, anytime her conscience struck the chord, and he would not have walked away. He might have forgiven her. Yet, even after everything, he was still there, standing in front of her. She lifted her eyes to his, those eyes were not dark any more. They held compassion, for someone like her. It went beyond the call of ordinary decency. This kindness, a token of his compromise to her, to save face, in front of those who would condemn her, reciprocated something in her, a reaction she never thought herself capable of.

'Nothing has to change,' she heard Ethan say, loud enough for everyone to hear, 'I am here for you. I always will be, and I will always think the world of you.'

He had not said the words that mattered. She realised now, she needed to hear those words, and she waited.

'I still want you in my life.'

It stung. He was not ready. To marry him now, it was not right. It did not feel right.

She took the ring off her finger, slowly, painfully, placing it into his palm, she looked at him, her mind took a photograph of his face, those beautiful features, and it dawned on her that she might never have the right to touch them again, to share that space with him, that special closeness, that only gave room for one, her heart broke. She truly knew, in that single slice of slipped time, what it was like, to have her heart ripped out. Her shoes came off, those silly stilettos lost their value, she did not care any more about her curls, her stupid dress was too tight to give her a dignified exit, but it left plenty of time for Ethan to catch up with her. His footsteps were not the ones that followed hers. She knew it was too soon. His world had fallen apart. She had helped with that. Her selfishness came at a cost. As Matti ran after her, she knew her world would never be the same again.

CHAPTER THIRTY-TWO
ETHAN

He watched the little fellow as he ran after the ball. It was like watching a very young version of himself. Back then, his feet kept chasing the ball. It never stopped. He never stopped running, not until the childhood years had slipped by. He would never let that happen to his child. In one big stride, he scooped the child up, kissing him on his cheeks, his forehead, hugging him close. This child, this extended part of him, was all he lived for. He looked ahead, into the distance, knew that a decision must soon be made. But for now, he wanted something else. It came to him in his child's laughter.

Both Miss Nan and Ania stood by, watching them. He did not need to look up to see the affection in their eyes. He was grateful for it. Then Ania said something very unusual, 'The next Mynah,' and her eyes were fixed on the child. Something resembling a smile could be seen in her features, her dark eyes mirrored those of his, and her grandchild. They were all connected, the three of them, he knew that. Only time would tell just how much. Only time would bring home a wife for him. For now, things hung in the balance between the two women in his life. He smiled to himself and thought about what Francis had told him on the day he was to be married. Well, he did not have a wife yet, but he heard both names at the back of his mind, whispers, each bringing home something different. He knew he must decide soon.

Tomorrow would be a new day.

SPECIAL NOTES ON THE TEXT –

- *Page 10: Kwa-Zulu Natal – a province in South Africa*

- *Page 17: Karumpu – Fictional village*

- *Page 17: Tongaat – Town in South Africa*

- *Page 46: Port Elizabeth: City in South Africa (Eastern Cape Province)*

- *Page 46: Cape Town: City in South Africa*

- *P69: Eleutheria – Fictional town*

- *P249 Kimberley Diamond Mine – located in Kimberley*